Enchanting the Fae Queen

By Stephanie Burgis

Wooing the Witch Queen
Enchanting the Fae Queen
Melting the Ice Queen

Enchanting the Fae Queen

Stephanie Burgis

BRAMBLE

First published 2026 by Tom Doherty Associates / Tor Publishing Group

First published in the UK 2026 by Tor Bramble
an imprint of Pan Macmillan
The Smithson, 6 Briset Street, London EC1M 5NR
EU representative: Macmillan Publishers Ireland Ltd, 1st Floor,
The Liffey Trust Centre, 117–126 Sheriff Street Upper,
Dublin 1 D01 YC43
Associated companies throughout the world

ISBN 978-1-0350-6303-1 HB
ISBN 978-1-0350-6304-8 TPB

Copyright © Stephanie Burgis Samphire 2026

The right of Stephanie Burgis Samphire to be identified as the
author of this work has been asserted in accordance
with the Copyright, Designs and Patents Act 1988.

All rights reserved. No part of this publication may be reproduced, stored in a retrieval system, or transmitted, in any form, or by any means (including, without limitation, electronic, mechanical, photocopying, recording or otherwise) without the prior written permission of the publisher.

Pan Macmillan does not have any control over, or any responsibility for, any author or third-party websites (including, without limitation, URLs, emails and QR codes) referred to in or on this book.

1 3 5 7 9 8 6 4 2

A CIP catalogue record for this book is available from the British Library.

Interior art by Shutterstock.com

Printed and bound in the UK using 100% Renewable Electricity by CPI Group (UK) Ltd

This book is sold subject to the condition that it shall not, by way of trade or otherwise, be lent, hired out, or otherwise circulated without the publisher's prior consent in any form of binding or cover other than that in which it is published and without a similar condition including this condition being imposed on the subsequent purchaser. The publisher does not authorize the use or reproduction of any part of this book in any manner for the purpose of training artificial intelligence technologies or systems. The publisher expressly reserves this book from the Text and Data Mining exception in accordance with Article 4(3) of the European Union Digital Single Market Directive 2019/790.

Visit **www.panmacmillan.com** to read more about
all our books and to buy them.

For Patrick, my own perfect partner. I love you!

Enchanting the Fae Queen

1

In a palatial, centuries-old villa in the heart of Fiora, capital city of the Serafin Empire

Twenty-five years ago

Gerard de Moireul was eight years old when his grandmother summoned him to witness his parents' execution.

He didn't realize, at first, why the servants were bothering to wake him at all. It had been weeks since he'd been left at his grandmother's villa, and in all that time, he had never met her nor been attended in his room by any of her household staff. After the first long day without any food, he'd finally found his own way to the kitchens, where a grim-faced older man had grudgingly served him a breakfast of plain, unbuttered toast and a small clay cup of well water.

Under the judgmental gazes of all the kitchen staff, Gerard hadn't dared ask for any more, no matter how loudly his stomach rumbled. From then onwards, though, he'd made a shamefaced pilgrimage to the kitchen twice a day, eating his meager portions as swiftly as possible and trying to ignore the way the room went deafeningly silent every time he entered. He'd spent the rest of his hours wandering the long marble galleries, all of them lined with impressive busts and statues but devoid of human life.

He couldn't even look out through the windows at passersby, as every single pane of glass in the villa had been covered and sealed by immovable black silk curtains before his arrival.

When hard, impatient hands shook his shoulder early one morning and harsh voices demanded that he wake, his first, desperate hope was that his parents were finally back from whatever urgent trip had taken them from him for the past two weeks. He didn't argue when he was presented with bright white, ruffled clothes, the sort that might be worn for one of his mother's famously luxuriant parties, where Imperial archdukes and the Emperor himself often mingled as guests with scandalous opera singers and heroic generals.

Curly hair tamed by a ruthless comb and unfamiliar clothes stiff against his skin, he scrambled thankfully into the grand carriage with curtained windows that waited inside the villa's sheltered outer courtyard...

And then stumbled to a halt as he took in the apparition who waited for him there. Dark eyes glittered with fury in her pale, stretched-thin face. Giant ruby clips studded her white hair, and even more jewelry flashed on every patch of skin exposed by her low-cut, celebratory gown.

"*This*," his grandmother hissed, "is the price of weakness and treason. Keep your eyes open, show no sorrow, and *learn it well*, or I will end this shameful family line forever."

Gerard might not yet know about the scandal that had swept

the continent for weeks—the bribes accepted, the secrets sold to enemies of the Empire, the soldiers' lives lost in consequence—but even at eight years old, he could sense the deadly truth in his grandmother's hissed warning.

So he kept his eyes open through everything that followed. As the Emperor's own personal executioner read out the list of treasonous crimes that had been committed, the crowd bayed with ravenous hunger and rage, and his parents were beheaded in front of him.

Under his grandmother's icy gaze, he didn't dare shed a single tear.

By the time he returned with her to his new home, Gerard thought his head and heart were both completely numb. Then, the next day, he was woken once again—this time, to be sent away to a military academy where every student and teacher knew exactly who he was and what his parents had done.

Perhaps his grandmother hoped that his classmates would fulfil her own deepest wishes, so he would not survive to shame the family in his turn. But Gerard had listened and learned his lesson well.

He would never forget it.

He was twenty-two years of age when he found himself unexpectedly in charge of a full battalion. All three of his commanding officers had been shot, and he and his men were left boxed within a valley with no options for retreat. However, Gerard had spent years studying military history and strategy in the dusty academy library that had been his refuge when he was younger. He could see exactly how to turn this seeming trap into a bottleneck for their opponents—and the astonishing, turnaround victory achieved under his command was the first step in an inexorable progression.

By the time he was twenty-five years old, court gossips and newspaper reporters alike were calling him the Empire's Golden Beacon. Breathless reports crossed the continent—both within and without the collected archduchies of the Serafin Empire—with news of his unstoppable triumphs in battle, paeans to the shining, golden hair that (according to one influential poet) symbolically *lit his men's way to victory*, and his relentless, ascetic self-control in every aspect of his life. By twenty-six, he was a multi-awarded general; at thirty years of age, he became the youngest ever high general of the Serafin Empire. He was appointed to the post by Emperor Otto II, son of the very same emperor who had attended Gerard's mother's parties and then decreed her bloody execution.

Now, as the Imperial high priest serenely wafted an incense burner over Gerard's head to signify the pantheon's blessing upon him as the Empire's chief defender and sword of justice, Gerard breathed in the heady scent and gazed across the packed audience of clapping royals, aristocrats, military officers, and newspaper journalists.

No matter how desperately they tried, none of those gathered reporters or court gossips had ever managed to attach a single scandal to his name.

They never would.

His grandmother was no longer alive to witness the event, but he could still hear the last words she had uttered when he'd attended her final bedside ten years earlier.

"It's up to you now," she'd rasped, her dark eyes as fierce and as furious as ever despite the physical agony wracking her body. "You're all that's left of our family line. *Make it matter*."

He fully intended to . . . no matter how provoking, dangerous, and unsettling the nemesis who had chosen to plant herself in his path, doing her reckless best to ruin everything.

In the archducal palace in the Archduchy of Savelberg, at a celebratory ball

Seven years ago

The first time Queen Lorelei of Balravia saw the Golden Beacon, it was across a glittering ballroom full of enemies.

Lorelei adored popping into her enemies' parties, and she never bothered to wait for an invitation. After all, there would be no fun in being a scandalous fae queen, sung and gossiped about nonstop, if she didn't make use of the fabulous portals at her fingertips to flout official borders and skip every invitation checker at the gates.

So she erupted into the ballroom in a shower of rainbow sparkles, wearing a gown of gauzy, shimmering scarlet chiffon and her most brilliant grin.

"My darlings!" she caroled as the string orchestra in the corner shrieked to a halt and every conversation broke off in shock. "We've finally arrived. Now the party can begin!"

Behind her, she could feel her favorite cousin's smirk even though she couldn't see it. "Let's hope the wine here is better than at the last Imperial party you dragged us to," Katrin drawled.

"It can't be worse," Lorelei's second lady-in-waiting retorted. "I'd drink sprites' spit before I tried that one again."

"Oh, Ilse, that doesn't count as an insult." Katrin sighed wearily, still not yet reconciled to the lady-in-waiting who'd joined Lorelei during Katrin's own time away, two years ago. "You drank sprites' spit for fun *both* of the last two times we visited the fae realm. No one believes that that's a burden for you anymore!"

"Hush, now." Lorelei beamed ferociously at the wide-eyed, staring mortals all around them and clasped her dimpled hands beneath her chin. "I'm quite certain our hosts have assembled a *fabulous* feast for such a momentous celebration. What *are* we all celebrating, again? Oh, wait, now I remember." She tilted her head, letting her gloriously unbound blonde curls cascade over her gleaming, bare right shoulder. "You just won a little skirmish, didn't you? *So impressive*... especially when you consider that it was fought against a perfectly righteous group of dissidents in a *separate kingdom*, not even part of your empire to legally maintain." Her upper lip curled with a fury she couldn't quite hide.

As the ruler of one of the worryingly few kingdoms still clinging to independence on the fringes of their continent, she could not *believe* the stupidity of the neighboring king who had invited the Empire's help in settling his own internal issues. Had he paid no attention to the shifting tides of politics? The elderly current emperor, after his own early expansion, had been content to leave the Empire's borders where they were; his only son, soon to become Otto II, had far more dangerous aims in mind.

No independent kingdom would survive if they gave in to his schemes.

"Your Majesty." The Archduke of Savelberg was still hanging back, gaping like a particularly unattractive fish, but his wife was clearly a stronger soul. The Archduchess stalked forward now in her bustled and brocaded gown, stiff white lace framing her high neckline and her expression rigid with dislike as she swept a tight, reluctant curtsey. "How kind of you to honor us with your attendance."

"But of course. I knew you must have *intended* to invite me, even if you did somehow mislay my invitation." Lorelei smiled sweetly and felt every human guest around her cringe at the sight. "How could my ladies and I possibly stay away? In fact..." She clapped her hands together in theatrical delight. "Why don't we liven things up a bit with a party game? I seem to recall that, for some bizarre reason, your husband recently chose to expel every one of your fae citizens from Savelberg's borders... so why don't *we* make up for everything you've all been missing since then?"

Glancing over her shoulder, she sent a sparkling grin at her attendants. "Shall we, ladies?"

Katrin shrugged with the same easy grace that made her an excellent swordfighter. "It *would* make tonight more interesting..."

"...And I *have* been longing for another treat." Feral gold flashed in Ilse's green eyes, and her teeth sharpened in anticipation.

"Wait!" The Archduchess started forward, lifting one lace-bedecked arm as if she actually hoped to stop them.

She should have known better. Mere humans could never act as quickly as a powerful fae queen and her most trusted inner circle. It only took a single wrinkle of Lorelei's nose and two high, eerie whistles from her attendants before the familiar spell was cast and vibrant green vegetation surged up from the floor of the ballroom. Bejeweled guests started back with cries of raw fear as tall trees and giant, poisonous blooms erupted between them and their companions. Even more greenery fell in long, trailing loops of ivy and carnivorous blossoms from the crystal chandeliers, while tiny sprites shot through the room, darting in and out of elegantly piled hairstyles with gleeful, tangling mischief and sneaking stolen sips of aristocrats' champagne.

Shadows shifted and elongated in the corners, transforming into tall, spindly creatures made of branches and thorns, with drooping fingernails and sharp teeth that glistened wetly in the candlelight.

The wild, exhilarating scent of Faerie filled the air, and Lorelei smiled with perfect satisfaction.

"General de Moireul!" The Archduchess bleated the name like a prayer, spinning around and searching the vegetation-shielded crowd. Her voice rose above all the other panicked commotion in a screamed demand: "*General de Moireul!*"

...And there was the real reason Lorelei had chosen to grace this particular gathering with her presence. Her eyes narrowed as she prepared to finally meet the new enemy whose name had been popping up more and more often in worried whispers among the Empire's neighbors:

The Golden Beacon.

Ever since Lorelei had first claimed the throne of Balravia, spiting her late father's wishes and all of her male cousins' hopes, new Imperial generals had been appointed again and again across the border, spilling like brainless salmon from the dreary military schools where would-be officers were sent from across all the Empire's archduchies. They generally seemed interchangeable to her—but there was something different about the way she'd heard this one discussed.

As Lorelei had learned since her own ascension, there was a magical point where songs and stories tipped into legend and took on a whole new power of their own, overwhelming every detail of the tedious truth with their own irresistible, infectious appeal. Right now, "the Golden Beacon" was still only a name. All too soon, though, it could become a symbol and a rallying cry that spoke doom to every kingdom still clinging to freedom . . .

Unless someone clever, strategic, and full of magic stepped in just in time to tarnish that golden gleam.

Lorelei's target stepped through the crowd of panicking aristocrats and greenery, and her smile deepened. Sylvana be praised, he looked like a mountain in a uniform! She couldn't kill this man without making him a martyr and inspiring a bloody war of retribution—but corrupting him for the sake of her kingdom? That might not be the chore she'd expected, after all, but a genuine *pleasure*.

"General de Moireul." The Archduchess sagged with relief as he joined her. "Thank the gods, you're here to save us all."

"I beg your pardon, Your Highness, but . . . from what, exactly, do you require rescue?" The man's voice was deliciously deep and rumbling. Still, as he turned from the Archduchess to look at her, Lorelei's chest tightened with sudden, instinctive warning.

Those wolf-like amber eyes were *far* too keen. They bored into her as if he could see all of her hidden secrets laid bare before him, through every layer of glamour and gossip that functioned as her shields—and his grave, unhurried question showed no hint of the alarm he should have felt.

"Well—but you can see—just look around you, man!" The

Archduchess flung out one sweeping arm to indicate the feral, fae wildness that had overwhelmed her ballroom.

Clasping his hands behind his back, the Golden Beacon nodded thoughtfully. "As I understand it, bringing a gift—such as this decoration—to any festivity is a point of courtesy for the fae. They *all* follow the laws of hospitality without fail. Having publicly announced herself as your guest, I am quite certain that Queen Lorelei would never allow any actual harm to come to you or any of your guests this evening."

Well... *fuck*. Lorelei's smile didn't lessen, but she purred her next words with sickly sweetness. "A soldier who's paid attention to his studies! How marvelously unusual." Sweeping forward, she closed one hand as far as she could around his absurdly over-large, muscular arm and fluttered her eyelashes at him. Colorful sparkles flew free at her command to dust possessively across his uniform coat and medals as she breathed in the pleasant combination of scents created by his soap, shaving cream, and sweat. "Your Highness, you must allow me to claim this man as my escort for tonight. I'm sure he'll keep *all* of us wonderfully safe."

"Oh, very well." The Archduchess snapped out her fan and wielded it before her flushed cheeks. "I hope you and your ladies will all enjoy your evening *as our guests!*"

"How could we not?" Lorelei watched, still smiling, as the Archduchess turned with a sharp flick of her fan and marched into the crowd to attempt a belated reconquest of her party.

Lorelei couldn't care less about that battle, nor about any of the aristocrats milling in a wide circle around her now, whispering excitedly and visibly debating the risks of swarming the infamous Fae Queen of Balravia while she stood within their midst.

She would leave Katrin and Ilse to find their own personal triumphs in that crowd. Tonight, she had a far more important battle to fight.

"So... the famous Golden Beacon." She tipped her head back to meet his amber eyes. The impact of that piercing gaze was just as much a shock to her system this time as it had been moments before—but that was the effect of mere physical charisma, to which she'd learned bitter immunity years ago. "We meet at last."

"Your Majesty." He nodded respectfully, his features as impassive as if she weren't casting the delicious scent of just-opening roses from her skin. He should have been leaning closer to subtly breathe it in by now, even if he didn't want to shatter his dour affect by smiling—but he held his arm as stiffly within her clasp as if he were standing in a military parade. "Would you care to be escorted to the refreshments table?"

"Truly, I would *prefer* to dance with you." She leaned in confidingly, adding the first breath of spring to her scent and allowing a gurgle of laughter to enter her voice, as if she were sharing secrets. "Perhaps I should have left a single open clearing in the ballroom, just big enough for the two of us to share."

"Alas, I do not dance." His features didn't even twitch. "However, I would be happy to introduce you to any number of fine dancers in attendance."

"No dancing at *all*? Ever?" She made a face, only half theatrically. "Don't you allow yourself a single pleasure, General?"

"I enjoy serving my empire."

Sylvana's tears! Was any man truly so dreary? She tilted her head, lowering her voice into a husky drawl as she trailed one finger across his uniformed sleeve and let her magic tingle through that barrier to tease against his skin. "Perhaps I could teach you a few new pleasures tonight."

"Your Majesty." He kept his voice too low for any onlookers to overhear, but his words dropped like heavy stones into the air between them. "You are far too intelligent to waste any more of your time."

"By spending it with you?" She blinked up at him with innocent, vacuous shock. "General, you must have heard at least *some* of the stories about me by now." If nothing else, the latest play based on her scandals was being performed to a sold-out theatre in this very city tonight. "How better could I possibly entertain myself than by conversing with such a delicious military man? Everyone knows I care for nothing but my own selfish pleasures."

"Forgive me my bluntness," he said quietly, "but I know nothing of the sort—and regardless of the reason why you've sought me out tonight, you will not lure me into any indiscretions that might lessen my position, tonight or ever." His amber eyes held hers with implacable conviction. "I will never falter in my duty to the Empire, no matter what the provocation. You will *never* turn me from my path."

Oh, gods! Sudden insight flashed through Lorelei, and she sucked breath in through her teeth.

No wonder he'd seen through her so clearly.

She'd come prepared for yet another mortal general swept through life by natural charisma, noble birth, and a reasonably muscular build. But in this man's eyes, she glimpsed the inexorable flames of divine fire that fueled epic, world-shifting victories in his future. In his voice, she heard the unmistakable echo of a destiny being written by the gods of the Imperial pantheon themselves.

Lorelei released his arm as if it had burned her like the magic-repelling iron rails currently being planned by Imperial engineers to crisscross the vast Empire—part of the mortal world's endless, vicious fight to extinguish the life and color from every corner of the continent. Meanwhile, the god of war and justice who stood at the head of the Imperial pantheon, Divine Jovar, smiled in benevolence upon His chosen few . . .

Including the man who loomed before her now, certain and protected in his god-touched path of conquest.

Unfortunately for him, Lorelei had her own divine sponsor—and more than enough personal stubbornness to move mountains.

"General de Moireul." She swept a curtsey so deep, it went beyond respect into the deepest and most blatant public insolence. Then she smiled up at his beautiful, impenetrable face with all of her own goddess-blessed ferocity and brilliance for once unhidden . . . and she had the satisfaction of seeing his eyes flare wide in sudden, startled acknowledgement. "I hereby accept that challenge."

2

In a darkened room, in an unknown location

The present

Even the most brutal of tortures could never force Gerard de Moireul to admit it, but it wasn't unusual for him to dream of Balravia's queen. After all, the woman had haunted his waking life for seven years.

She was an incorrigible *menace*.

The rest of the Empire might delight in salacious stories and songs of the countless lovers Queen Lorelei had publicly discarded—or executed—in the course of her scandalous reign, but he could only *wish* more of her time was spent that way. Instead, she seemed to take delight in tormenting him, specifically and untiringly, for no logical reason that he had ever been able to fathom . . . and not only when they met face-to-face, which happened far too often for his peace of mind.

If he marched his troops to a carefully planned battle only to find that the other side had somehow mysteriously vanished into thin air, he was certain to find her telltale rose-blossom fragrance taunting him from his pillowcase when he returned to his private quarters afterwards.

Whenever Emperor Otto II held a grand new ceremony to award him with another hard-won medal of achievement, rather than taking pride in the Imperial affirmation, Gerard found himself bracing and holding his breath throughout, just waiting for a new, impossible catastrophe to hit. Once, a sharp-thorned rosebush erupted beneath him just as he was lowering himself onto what *had* been a plain wooden chair only a moment before. On a different occasion, the sudden stench of rotten fruits overwhelmed his senses just as he was drawing a deep breath to deliver a meticulously crafted, diplomatic speech to an assembled audience of the Empire's highest nobility. Only the most rigorous, lifelong training in self-control had saved him from collapsing into a sneezing, choking fit that would have made him the laughingstock of every newspaper report.

Of course, there was never any evidence left behind to prove the culprit to any outside observer, much less to provoke the kind of official Imperial reaction that could only too easily crush her small, impudent kingdom . . .

But most maddeningly of all, Queen Lorelei always made certain to leave a calling card just for him, whether she conveyed it through the lush scent of fresh roses or via a shimmer of dancing, rainbow-colored sparkles that melted as soon as he—and he alone—had spotted them.

What was she trying to provoke?

Obviously, it was a useless effort on her part. He knew his duty well, and his goals were set in stone. He would never allow such absurd and childish teasing to distract him. Still, he found himself turning the question of her motives over and over in his thoughts at night ... and then dreaming horrifyingly intense, shocking scenarios where he pinned her down on his bed to *force* her to finally answer all of his questions, while she laughed shamelessly up at him and then ...

No! He would not remember those dreams. Even Gerard couldn't exert control over his own subconscious while he slept. He could only resist lingering over those reprehensible fantasies in the light of day.

So it wasn't a surprise when he awoke in pitch darkness, aching with unforgivable heat once again. Damn it, why couldn't he ever get her out of his mind for long? And why did his sleeping mind somehow turn her ceaseless, mocking torment into irrational *temptation?*

Only yesterday, he'd come face-to-face with the fae queen on a snowy battlefield where she'd stood, barefoot and reckless, allied with two other powerful, independent queens in open defiance of the Empire. It had taken all of Gerard's diplomatic efforts, combined with those of Estarion's surprisingly pacifistic Archduke and the icily calculating Queen of Nornne, to prevent a war that none of them actually wanted ... and Lorelei's impudent provocations had come dangerously close to evoking a personal reaction that Gerard couldn't afford.

Perhaps he should have expected her to invade his dreams afterwards.

This time, mimicking real life, he'd dreamed that he was sleeping on the thin cot in the small, plain tent he always used for marching with his troops. When the decadent, unmistakable scent of her perfume had awakened his dream-self, he'd stiffened, his eyes snapping open ... and found the notorious Siren of Balravia smiling mischievously down at him, lit in the darkness of his tent by a circle of golden fae lights that danced around them both, enclosing the two of them in a warm, intimate circle.

"Shh, darling." She tipped one palm to scatter shimmering silver dust across the exposed skin of his face and throat before he could rise. "There's no need for you to wake or worry now. I'm taking care of absolutely everything."

Even his dream-self knew that was patently absurd. Between the troops he commanded, the dangerously narcissistic Emperor he served, the perilously shifting streams of politics, and the endless weight of his own family legacy, Gerard *always* had to worry. It was his responsibility and the choice he had made and ... and ...

And yet ...

As the silver dust settled and melted into his skin, warm, irresistible lassitude overcame him, and he found his eyes falling inexorably shut. Lorelei's small, soft fingertips stroked lightly across his cheek, leaving tingling trails of sensation in their wake, and despite everything, his rational objections sank too deep to be rediscovered.

It was only a dream, after all. No one could blame him for taking pleasure in a dream. Only a dream ...

And he reminded himself of that, again and again, for several agonizing moments after he woke, spread-eagled and panting, his senses still full of that aggravating scent of roses and his body burning with a heat he utterly refused to identify.

Enough! His mind still fogged with sleep, Gerard set his teeth together and turned to roll out of bed for his usual, punishing round of morning calisthenics. They were designed specifically to expel all such distracting nonsense from his head ...

But the moment he tried to move, he found himself tethered by strangely soft—yet implacable—chains that fastened across his chest, his arms, and his ankles to hold him firmly in place, splayed out across a wide, soft mattress.

Was he still dreaming after all? This wasn't his thin, hard traveling cot. And how could the air feel so luxuriantly warm in the middle of a snowy mountain pass?

Gods above. He sucked in a sharp breath through his teeth as the outrageous truth finally hit him.

No wonder he could still smell roses!

"*Queen Lorelei.*" It was a snarl of disbelieving fury—and the most uncontrolled outburst he'd allowed himself in decades.

Rainbow sparkles erupted in the darkness before him as if he had uttered an invitation.

"Finally!" The Queen of Balravia burst out of one of her fiendishly unstoppable fae portals, clothed in a low-cut, gauzy, gold concoction and beaming triumphantly. As she emerged, the blanketing darkness lifted from the room around them to reveal a large, airy bedchamber wallpapered in shades of forest green and lit by midday sunlight. There must have been a window somewhere to allow in so much light, but the full force of Gerard's attention was fixed on the fae queen's deceptively lovely face. She clasped her hands as if with rapture under her pointed chin and regarded him from the floor beyond his prison-bed, her periwinkle-blue eyes glinting with mischief. "I thought you'd never wake up, sleepyhead. I've been waiting for *ages!*"

He could not allow himself to lose control and bellow, no matter what the provocation. But it took all of the willpower he'd learned across his lifetime to keep his voice steady and uninflected. "That, Your Majesty, would be because when you kidnapped me from my tent in the middle of a full Imperial army encampment, you laid an illicit sleeping spell upon me. The number of international laws you have just flagrantly broken—"

"Oh, that was just a tiny little enchantment, not a *spell*. Honestly!" Rolling her eyes, she flicked one dimpled hand in dismissal. "If *that* was all that was keeping you asleep, you would have woken up hours ago, as I'd expected. No, I think you must have been exhausted, poor thing. You do work yourself terribly hard, don't you, running around every day, trying to satisfy all of Otto's demands? Really, you ought to be thanking me right now for whisking you away on this lovely vacation."

"*Vacation,*" Gerard repeated flatly. Incredulity mingled with righteous outrage—a reaction that had become intimately familiar across the past seven years of their acquaintance.

Was she actually trying to drive him into madness? Had that been her plan for him all along?

As she glided towards him, the shimmering golden fabric of her gown brushed softly against the sides of the bed, and he found himself intensely, unavoidably aware of his own position, splayed across the silken covers of the mattress and bound by impossible chains of flowers. He'd already felt their magical implacability; he wouldn't humiliate himself by fighting against them now and failing under her delighted gaze.

Thank all the gods that it had been too cold in his tent last night to sleep unclothed. He was still missing his polished boots, vest, cravat, and uniform coat, but at least his chest and outstretched arms were fully covered by a long-sleeved, high-collared cotton shirt, and his legs were safely sheathed in woolen trousers.

There was no actual, practical possibility that he could feel the heat of her lingering gaze through those layers.

But there was one certain truth he'd understood about the Fae Queen of Balravia from the moment of their first meeting: She excelled at throwing her opponents off their guard. So Gerard used decades of experience to separate himself, now, from the weaker impulses of his body and gaze up at her with the unaffected demeanor he'd perfected long ago. "I wonder, Your Majesty: What do your good friends and allies, the Queens of Nornne and Kitvaria, think of this supposed vacation you've arranged without my permission? Did *they* agree to this political decision?"

Queen Lorelei didn't flinch, of course. Her shields were far too polished for that—and despite what the rest of the continent might imagine, Gerard had understood for years that she was more dangerously clever and less emotionally driven than she wished any of her enemies to realize. He had been teaching himself her tells for years, though, so he savored the brief flicker of her sparkling eyelashes despite the condescending curl of her lips an instant later. "My dear general," she purred, "I know you're on vacation, but surely you haven't already forgotten the rules of successful political alliances? We Queens of Villainy would hardly have chosen to band together in the first place if we couldn't trust each other to keep the details of our private meetings *private*."

Aha. "So you haven't warned them what you're up to." He cocked a single eyebrow in rebuke. "I would have thought you owed them more loyalty than to leave them wrong-footed when the Empire responds—with force—to this direct attack upon its highest military leader. Both of your allies were witnessed at your side only yesterday by a multitude of reporters as well as my own troops. They will both share in the blame, and Emperor Otto's response to all *three* nations, when he hears the news of my abduction at your hands—"

"Why do you think I bothered to steal you in the first place, darling?" Her voice was light, but her eyes glittered with rare temper—another victory for him to mark on their personal battlefield. "You may have a terribly pretty face, but I hardly need to kidnap my playthings. They offer themselves to me on a regular basis without any effort on my part."

That, he did not doubt—and there was no good reason for hot irritation to flare through him at the reminder. So he ignored his own irrational reaction to focus on the unlikely clue she'd tossed him. "You actually *want* the Empire to attack? You can't possibly think Balravia would survive that invasion—not with both of its allies busy repelling simultaneous attacks on their own lands." If she had any idea just how hard he'd been fighting to temper the Emperor's increasingly disturbing ambitions in that direction . . .

"Not yet." Her eyelashes lowered as a wicked smile played at her lips. "Don't worry, darling, I'm not quite so careless as you seem to imagine. I *can* glamour your handwriting, you know—and set a very convincing scene. According to the note you left behind, you're trusting your closest officers to maintain your privacy and allow no one else into your tent while you pursue a secret, urgent quest elsewhere for the sake of the Empire. By the time little Otto finally realizes you're gone—much less who was bold enough to take you—it'll be *far* too late."

"Too late?" A wave of foreboding rolled through Gerard's bound body as he looked up at that wicked grin. "For what, exactly?"

"Seven years ago," said the fae queen, "you set me a challenge. By the end of our visit, General de Moireul, I plan to finally win it."

3

In the Queen of Balravia's private hunting lodge, hidden deep within the darkest and most ancient woods in the heart of Balravia

Lorelei had always excelled at the dramatic art of timing her entrances and exits. Even as she spoke those final, taunting words, she was silently summoning a portal; she had the satisfaction of seeing the Golden Beacon's mask of indifference crack with a single twitch of one eyelid as she offered him a jaunty wave and stepped away the victor in their conversation, leaving only sparkles behind to remind him exactly who was in control.

Then she landed in her pink-and-white morning room, on the other side of the lodge, and released the shriek of frustration that had been building within her all throughout their encounter. "*Argh!*"

"So the two of you had a pleasant catch-up?" Her cousin Katrin was practicing sword-play on the far side of the room, having pushed all of the couches out of the way and rolled up the long sleeves of her gown. She rose smoothly from a flowing lunge to aim a wry glance over one strong shoulder.

Lorelei said, "That man is the most hardheaded, arrogant, maddening—"

"He *is* rumored to be unstoppable," Ilse mused. She sat curled up on a couch by the tall windows, reading the first of a pile of novels propped on the plush golden cushions beside her. "He is rather yummy looking, though, isn't he? I wonder if the stories are true and he's still a virgin. Is that even possible?"

"Don't even think about it." Lorelei's eyes narrowed. "He certainly won't be seducing anyone here to escape!"

"Oh, no," Ilse said with perfect innocence, turning another page in her book. "I wasn't saying that out of any interest for myself. I was only thinking of you, Your Majesty!"

At that, Katrin gave a muffled snort of disloyal laughter—but she was, at least, sensible enough to hide it in a cough and immediately resume her exercises. Lorelei swept a dangerously narrowed gaze from her cousin's tall back to her second lady-in-waiting's perfectly oblivious face.

She *was* glad that they had learned to get along so well over the years. She even wished them well in the promising new flirtation they'd been engaging in for the past few months when they thought she wasn't paying attention.

Every so often, though, there was a downside to their new amity. Surely none of the other Queens of Villainy's attendants felt so free to mercilessly tease their own queens.

"That eventuality," she promised them both, "will never happen." Once, a long time ago, Lorelei *had* allowed more than one handsome man to soften her wits, gain her trust, and then humiliate her—but she'd risen like a phoenix from the ashes of those all-too-public early lessons and taken control of the narrative forced upon her. Physical lovers, she took happily and often, but she would never again make the mistake of allowing any man, no matter how attractive, into her heart.

Seven years ago, when she'd chosen to proposition the Golden Beacon, she hadn't known how dangerous he truly was; now that she knew him better, she would never dream of taking that risk.

. . . Even if he *had* looked like a fantasy plucked from her most decadent imaginings just now, spread out on that bed for her personal perusal. How in Sylvana's name had he managed to lie there, helplessly bound by chains of her making, and *still* somehow project the impression of a patient host in full control of the room and their conversation?

"Queen Ailana's been trying to get hold of you, by the way," Katrin reported as she made a complicated, spinning move. "Her latest message said that it was *extremely urgent*."

"Ugh." Grimacing, Lorelei threw herself across an empty sofa. "She must have worked out he's missing." That was the problem with making friends and allies with the most successful spymistress on the continent: Ailana knew almost *everything*. Her official magic lay in the powers of ice and snow that came from her aelfar heritage, but as far as Lorelei was concerned, Ailana's most terrifying power was her ability to coolly, calmly ferret out private information—and then turn her icy logic upon Lorelei's wildest schemes like the most disappointed older sister in the world.

Lorelei had never believed in wasting time on regrets. If she had sat around weeping about her own mistakes ten years ago, she would have been dead within days! Still, her most recent brilliant plan—to unite all three independent queens on the continent against the threat of Imperial expansion—had come with side effects she had not anticipated.

Somehow, both of her fellow queens, different though they were, had chipped their ways into her guarded heart. Clever, strategic Ailana of Nornne and grumpy, blunt Saskia of Kitvaria had earned her respect and affection as well as her loyalty... so the regret that Lorelei had felt this past week after mistakenly harming Saskia's lover had burned too badly to endure.

Felix, the softspoken Archduke of Estarion, was head over heels in love with Lorelei's friend, *not* a sneaking threat to Saskia after all. Lorelei had seen for herself how he'd stood for all three queens on that battlefield yesterday when he'd ordered the Golden Beacon to remove all Imperial troops from Estarian land and call off the planned joint invasion of Saskia's nation.

Even the Empire's high general couldn't refuse to follow that archducal order, with no higher authority present on the field to contradict it. However, the moment the Golden Beacon returned to Fiora to report that interaction to the Emperor, Otto II would react with murderous fury to the ruination of his plans. Whether he sent hired assassins, made up an act of Imperial treason to call for Felix's public execution, or simply broke the constitution of the Empire to have his way on that longed-for expansion, his response would be immediate, punishing, and brutal.

Obviously, Lorelei had needed to do *something* to help and make up for the harm she'd already done to Saskia's beloved...

But she knew exactly how Ailana would react to the path she'd chosen.

"*Ugh*," she repeated and closed her eyes, drawing up chains of ivy from the ground beneath the floor to cover, surround, and shield her in a softly rustling, green cocoon of peace. "I need a nap before I can even think about that conversation."

It was absurd that she hadn't managed to sleep earlier, after so many days and nights spent wide awake, dealing with crises. By rights, she should have fallen into bed the moment she had the Golden Beacon safely in her clutches and then slept as peacefully as a dryad in winter. Instead, once her initial enchantment upon him had faded, she'd paced her lodge for hours with skin that prickled as if it were being poked by invisible needles, waiting for him to finally wake up.

No, worse: *worrying* about why he hadn't.

Ugh!

Ailana didn't know everything. She couldn't. Even *Lorelei* didn't understand the storm of feelings that had overcome her yesterday as she'd stood shoulder-to-shoulder with her closest allies and watched the godsblessed Golden Beacon, after seven full years of private sparring, victories, and defeats, calmly announce that he would be passing on every detail of their meeting to the Emperor Lorelei despised . . . and then following Otto's selfish, greedy orders, however misguided they might be and regardless of his own personal feelings on the matter.

It was unbearable. That was all she had known, with a burning conviction that had overruled all logical objections. It was *wrong* to hear him say that. She owed her loyalty to her fellow queens, not to her enemy's high general—but she still had to save him from his own misguided sense of duty, no matter what either of her allies thought of her methods. Even if her quest was irrational—impossible!—she had to *try* to turn him off that dark path in time, before he could do anything truly unforgivable . . .

. . . And even if she didn't understand *why* she had to do it, she knew her instincts almost always led her in the right direction.

Unfortunately, when the buzzing swarm of worries and schemes in her head finally subsided enough to allow her to slide into sleep in the shelter of her private green cocoon, her dreaming mind transported her directly back to the moment when she had first discovered that her instincts couldn't always be trusted.

If Lorelei's instincts were always right, she would have known to hide when her father first arrived in the fae realm. But she had been raised in her mother's court, the cosseted mortal daughter of Efaelen's immortal fae queen, and at ten years of age, she hadn't yet been included in any political councils.

It didn't even occur to her that she might be in danger when she heard the leaves around her start whispering the news.

"The King of Balravia... the King of Balravia has come..."

This was *wonderful* news! Lorelei had always wanted to meet her father, who lived far away in the mortal realm, cut off by an aetheric veil from the neighboring fae realm where she and her mother lived. He had never been able to visit her before because mortals couldn't cross through that veil on their own, but he must have finally found a friend to help him now—and she already knew that he would adore her when they met, just as her mother always had.

She would love him so much, too! She would show him all of her best magical skills, and he would look at her with pride and be thrilled to have such a remarkable daughter.

She danced her way to her mother's private rooms, so wrapped up in her own delightful plans that she was barely even aware of the raised voices shouting beyond her mother's door.

"If you think the nation will accept some flighty fae—"

"You cannot alter the magical contract—"

"Then I'll deal with her myself!"

The last words were bellowed by an unfamiliar male voice. The door was locked, but that was no matter: Everyone said Lorelei's skill at creating portals was truly remarkable for her age. She certainly couldn't wait long enough to knock before her grand entrance!

She appeared in a shower of lovely silver sparkles an instant later, beaming with anticipation, before a tall, dark-haired and -bearded human man with eyes the same bright shade of blue as hers. Those almost-familiar eyes widened in recognition as he saw her... and then his face contorted into something ugly and unfamiliar as he lifted his gaze to look past her. "I'll just take care of the matter now, shall I? And then we'll see about your precious magical *contract*!"

Lorelei barely heard her mother's wordless shout behind her as her father's big, hard fingers closed around her throat and *squeezed*.

The next few moments were a nightmare of shock and pain and confusion. Alarms shrieked through the air, her mother's ancient green magic lashed past her, and as Lorelei's gaze blurred and then went black, every clawed and sharp-toothed guard in the court descended around them.

When she finally came to herself once more, she was lying cradled on her mother's lap with her mother's handmaidens gathered around them, every fae and dryad and hag murmuring unhappily over her.

"Mama?" Lorelei croaked.

Her throat hurt too much to say any more, but the single word was enough. Her mother's face tipped forward, her fathomless green eyes burning with intensity. "Shhh, my darling. Rest your voice until you've recovered."

"That *man*—!" Her mother's oldest and dearest handmaiden muttered the words as she smeared cooling salve across Lorelei's bruises. "I swear, if we were allowed to lay claws on him, I would wring *his* neck, and then—!"

"We are not." Her mother's voice was colder than Lorelei had ever heard it. "Rest assured, he will never be allowed to forget this moment. But I count myself to blame, as well. I have indulged myself for far too long."

As she looked back down at Lorelei, her body stiffened, soft comfort hardening into unyielding determination. "It's become too easy for him to forget the promises he made when we signed our marriage contract. I was selfish, keeping you here so long to myself. I cannot indulge in that luxury any longer."

Wait. Panic began to beat against Lorelei's throbbing throat. She couldn't mean . . .

"We'll wait until you've fully recovered," said her mother, "but then it will be time, my love, to finally take your place where you belong, in the mortal realm. *No one* in Balravia will ever again be allowed to forget that you are the rightful heir to your father's throne."

"But—!" The word was an anguished croak as Lorelei suddenly struggled in her mother's arms.

They tightened firmly around her. "The goddess Sylvana Herself, mother of the trees and flowers, guided me to this point, my child. This is what must happen—what *always* had to happen, if the fae were to have any chance of survival in the decades and centuries ahead. Balravia must have *you* upon its throne to fight for our people's future in the mortal realm. She saw that truth and shared it with me."

The Queen of Efaelen's voice was steady, but for the first time that Lorelei could remember, her green eyes shone with tears. "I'll send my best guards with you to ensure that you will never be harmed by that man again. And remember: you are worth a thousand of him and his grasping nephews. You stand for all of us from now on. You even stand for Sylvana Herself! With Her blessing, you will claim your place and your throne with your head held high, and you will *never* apologize for who you are, no matter what any mortal fools may say."

Lorelei was too desperate to care about the pain as she scraped the frantic question through her throat. "Won't you come, too?"

"Oh, my darling." Her mother shook her head in a slow, heavy movement of defeat. "I am bound by that contract, too . . . and I had to make my own sacrifices for this great chance. The mortal realm has not allowed my presence since the moment of your birth."

Everything hurt. Everything was *wrong*. "I don't want to go anywhere," Lorelei whispered.

"I'm afraid," said her mother, "it is time for you to learn that, as queens, we do what we must, not what we would prefer."

Lorelei burst into tears and buried her face in her mother's soft chest, surrounded by the fierce care of her mother's attendants, in the last safe display of anguish she would be granted for many perilous years to come . . .

And came awake, panting, back on her own sofa, a grown woman with her mother's reminder still ringing in her ears:

"*We do what we must, not what we would prefer.*"

Opening her eyes, Lorelei gazed sightlessly up at the green covering of ivy she'd built for this moment of privacy and accepted the unpalatable truth.

She was, as her mother had promised, a queen. She was blessed by the goddess Sylvana with a divine mission, for the sake of everyone and everything she loved.

So she would have to set aside all of her misfiring instincts and kill the Golden Beacon without a moment of hesitation if she failed in this challenge.

4

The ropes of flowers were, as Gerard had already surmised, unbreakable. Fortunately, his success at warfare had never relied upon brute force, and he'd been practicing calisthenics for decades.

He'd had to find his way out of more than one set of knotted ropes at the military academy... and not only as teacher-sanctioned training exercises.

It took nearly an hour of patient work, but he finally managed to wriggle his second wrist free of its scented binding, shift with painstaking care underneath the chains that had secured his chest, and contort himself upwards into a seated position on the bed.

An instant later, a door appeared in what had,

until then, been an unbroken stretch of wall directly in front of him. Gerard stiffened, every sense flashing vividly alert. The door opened to reveal a tall figure with a silver platter in her arms... and he let out a silent breath.

It wasn't Lorelei after all.

The feeling within him was, of course, *not* disappointment. It was only the natural sensation of emotional letdown that occurred whenever an anticipated battle was postponed. Still, he could hardly pretend that he was safe now—especially as he recognized the woman walking into his chamber. "Lady Katrin, is it not?" He couldn't bow from his awkwardly restricted position, ankles still fastened against the corners of the bed, but he gave her a respectful nod, as befit the Queen of Balravia's most favored cousin.

He'd never before seen a sword hanging from her belt, but the sight did not surprise him now. Whenever he had witnessed her attending Lorelei in public, she'd moved behind the queen with unmistakably predatory grace, her green gaze sweeping the crowd with unceasing vigilance.

That gaze landed on him now, seated atop the soft chains he'd escaped, and her lips quirked. "You just won me a bottle of fae wine from Ilse." Striding across the room, she set the silver tray between his feet, just close enough for him to lean forward and take it if he stretched—but far enough that he couldn't grasp her arms as she set it down.

Gerard left it untouched as he regarded her steadily. "I am honored that you're serving me yourself, my lady... but may I ask whether there is anything I should be aware of before I consume the food here?"

"What, because of the old stories?" She snorted. "Trust me. If any mortals ever grew so addicted to fae food that they couldn't stomach what they found at home afterwards, it was because, unlike some people on this continent, we believe in *flavor*. There's nothing magical about it."

"I see." That was clear enough—and full-blooded fae like Lorelei's cousin could not utter lies. He stretched forward to pull the tray closer. "I"—the phrase *thank you* was forbidden among them, was it not?—"appreciate both the reassurance and the education."

The fragrances drifting upwards from the tray were enticing, especially as compared to the plain rations he'd shared with his troops over the past few days of marching. As he breathed them in, his stomach made it known exactly how long it had been since he had eaten even that dried meat and tasteless porridge.

Lush noodles in a creamy, garlicky sauce were interlaced with delicate mushrooms and a few savory herbs he recognized, along with vivid green-and-red leaves that were unfamiliar. Taking a bite, he closed his eyes for a moment of true appreciation.

When he opened them, he found the queen's bodyguard watching him with a wary crease between her dark brown eyebrows. "Shouldn't you be trying to bribe or threaten me to gain your release?"

"Would there be any purpose in that attempt?" Gerard asked mildly. "From what I understand, you've been attending your queen for at least a decade and a half. If you'd had any interest in betraying her, I imagine you would have had more than enough opportunity when she first fought to claim her throne."

Lady Katrin might have been known under a masculine name, figure, and title when she'd first arrived at the Balravian court fifteen years ago, but it was common knowledge that fae could change their appearances with ease—and her familial relationship with the queen had been warmly acknowledged in both male and female forms.

"Most people would have guessed less than a decade," Lady Katrin said thoughtfully. "You've been thorough in your research."

He scooped up a second bite, twirling the pasta around the tines of his elaborately ornamented fork with care. "It seemed sensible, under the circumstances."

"Planning how best to mount an invasion on your emperor's behalf, you mean?"

"No," said Gerard. He left his answer at that as he lifted the mug of bubbling cider from the tray to his lips. It tasted of apples and autumn and something wild, sweet, and undefinable.

Lady Katrin's glance flicked momentarily from his face to the plain wallpaper to the left of the bed before she turned back to him with a smile that was anything but friendly. "Well," she said, "I *was* told to loosen your bonds after you ate, so that you could make use of the water closet." She tipped her head at the door to his right—the only door that had been visible until her arrival. "Based on what I've seen so far, though, I'll wager you can manage that by yourself. Still, we shall meet again soon."

"No doubt." Gerard watched her stride back out the outer door . . . which sealed shut into an unbroken wall once again in her wake. *Interesting.*

He chewed through the rest of his meal with methodical precision, fueling his body for the next steps as he considered his options.

The fae were notorious for their use of glamours to distract and fool humans. That door might be magically sealed against him if Lorelei had asked for help from her friend the Witch Queen of Kitvaria, but it seemed far more likely that it was merely hidden from his view.

As it happened, Gerard had an excellent visual memory . . . but Queen Lorelei, for all her theatrics, was rarely careless. If she hadn't wished him to know the location of that door out of his carpeted prison cell, she would have used one of her infamous portals to transport her cousin back and forth.

If he simply walked out the same way Lady Katrin had, he would no doubt step into another, waiting trap. On the other hand . . .

It took him far less time to free his feet now that he had the use of both hands. Once he was up and had done enough stretches to loosen his cramped limbs, he turned to the door on his right that had been visible all along. It would be foolishness to take anything he was told by Lorelei's handmaidens at face value.

The handle turned easily under his touch, and the door swung open to reveal a surprisingly large and airy room with a modern, flushing water closet as well as a marble sink and a luxuriantly proportioned bathtub decorated in images of frolicking water sylphs. Of course the Queen of Balravia would accept only the best and most lavish features in her palaces... even for the rooms where she kept her prisoners. Had the woman ever acknowledged a single limit to her own personal pleasures?

It was only too easy to imagine Lorelei draped in that bathtub among the painted water sylphs, her golden curls trailing over the rim of the bath, no doubt indulging in lushly fragranced bath salts and—

Gerard's jaw clenched, and he closed the door firmly on that irrelevant image.

There would be no safe exit through that antechamber, nor through the door that Lorelei had allowed him to see. Still, he remembered that swift, telltale flick of Lady Katrin's gaze when she'd looked past him and seen something different from what she'd expected.

Ignoring the door that she had used, Gerard strode around the bed and ran his hands with methodical care across the wallpaper from the front to the back wall of the room, working from the ground upwards every time. No helpful doorframes or handles pressed against his skin... but when he shifted his search upwards, the unmistakable ridges of a window frame pressed against his fingers.

Aha. He'd known there must be a window somewhere, to light this room so well! Fierce satisfaction rippled through him as he explored the surface beneath his fingertips. No iron bars were to be found here, of course; no fae could ever bear their touch. Once he escaped, he'd have to remember to start sleeping with iron on his own skin, now that he understood the reckless lengths to which Queen Lorelei would go.

But in the meantime...

His fingers closed around the long window latch, and he let out a hissing sigh through his teeth. Naturally, the latch was locked into place. Gerard had no key to fit into its hole, nor any helpful pins on hand to pick the lock—but he was no foppish aristocrat to despair at that discovery. A controlled, hard yank in exactly the right direction made a pained *sproing!* sound within the latch's pivot point. Incipient victory surged within his veins, adrenaline urging him to push the window open and hurtle towards freedom before the ticking clock could doom him . . .

But long experience made him pause, breathing deeply through the pounding in his veins. The fae queen was wily and cunning, and she knew his strengths all too well. Any true escape couldn't possibly be this easy.

His eyes narrowed on the still plain-looking wall. The lock itself was broken . . . but what *would* happen to any victim foolish enough to think themselves already done?

Pulling his hands back, he took a painfully long moment to think it through. Then he stepped even closer and, knotting his hands behind his back, leaned forward to use a different set of senses.

Lorelei's own floral scent still caressed this room, teasing and flicking at his attention as he sniffed his way across the window, taking care to stay a careful inch away from the illusion. Mingled with that arousing—no, *annoying*—hint of roses was a faint pine scent that could have come just as easily from cleaning materials or from any deep woods beyond his prison. But what tingled at his senses next . . .

Jovar's scars! Gerard jerked backwards just in time as he recognized the next scent in his olfactory search.

That was elfshot in its purest form . . . and if he had so much as brushed against it with his bare skin, he would be lying on the floor now, knocked unconscious, only to wake hours later with a rash that burned for days.

Damn it, Lorelei—!

He drew a deep breath through his nose and then released it.

"*Giving in to your emotions will never aid you.*" One of his teachers had told him that decades earlier, when he'd found a young Gerard raging and panicked after stepping into a painful trap designed by his classmates. It was a lesson Gerard had put to use again and again across the years, and it helped him find his way again now.

The serving tray with his empty dishes and silverware still sat neatly on the bed beside the abandoned ropes of flowers. He retrieved the long silver spoon and fork and held them before him like twin spears as he approached the wall once more.

All in all, he found three different spots where long, sticky vines of elfshot had been plastered against the windows. He scraped them all into a pile in one corner of the room, well out of stumbling range. Then he filled his empty cider cup with hot water, making use of that decadent bathtub after all . . . and imagining with grim satisfaction how annoyed Queen Lorelei would be by his discovery.

It took three thorough rounds of hot splashes across the wide stretch of glass, followed by a careful scrubbing with lilac-scented soap and layers of the bed's silk sheet wrapped around his hand as a shield, before he could be certain that the danger was fully removed. By the time he finished, simmering impatience had risen to a hot boil in his gut, but he could finally sense his victory ahead. Only a few more minutes, and he would be free.

He pushed both invisible panes of the large window firmly open, leaned forward through the illusion of wallpaper, and felt triumph settle through his veins. Snow-covered flat ground waited for him scarcely eight feet below the windowsill, lit by a low, late-afternoon sun. Beyond that patch of snow loomed tall, equally wintry trees in an unbroken line to the horizon—but Gerard had trained for combat in forests, too. He would find his way without trouble.

. . . And oh, once he was safely back in civilization, Queen Lorelei would come to regret her impulsive abduction! He might not choose to report this foolish incident to his emperor, but Gerard would know—and better yet, *she* would know!—that he had outwitted her and won this latest and most outrageous round of their endless, circling challenge.

Ah, how that defeat would burn! Savoring the image of Queen Lorelei's furious chagrin—her bright blue eyes flashing with rage, her chest heaving—he wrapped the thick duvet from the bed around his shoulders. Very nearly smiling, he set both hands on the bottom of the window frame for balance, swung his legs through, and dropped lightly down towards that soft, waiting snow and freedom . . .

Only for the world around him to abruptly *shift* the instant he released the wooden window frame.

Instead of landing on cold, crunching snow, he landed on soft, sucking green moss. The building he'd just escaped was nowhere to be seen, and the duvet around his shoulders was suddenly far too hot for comfort.

At least five different types of pine trees speared upwards from the dark, shaded ground around him, mingled with beech and oak. All their scents combined with something deeper, wilder, and unfamiliar that made the back of his neck prickle with a warning of grave danger.

As he turned in a slow, defensive circle, the scent of fresh roses arrived to overwhelm them all.

"*Finally!*" Queen Lorelei landed on the moss before him in a shower of rainbow sparkles and clapped her hands as if he were an actor in a private play for her entertainment. Her smile was so infuriatingly condescending that he almost forgot how to breathe as he stared, open-mouthed, at her. "I *knew* you'd find your way here eventually if I waited long enough. Come along, now, General. No more dilly-dallying, if you please. We're already running late for our adventure!"

5

It was astonishing just how easily Lorelei's mood could be uplifted by that look on Gerard de Moireul's face. The amount of incredulity and outrage expressed by an infinitesimal widening of that man's eyes and a single pulse of a blood vessel in the left side of his forehead was enough to set her up for *days* with delight. She would be feasting on this memory for weeks to come!

But she knew she had to move fast, before he could recover his legendary equilibrium. Fortunately, she'd woken from her earlier nap with a brilliant new idea, and she had sent off an urgent missive in preparation just before her magical defenses had shrieked in warning that her prisoner was about to escape . . . a full quarter hour earlier than she had expected.

Even so. It was all going to work out perfectly.

"This way!" she said brightly and turned to skip through the soft green pathways between the trees.

"*Careful,*" those trees all whispered to her. They leaned close and rustled their warning to her through their needles and leaves with a tingling breeze that tickled her skin in warning. "*Danger. Enemy. Close.*"

Of course the Golden Beacon was her enemy. She'd known *that* for as long as she'd known of his existence. But Lorelei had no fear of anything he could do to her here in her own natural domain. If he had even half the common sense she credited him with...

There. Her lips curved into a smirk of satisfaction as she heard his hard, impatient footsteps catching up to her. She'd known he would be too wise to attempt any escape through these particular trees.

"Tell me where you've brought me, Your Majesty." The inclusion of her title was a mere formality; he'd rapped out the demand in the tones of any longtime general demanding a report. That thick duvet he'd worn like an improbable cape was gone now, left behind as they'd left behind the chill of a winter afternoon to step into this warm, autumnal morning. He shifted out of the way of a curious copper birch just before its questing leaves could brush against his shoulder and aimed a quick, wary glance around them. "I've never in my life seen any woods so thick with magic."

"Welcome to the fae realm, darling—and to the glorious kingdom of Efaelen, in particular." Reaching out, she gently stroked those trailing, copper-tinged green leaves that he'd snubbed, humming over them in consolation. "Don't worry, I'll protect you from the trees. As long as you don't share your true name with anyone here, you'll be perfectly safe. You are my guest, after all."

"Your *prisoner,*" he ground out.

Goddess be praised, she really had gotten to him this time, hadn't she?

"We-e-ell..." Drawing to a halt, Lorelei laid one hand on his closest broad shoulder and batted her eyelashes up at him, teasing rainbow glitter into the air—and onto his white shirt—with malicious intent. "Of course, it's entirely up to you how you think of our relationship, my love, but you *may* wish to clear your head a bit before you make any firm decisions . . . or describe our situation to anyone else we meet. After all, if you're my *guest* in this realm, then obviously, I couldn't allow any harm to befall you. All of my fellow fae will understand *that*. But if you're no more than my prisoner and an enemy to boot . . . ?"

She lifted her shoulders in a careless, taunting shrug, allowing the implications to rest unspoken between them. The heat of his skin radiated through the cotton of his shirt into her palm like a furnace. She tried not to take note of it . . . but oh, Sylvana help her, that thin cotton was *useless* as a shield! Why couldn't he have kept the duvet wrapped around him on their journey, for her sake? Lorelei could feel each tightly bunched muscle in his shoulder now *so* clearly that she had to bite the inside of her cheek to prevent herself from stepping back in self-preservation . . . or falling forward into madness.

Gerard didn't shift away from her touch, but his amber eyes narrowed dangerously as he gazed down at her. "Do you even have a fixed plan at the moment, Your Majesty? Or is this all one more series of reckless leaps into the dark?"

"Darling! Don't you wish you knew?" Laughing, Lorelei retrieved her hand and blew him a taunting kiss before dancing ahead through the welcoming trees, out of reach of any more too-perceptive questions. It took very little effort to persuade these old friends to lean even closer behind her, stretching their branches in his path.

As he slowed to manage the obstructions behind her, she braced herself for the next step of her challenge. Whether or not anyone else believed it, Lorelei *always* had a plan . . . but occasionally, it did include worryingly unreliable components.

If *she* were truly sensible, she would kill him now and be done with it. She'd held off seven years ago for fear of sparking war; now, that fate was on its way regardless of her actions here. None of the other generals under Emperor Otto's control could lay claim to even half of the Golden Beacon's strategic brilliance; none of them would be as lethal in the battles soon to come. But every instinct in her body whispered that she *needed* him alive and at her side—no, not *at* her side, of course, that was silly, but on *their* side, the side of all three Queens of Villainy and every vulnerable magical citizen they were desperate to protect.

Turning the Golden Beacon's allegiance might sound like an impossible goal, but then, what kind of scandalous fae queen would Lorelei be if she didn't ignore accepted rules and fight the battles that no one else even dared to attempt?

Without any fae blood in their veins, no full human could navigate the aetheric barrier between the fae and mortal realms. With Lorelei as his guide, though, Gerard would finally see for himself the true wonder and beauty of fae magic—and the vibrancy of the people his emperor wanted to erase from the mortal realm.

Better yet, when it came to changing sides in the battles to come, what could be better than for Gerard and Lorelei to bond in the face of shared peril and prove exactly how well they could work together? It was an idea stunning in its simplicity . . . even if it did mean encountering Efaelen's immortal ruler for the first time in years.

Something twisted in Lorelei's chest at that reminder. It wasn't homesickness—how could it be, when these very trees had sheltered and guarded her since earliest childhood? But when she thought of everything that had changed since then . . .

Enough. Phoenixes didn't roll around in the ashes of *their* past lives; no more would she. By the time she led her reluctant guest out of the woods into a gloriously bedecked and sunny field five minutes later, Lorelei was beaming as if she'd never for an instant doubted her welcome.

The sight ahead lifted her spirits immediately.

Colorful ribbons made of sparkling magic floated through the sunlit air above three improbably large, gauzy tents made of spider-silk. Their doors were all drawn open in invitation—and a glittering flood of fae of all descriptions came flying, crawling, and stalking in and out of them and across the wide, flat field beyond like a parade of magical delight and wonder. Tiny sprites with iridescent, insectile wings darted through the air above slime-covered, dagger-toothed swamp fae and past giant, striding figures whose watchful dark eyes peered out at the world from behind their branches of abundant red and gold leaves and dangling acorns.

It had been *so* long since Lorelei had been able to attend a proper fae festival! She'd almost forgotten the thrill of so much gathered wild magic charging the air, like a wildfire just waiting to be lit.

"Darlings!" Clapping her hands together, she let go of every petty rule that tied her hands in ordinary life and, for once, allowed her full power to burst forth without any leash, showering the entire crowded field with an impossible rain of crimson leaves and golden glitter.

Fae across the field shouted in delight, vying to catch those gifts on their own skin—and each caught offering melted into its recipient's scaled, furred, or hairless body to leave behind the golden mark of Lorelei's own personal kiss and her powerful magical blessing. Hunting horns sounded at her command, high and achingly bittersweet, calling on every assembled fae to welcome home the only daughter of their ancient queen, the former princess who had—although they couldn't be allowed to know it—devoted her life to fighting for all of their sakes in the mortal realm.

An answering roar of feral, wordless joy rose from the crowded field. Every figure dropped to the ground in her honor . . . except the one silent, unmoving ruler who sat on a tall silver throne at the far back of the field, where they had been hidden from Lorelei's sight until now.

She felt the Golden Beacon step up behind her, but she didn't turn to take in his expression. She couldn't. Every muscle in her back was suddenly knotted tight, ignoring the commands of her better judgement, as she peered through the still-falling shower of leaves and glitter, trying with all her might to make out those final details.

The person who sat on that throne wore autumn's colors in their flowing robes, just as she'd expected. Their traditional Crown of Autumn glowed fiery gold through every glittering obstruction in the way. But something about those angles . . .

Aha. As a tall, straight figure rose from the throne, Lorelei's shoulders sagged with both relief and piercing, irrational disappointment. She might not be able yet to make out his face, but that was an unmistakably male figure.

Queen Morgana was *not* in attendance after all.

Biting back a sigh, Lorelei lowered herself into a respectful curtsey. Her mother's latest consort, Lord Reynard, might be depressingly tedious, but he was also quite harmless. All she need do was make a bit of polite small talk and share a public embrace, and she would have everything needed for her plan.

Unfortunately, before she could rise from her curtsey, a different male voice rang out across the field and proved that she had been far too rash in more than one of today's assumptions.

"*Dear* sister." Lorelei could hear the repulsive smirk in that voice even before the last of her falling leaves dissolved to show it on an all-too-familiar fae nobleman's perfectly handsome—and viciously untrustworthy—face. "How kind of you, for once, to deign to join us in our festivities."

Fuck. What was Reynard's son Oberon doing here, wearing the Crown of Autumn as host? Things hadn't changed *this* much since she'd last visited Efaelen, had they?

The Golden Beacon's voice rumbled behind her, pitched too low for anyone else to hear but vibrating through her bones. "I wasn't aware you had a brother, Your Majesty."

"I do *not*," she gritted, pulling herself together.

. . . But she had misunderstood the trees' earlier warning of an enemy lurking nearby.

Lorelei beamed her most glorious smile across the field at the loathsome son of her mother's consort. Their parents might currently be entangled, but Oberon certainly *hadn't* used that fraternal form of address the last time she'd been forced to interact with him, nearly six years earlier. Back then, he'd made a slithering attempt to seduce her by trickery and thus attain a queen of his own to match his father's accomplishment.

If only Oberon had chosen to follow his father's example in any other ways—from Reynard's occasional acts of real, if whimsical, kindness to the simple courtesy Reynard extended to even the lowest fae—Lorelei might not have bothered to humiliate him quite so soundly for it in front of the assembled court.

She couldn't *believe* her mother had allowed him to wear the Crown of Autumn for such an important cultural event . . . but she *would not* let him think it gave her any pain to see it.

"How sweet to see my mother is indulging you so, Lord Oberon," she cooed across the field of fae that lay between them. "You must have been *wonderfully* well-behaved ever since she finally allowed you back into her court."

Lorelei might have been too busy to visit Efaelen during the last few years of increasing turmoil in the mortal realm, but she still had her own sources in that court—and she hadn't missed any of the gossip when her mother had risked her consort's sorrow by exiling Oberon for an unheard-of four full seasons following a series of unforgivable public exploits.

Lorelei thoroughly enjoyed the fury that flashed across his expression at the reminder of his past punishment. Did he not understand how many *far* more competent villains she had squashed beneath her heels to win her own throne in the first place?

Rapidly revising her plans for the next few days, she said, "*What* delightful serendipity it is that we stopped by in time for this rare and momentous occasion. I should have hated to miss the sight of you looking so very . . . well . . . *exceptional* in a crown! But we are, I'm afraid, only passing through on our way to—"

"'Passing through'?" Slowly, tauntingly, Oberon raised a familiar sheet of pale pink notepaper that he must have been hiding, until now, within the sumptuous folds of his robes. "My, my, our former princess. What a way to describe taking on our people's most sacred challenge! Perhaps you've forgotten even more than I'd realized in all your years of running away to play house with the mortals."

Lorelei was no longer a princess but a queen—and it was only the thought of her own kingdom, and the people there who relied upon her, that saved her now. They would all suffer along with her if she murdered the son of her mother's consort in public, especially while he wore one of Efaelen's most ancient symbols of authority.

With an effort, she kept her voice as sweet as honey and batted her eyelashes at him. "Goodness, dear, you really *must* be bored if you've had to turn to reading other people's private correspondence for your amusement!"

"On the contrary. After Queen Morgana was called away on an urgent matter, I was named her proxy. Thus, it is my duty to open missives addressed to her . . . at least when they are clearly labeled 'urgent.'" Oberon smiled back with unmistakable, hateful triumph. "Don't worry, Sister. Despite the lateness of your plea, I will be *more* than delighted to accept you and your"—he flicked a disdainful glance at Gerard's silent, looming figure—"*mortal* into this year's Tournament of Leaves, just as you begged in your letter. I see here that you swore to complete it with honor—and never fear, you are just in time to enter."

With a decisive nod, he gestured for the assembled fae to rise back to their feet and clear the battlefield for combat.

Lorelei swallowed hard. Option after option tumbled frantically through her mind—but she discarded them, one by one, with sickly inevitability.

A public oath could *never* be withdrawn in the fae realm . . . not without losing her entrance to Efaelen forevermore.

"*Tournament of Leaves*, Your Majesty?" Gerard asked quietly, his breath brushing against Lorelei's hair.

She shook her head—a quick, jerky movement—in answer but didn't dare shift her gaze from Oberon's victorious figure as fae hurried to follow his commands. On one side of the field, a handful of healers gathered by the tent that was prepared to store any necessary bodies along the way.

One or two combatants *were* killed in these games every year, it was true. But when Lorelei had come up with her brilliant plan, she'd done so with the understanding that neither her mother nor Reynard would allow any such fate to befall either her or her tournament partner. She might have been discarded from the line of Efaelen's royal succession, traded away to Balravia like a royal chess piece; her mother might barely even remember her most of the time, their early attachment lost long ago; but both of those judges would have scrupulously honored Lorelei's dual relationships to Efaelen, both by blood and by vital political alliance.

Entering the tournament with Gerard as her partner, today, was meant to be a mere *simulation* of peril to prove that they could fight together as allies, not an actual exercise in mortal danger . . .

But from the smirk on Oberon's face, Lorelei knew that the rules of combat had just shifted.

He must have been waiting all these years for such a perfect opportunity for revenge.

"*Players, assemble!*" Bells jangled in glorious accompaniment to his command, and Oberon raised his robed arms high, the Crown of Autumn glowing upon his head like a victorious taunt. "It is time for the games to begin!"

6

Gerard had spent the last fifteen years of his life dominating brutal battlefields. He knew one now when he stood atop it, no matter how many magical, festive fae adornments swirled around it. By the time Lorelei finally turned to face him, she wore a smile full of confident, dazzling mischief...

But he'd been studying her for years, too.

"Precisely how much danger are we in?" He had to lean tantalizingly close to ask the question under his breath. The assorted members of the crowd were giving the two of them space at the moment, but he wasn't fool enough to underestimate fae hearing—or the hatred on that ruling fae lord's face. "I take it you had *not* factored Lord Oberon into any of your clever plans?"

For once, he managed to provoke a visible reaction; Gerard savored the brief, telltale twist of her lush lips and the flash of frustration in her impossibly blue eyes. But of course this woman would never allow him an easy victory. Instead, she tipped her head back and batted her eyelashes up at him with saccharine pity. "My, my, General de Moireul. Are you actually afraid of a little physical challenge? All those stories in the newspapers made you sound so fit and agile—but then, ever since you took up command years ago, you've never had to risk your *own* skin, have you?"

Jovar save him, how did she find every gap in his armor with such pinpoint precision? Gerard would *never* be one of those smug, careless generals who hid behind their medals or risked their men unnecessarily! His jaw tightened at the accusation, but he forced himself onward. "What is your true relationship with Lord Oberon?"

"Isn't that patently obvious?" She rolled her eyes. "Deep contempt, of course. Have you *seen* the pattern on his robes? I could never approve of anyone so lacking in good taste."

The Queen of Balravia herself was notorious across the continent for showering rainbow-colored sparkles everywhere she went without the slightest regard for good taste, decorum, or royal dignity . . . but Gerard chose not to follow his tormentor down *that* temptingly laid path of distraction, either.

"What makes him consider you his sister, then?"

Her eyelashes flicked mocking glitter at him. "Oh, trust me, darling. No matter what *dearest* Oberon may say now, neither of us has ever thought of it as a fraternal connection." Her voice was poisonously sweet, but he caught a note of real tension underneath.

Ah. One of her many former lovers, then. Gerard's muscles tightened instinctively as he lifted his gaze once more to look across the rapidly clearing battlefield.

The man who sat atop a gilded throne on the open grass was, of course, a perfect specimen of aristocratic fae beauty, from his shining locks of long, bark-brown hair to his tall, spare figure, which looked as lean and tensile as an arrow string. No doubt he and

Lorelei had made a striking pair for whatever length of time she'd indulged him in her bed.

No wonder he was so bitter now, witnessing what he had lost.

Gerard took in the hungry gaze still fixed on Lorelei—and felt a sudden, almost overpowering instinct to shift between them and turn his own bigger body into a wall to protect his nemesis's small, curvaceous figure from the other man's view.

Utter madness. Lorelei was Gerard's captor; his *enemy*. She would never need or want any help from him. He certainly shouldn't want to give it.

Still, it took all the willpower he had to lock himself in place and keep his voice low and uninflected. "Will you at least tell me the rules of this tournament you've chosen to enter us into? It seems unnecessarily complex as a method for disposing of your prisoners."

"Oh, but you're not my prisoner while we're here, remember?" Her glittering eyelashes fluttered low, hiding her eyes.

Gerard raised a single, pointed eyebrow. "Then I may turn and go home now?"

"And abandon me to fight alone?" She gave a dramatic pout. "*That* would hardly be noble or gentlemanly behavior from the famous Golden Beacon."

A wave of exasperation rolled through Gerard's body as he gazed down at her. Was she really so certain of her control that she didn't even feel a need to leverage her most obvious and effective threat? They *both* knew he could never find his way back to the mortal world without a fae guide . . . and judging by her earlier conversation with Lord Oberon, she was clearly bound by some ancient fae rule of etiquette not to back down from this ridiculous venture.

"*Enough.*" He infused iron into his voice. "Just tell me: Have we any chance of actually winning this tournament?"

Her lips twitched as her eyes flashed open with what looked like sudden, real amusement. "*Of course* you want to win, even now. I should have known the Serafin Empire's most famous general wouldn't limit his competitive urges to the mortal realm! You just can't bear to lose at anything, can you?"

If Gerard had ever in his life met a more competitive creature than the woman who stood before him now, he might have allowed that insight to discompose him. As it was, he pressed onward. "What sort of challenges are we about to face? And which weapons are we allowed, if any?"

Sighing, Lorelei finally deigned to answer one of his questions. "There should be an assortment of challenges across the next few days, ranging from—"

"*Days?*" How many days could Gerard's men hold their camp in that remote mountain pass without alerting the Emperor to his predicament? He didn't doubt the loyalty of his officers; if that note Lorelei had left in his handwriting was even half as convincing as she'd claimed, they would all fight to keep his "secret quest" safe from even the most official of inquiries.

But he also knew his emperor's impatient nature. Back in Fiora, Otto would be seething with bitter fury and humiliation after the anticlimax of his armies' long-awaited march to the Kitvarian border. There, Gerard had officially agreed to a peace rather than an invasion as Otto had commanded, to seize a new territory and officially expand the Empire for the first time in decades. Under the unexpected circumstances that had arisen at that border, Gerard *couldn't* have done otherwise without flouting Imperial law—but when it came to Otto's increasingly bellicose ambitions and recent purge of the more peaceable and thoughtful advisors from his side . . .

May Jovar light me a way back soon!

"Oh, do stop fussing so much!" Lorelei wafted a handful of rainbow sparkles through the air as she waved away all of his serious concerns with a careless flick of one hand. "After all your studies, you must understand that time passes very differently here. Why, for all you know, we might return to Balravia less than a minute after our departure!"

"And for all *you* know . . . ?" he prompted tightly.

"Darling, just relax your pretty head and let me worry about all of that. I have everything under control, remember?"

Would she ever stop trying to push him into madness? Gerard's teeth ground together, his own control close to the breaking point . . .

And she returned seamlessly to her earlier explanation. ". . . *Ranging from general challenges of wit and magic to paired duels against a variety of opponents. We're allowed to use any weapons we bring with us.*"

This time, Gerard didn't even bother with a response. He only looked down at her with weary patience.

"Oh, very well, if you *will* be so humorless about it!" Reaching behind her neck, Lorelei pulled out—apparently from nowhere—the sheathed sword that had lain beside his bed when she'd abducted him. "You may have it back for now, if you'd like."

"How very generous, Your Majesty." He gritted the words through his teeth as he reached for his stolen weapon, the air between them almost palpably vibrating with tension.

She offered it to him by the hilt—and as he took it, his larger hand closed around her fingers. It was the first time he had touched his maddening, infuriating, mischievous captor in all their seven years of circling.

It felt like a flint being struck.

Lightning sparked against his skin where it touched hers, and then it spread like a fire that had to be smothered immediately, before it could devastate *everything*. Gerard braced his muscles against the sparking heat and light and dug his booted heels against the grass, fighting to keep his face under control as he drew his hand away. He could *not* let her see or guess how powerfully she'd affected him . . .

And then he saw that her own eyes had flared wide, and she was breathing quickly.

Seven years ago, she'd taken his arm in hers and pressed her lush figure shamelessly against his side, but she'd done it with cool control as part of a calculated seduction, and she'd been a stranger to him. Her touch hadn't affected him in the slightest.

This time, his hand had closed around her fingers only for a moment—but her responsive swallow was a visible flex against her soft throat, as if his impossible, incorrigible nemesis was fighting *exactly* the same battle as him, after all.

... As if he wasn't the only one who'd been burning up from the inside out from the moment he'd seen her this morning ... and across so many years of private, intimate battles.

The tip of Lorelei's tongue swept out to moisten her upper lip, her dilating gaze clinging to his—and for the first time he could remember, Gerard acted without a thought, shifting forward into her space by pure instinct. As he claimed the inches between them, his fingers tightened around the familiar leather grip of his sword.

A crack in the leather scraped against his palm, *finally* breaking through his mindless haze.

Jovar save me. How could he have forgotten?

Gerard hadn't felt so much as a hint of his sword's presence earlier, even when he'd stood nearly close enough to touch Lorelei's back. The leather grip's familiar, comfortable solidity in his hand was a staggering reminder of the fae queen's powers of illusion.

No matter how desperately his body might try to pull him towards her; no matter how open and unguarded she might *appear*, with her blue eyes so helplessly wide before him now ...

He would *never* be able to trust anything she showed him. It could never be anything but deception. Worse yet, trust would signal betrayal of every oath of loyalty he had sworn to the Serafin Empire.

It would make him *no better than his parents*.

That realization was more effective than any blow. Breathing hard, he yanked his gaze free and took a long step backwards, rebuilding his self-control stone by stone until he was as hard and emotionless as any of the cold, grey statues that had lined the galleries of his grandmother's villa in Fiora.

When he finally met Queen Lorelei's gaze again, he felt *nothing*: no reckless warmth, no dangerous yearning, and not the slightest trace of shameful temptation. His vision was focused and clear, as always, and she was only one more challenge to defeat as he had so many others.

"Regardless of what you may be scheming, I can be pushed only so far," he said evenly. "I will agree to fight by your side in every trial in this tournament that I am called to—but only if *you* agree that you will return me to the mortal realm immediately after our final challenge. Otherwise, I will lay down my arms now and refuse to move another step."

Her glittering lashes swept down to cover her eyes for a long, silent moment. Then they flicked open, and she gave him a smile of pure, undiluted condescension, with no hints of openness or vulnerability anywhere to be seen. "Very well," she murmured. "I accept your bargain."

At her words, a hot shock of magic suddenly charged the air between them, like a fire catching light. It burned against his skin for a single, scalding instant and then vanished . . . but its message lingered in his still-tingling skin and twisted gut.

Bargains were far more than mere words of commitment in the fae realm, apparently—and on this magical battlefield, for the first time in years, Gerard was well out of his depth.

Hundreds of miles away and in the mortal realm, another battle was about to erupt in a snowy mountainside camp. Ten feet away from a massive boulder coated in transparent ice, ten armed soldiers stood guard before their commander's tent, facing off against five others, who flanked an official Imperial messenger. Raised voices rousted even more soldiers from their tents, while white-and-gold-cloaked Gilded Wizards clustered in a separate group nearby, watching and whispering worriedly to each other.

The Imperial messenger's irate voice carried the accent of the highest court and lashed his gathered audience like a whip. "Your precious Golden Beacon may have given you *his* orders, but His Imperial Majesty will not be denied! He requires the attendance of your general *now*, by swiftest course to the capital, with no more cowardly lagging along the way. General de Moireul *will* be on the train that leaves Kölnir station tonight, or he will be declared guilty of disobeying Imperial orders . . . again!"

Angry muttering sounded through the crowd of watching soldiers as they edged closer.

The five soldiers who stood behind the messenger dropped their hands to the hilts of their swords in rolling unison, like a wave of impending violence.

Unseen and undetected by any of them, the distant observer who watched it all through the boulder's thin coating of ice winced in pained anticipation . . .

And then one of the cloaked Gilded Wizards stepped forward, pushing back her hood as she interrupted the standoff. "Wait!" Turning from the Imperial messenger to the officers who led the human shield before the general's tent, she said loudly, "We think you should all know. One of my colleagues walked past the Golden Beacon's tent yesterday morning . . . and he's certain he sensed the remnants of fae magic coming from inside it."

The crowd erupted into a new kind of chaos at that news . . .

And, seated far away in her efficient royal office in her cold, northern capital city, Queen Ailana of Nornne let out a low groan, closing her eyes for a brief moment of respite from the scenario playing across the sheet of ice on the silver tray set on the desk before her.

"Oh, Lorelei," she murmured wearily. "What have you done now?"

7

The moment that the first round of the Tournament of Leaves began, Lorelei found herself swept away from the open playing field and confined, alone, within a dark, freezing cavern with no breaks in the damp walls around her and no sign of her reluctant partner anywhere.

Luckily, she was confident that she could find her way out of this trap—within a minute at the most!—if only she could keep her racing mind on the challenge... and away from that terrible, treacherous moment when she'd nearly lost her head over a man for the first time in years. Not just any man, either: It had been the godsdamned *Golden Beacon*, of all the worst possible choices! What would her fellow Queens of Villainy say if they ever found out about *that* mortifying misstep?

At least Lorelei had had some excuse to be surprised by betrayal when it had come from her first two lovers. Back then she'd been young, lonely, and naive, and both of them had sworn loyalty to her on their knees.

Stiff-necked, stubborn Gerard de Moireul saved all of *his* loyalty for the emperor who wanted to march heartless armies across the continent and turn Lorelei's beautiful, unique Balravia into one more flat and soulless Imperial archduchy covered in iron rails like a cage. Every magically gifted human would be forced into the regimented Gilded Wizards, and not a single wild fae influence would be left at all.

... And for all she knew, Gerard might be trapped in a nest of venomous flying serpents now, surrounded and overwhelmed without her magical help, while she fluttered about this absurd cave fretting about unimportant *feelings*.

Curse it!

She had not expected to be separated from her partner in the very first challenge that was set. Still, if Oberon thought he could throw her off her game, he was very much mistaken.

Drawing a deep breath, Lorelei tipped her head back and purposefully set aside every years-old memory of burning poison and humiliation ... and the even more dangerous heat that had scorched the air between her and the Golden Beacon when he'd finally snapped his leash for a single, breathless moment.

He'd come so close to kissing her ... !

Lock it away. Breathing deeply and evenly, she turned in place and reached out with all her senses to absorb the illusion that enclosed her. Formed by some of the most ancient fae in her mother's kingdom, it was of unmatched quality; in other circumstances, she would have dearly loved to study its effect. From the irritating *drip—drip—drip* of a distant fall of water, coming from deep in the shadows of the cavern, to the overwhelming smells of moss and damp and the chill of slick stone ground against the bare soles of her feet, every detail felt unassailably real, solid and true.

Somewhere in the near distance, the fae audience must be watching, chatting and cheering, sharing snacks and laying bets with their friends and enemies over how long it would take her to find her way out. All that Lorelei could hear, though, was the endless drip that nagged at her ears as the cold, moist air pressed in against her bare arms, trying to force her to shrink into herself.

It wouldn't work—and the fact that he'd chosen it proved that Oberon didn't know her as well as he'd thought.

All across the continent, in the mortal and fae realms alike, ignorant followers of her escapades might agree that this must be her nightmare: to be trapped on her own, far from any glittering parties, handsome lovers, or adoring crowds. If she were truly the paper creature of their imaginings, she would panic at her solitude and discomfort and use herself up far too soon, rashly flinging all of her power at the illusion to shatter it in a full-blown attack.

But Lorelei had learned decades ago how to function alone behind her sparkling public image—and every battle or assassination attempt that she'd survived since then had helped teach her the exact limits of her magic.

So, instead of bracing herself to battle with magic, she closed her eyes and reached out—not with her fallible physical senses this time, but with something far deeper and more true: her ingrained link with the earth itself and all that grew from it.

I'm back, darlings, she called out in a silent, musical lure. *Why don't you come find me? It's been far too long.*

According to tales her mother's attendants had told, flowers had shot out from the ground to curl around her crib in blessing before she was even old enough to notice them. When she'd been expelled into the mortal realm to stake her claim at her father's court, that move had cut her off from every leaf and bloom in the fae realm, and the loss had felt like an amputation.

Now, she let her whole body relax, sinking into the damp chill of the stony ground without any apparent care in the world. She was clearly no threat to this illusion. It didn't have to fight to hold *her*. She wasn't even struggling against it! She was just being herself, silly and pretty and thoughtless, certainly not worth worrying about...

And as she felt the first soft, questing tendrils of vegetation slip across her toes, a dull roar began in the distance. It thundered into raucously approving cheers all around her as the fresh air warmed her skin once again. Lorelei tipped her head back to feel the true sunlight on her face, and the welcome scent of fresh green life filled her senses, that dank, chilly illusion shattered by a force far more powerful than any individual fae: the land that sheltered all of them as Sylvana's gift.

Thank you, Lorelei whispered with deep sincerity.

Then she sprang to her feet to rescue her infuriating prisoner.

At first, all she could see was the green field spread around her—far vaster, now, than the original clearing that had been crossed by every fae visitor before this tournament began. Now that the official games had started, that green area had been magically stretched and tugged in every direction until it spread, from each partnership's point of view, all the way to each horizon, while the spectators looked down upon it with a telescopic focus from their distant, newly erected stands of living willow.

Lorelei's first challenge had kept her trapped in one small section of that field; now, as she narrowed her eyes and looked again, more carefully, across that vast, seemingly empty area, her gaze snagged on a telltale blur of air only fifty feet away.

There!

She leapt forward, aiming herself at the spot where that translucent patch of air rippled above the grass so gently that she'd missed it in her first scan. *Something* was hidden behind that illusion—no, *someone*: Gerard, facing off against who-knew-what and fighting for his life without her.

Unacceptable. Lorelei wished with sudden, burning intensity that she had the wings of some of her mother's other subjects—or that she'd at least thought to bring her gorgeous riding gryphon, Bluebell, to speed her way through the tournament. As it was, all she could do was sprint across the soft grass, powered by fury and an irrational, growing panic.

No one was allowed to kill the Golden Beacon on her watch!

... No one apart from her, obviously. But that was *different.*

This time, she didn't pause to think through clever strategies or worry about magical conservation. She simply flung herself forward through that resistant magical barrier, *refusing* to allow it to stop her—

And as she broke through with a sparkling explosion of magic that blinded her for an instant, Gerard's voice rapped out:

"*Close your eyes!*"

That dungeon-deep voice, in that tone of command, could have sent an armed battalion to its knees. Lorelei shut her eyes in immediate, uncharacteristic obedience.

An inhuman screech of rage sounded only two feet away. Gritting her teeth, she didn't flinch. The sound was muffled an instant later, followed by a physical collision so close, it shifted the air against her skin.

Lorelei held perfectly still, with every muscle braced and every sense but her own cruelly denied vision flaring with agonizing awareness. Harsh pants of breath mingled nearby with thumps and snarls and something that sounded like a human grunt of pain.

Damn it, if he didn't release that high-handed injunction soon ... !

"Very well." Gerard's voice was ragged with breathlessness, but his tone was matter-of-fact. "You may open your eyes."

"How very generous of you." Dryly, she echoed his earlier words. However, they took on a different meaning as her eyelashes lifted and she finally absorbed the sight before her. "Oh, *my.*" Blinking, she fluttered a cloud of glitter into the air, hoping to distract him from the expression on her face.

Her strategy backfired as specks of rainbow glitter landed on one bare, muscled shoulder.

Lorelei choked back an involuntary whimper. *Sylvana, save me!*

This simply would not do. She was a scandalous rake of a queen, not some innocent to be gobsmacked. She'd seen *plenty* of handsome men's naked bodies in her time...

And yet, to see General Gerard de Moireul himself—always *so* very proper and correct—standing unexpectedly shirtless before her now, gleaming with sweat, his lightly furred, broad chest rising and falling from his exertions above his belt-free woolen trousers, so tantalizingly close that she could easily—

No! Just in time, she yanked back her right hand, which had begun to lift of its own traitorous accord. *Leave the pretty alone. Danger!*

Gathering her wits, Lorelei raised one disdainful eyebrow and prayed he hadn't noticed her gaping at him like a lovestruck fool. "Goodness, this really *is* my lucky day. Did you find it just too, *too* unbearably hot to remain clothed? It might earn us extra points in our challenge, but I should remind you, before you go any further with this delightful disrobing, that we do have an audience."

The look he gave her in return was distinctly unimpressed. "Perhaps, Your Majesty, if you look down by your feet, you might spot the answer to your question."

Ah. Yes, there was still a whole world around them, wasn't there? Embarrassingly enough, she hadn't noticed anything but him since her eyes had reopened. Now, she finally looked past that overwhelming, destabilizing, half-unwrapped temptation of a man...

And both of her eyebrows shot up as she took in the whole scene around them, from the narrow ravine that closed them between two tall and rocky cliff faces to the piled and curled-up mass of scaly brown-and-red muscle that lay sulking on the ground beside her, its big, lethal head covered in Gerard's missing shirt, which was firmly secured there by his belt.

"A *basilisk?*" No wonder he'd warned her to close her eyes! Meeting that reptilian gaze would have frozen her into permanent stone. But...

Her gaze dropped to the sword he'd abandoned on the ground behind him. "You didn't want to finish by slicing off its head?" Basilisks were vanishingly rare nowadays, so their decapitated heads raised staggering sums at auction when offered up by swaggering hunters.

His strong shoulders lifted in a deeply distracting shrug. "Now that it can't make eye contact, it can offer us no further harm. I doubt it chose to participate in this tournament of its own accord; I could hardly fault it for attempting to defend itself. And as you said I was allowed to use any weapon I'd brought with me into the tournament..."

"You chose your shirt rather than your sword." Lorelei swallowed down a groan of pure despair. "Of course you did." Gerard might be the soulless Emperor's most favored general and devoid of magic, but he was no callous brute, no matter how hard she'd tried to believe that over the years. *Damn it.* "You've done your research, again."

For once, her praise was sincere—but his eyebrows lowered into a frown of unmistakable discomfort. "There was an excellent library at my military school. It was only sensible to make use of it while there."

"Hmm." Based on the stories she'd heard of others' military school exploits, most of his fellow officers-in-training *hadn't* felt the same. But then... his parents had been notorious for some scandal or other, hadn't they? Perhaps, after that, the other students had stopped inviting him to join their more sociable activities.

Regardless of the reason, he'd clearly found his way into that library, studied all of the magical creatures Imperial soldiers were meant to hate, and grown into a man capable of commanding tens of thousands . . . but still soft-hearted enough to spare the universally reviled creature that had just tried to kill him.

As Lorelei met his clear amber gaze, something inside her chest twisted in one final act of resistance . . . and then subsided in defeat.

He truly was a good man, despite his misguided allegiance. And she . . .

Well. Fortunately, Lorelei was utterly heartless. *Everyone* knew that, and she thanked Sylvana now for that blessing . . .

Because if she hadn't been, right now, she would be in desperate trouble.

8

Queen Saskia of Kitvaria was feared across the continent for her vast magical powers, her notorious temper, and her unabashed wickedness.

So it felt decidedly unfair that *none* of the people who knew her best showed any compunction about interrupting her most peaceful moments.

"Ahem." Morlokk, her majordomo, cleared his throat meaningfully as he loomed over her comfortable wing chair in her cozy library of magic. "I believe you're wanted, Your Majesty, by Queen Ailana of Nornne."

"Is that what all the buzzing was about a few minutes ago?" Frowning, Saskia set down the book she'd been studying and glanced across the room at the magical mirror-box she'd set atop a half-empty shelf. She'd promised the other two

Queens of Villainy only last week that she would go nowhere without it, in case any new developments arose in the Serafin Empire's quest to make itself a nuisance and expand across their countries. Still, when she was deeply absorbed in work, she often missed such inconsequential noises... and she was far too close to success in her latest project to stop now. "Never mind. She can wait until later. I'm almost certain, if I just take the time to piece together these two different spells—"

"*Ahem.*" This time, Morlokk's throat-clearing was even more pointed—and when it came to the clearing of an ogre's throat, *no one* could ignore the strength of that rumble. "I'm afraid Queen Ailana thinks it too urgent for that."

Saskia rolled her eyes, entirely unimpressed. "Ailana can think whatever she wants, but we're not in Nornne, so—wait a moment." Narrowing her eyes, she looked up at her trusted advisor and surrogate father. "How do *you* know what she thinks? That box has been right here with me all afternoon."

"That box, yes." Morlokk gave a massive shrug. "However, Your Majesty, the Queen of Nornne was kind enough to offer similar devices to me and Mrs. Haglitz, as well. We can use them to make our orders for the household far more easily, even from a great distance—*and* come to your assistance when a message might otherwise be missed."

"Unbelievable." Ailana *had* asked Saskia to enchant several of the devices—but she'd certainly never mentioned using any of them in that fashion. Closing the book, Saskia shook her head at Morlokk. "You, of all people, actually allowed her to trick you into accepting a *bribe?*"

From the moment she'd first fled into hiding as a child under his and Mrs. Haglitz's protection, Morlokk had had the knack of looking down at her whenever she made a foolish statement with such weary patience that her shoulders hunched with guilt before he said a single word. Now, he let the silence linger for a long, painful moment before replying, "As you know, no one in this castle would *ever* accept a bribe to cause you harm. However, Mrs. Haglitz and I agree that the Queen of Nornne was being sensible to lay multiple paths of communication. After all, she has been a useful source of urgent information in the past."

"I suppose so." Saskia sighed and looked across the table at her consort. Felix had been keeping his head discreetly bent over his own reading material, but she glimpsed a rueful quirk of his lips as he looked down at the page. Of course, the last time Ailana had carried a warning, it had been in regards to *him*. "I don't suppose you—?"

"Forgive me, darling." Felix finally looked up, eyes gleaming with amusement as he shook his head. "This is your kingdom, not mine—and you're the one she wants to speak with. I'll handle the research for both of us while you're busy."

"Now you're just being cruel." Saskia glowered at him as she stood up. "You know I love researching with you."

"And I love you," he murmured, reaching for her hand across the table. His kiss was warm and soft against her skin; she couldn't help returning his rueful, tender smile. "Take heart," he added. "If Lorelei's still missing, at least Ailana can't use any fae portals to arrive in person with her instructions."

"*Instructions.* Pah! She needs to learn, and *soon*, that we're not members of her network of spies." Saskia had informed Ailana of that fact multiple times before—but the ice queen was far too used to being the cleverest, most strategic, and best-informed person in any room. It took all the stubbornness that Saskia possessed to maintain her own power in their trio.

As she started towards the door, already planning her upcoming lecture, Morlokk bowed respectfully. "Would you prefer to contact her from your tower, Your Majesty? Or shall I ask Mrs. Haglitz to send you a tray of coffee in the parlor?"

"No trays," she told him. "No coffee or treats! We are *not* going to settle into a friendly chat. This time, it will be a *swift* matter of business."

Five minutes later, though, when she opened the mirror-box and caught sight of her ally, Saskia was startled into personal conversation after all. "Gods, what's happened now?" she demanded. "I've never seen you look like this before."

Termed an ice queen for more than just the strength of her particular magical powers, Ailana of Nornne was famed for her unmatched elegance, perfectly composed demeanor, and nerves of steel. Only a few days ago, Saskia had stood at her side to face down Imperial armies at Kitvaria's border, and Ailana hadn't displayed the slightest anxiety about the outcome.

This time, lines of strain creased the light brown skin around Ailana's eyes, deep shadows tugged at the skin underneath... and her response spoke volumes. "*Lorelei.*"

"Ah." Sighing, Saskia sat back on the velvet couch she'd chosen, tucked beside a warm fire in the small second-floor parlor. She should have ordered coffee, after all, to brace herself if their unpredictable fae ally was involved in whatever new crisis had arisen. "Has she already popped up again, then? Felix and I have both been working to design a spell that might break through her defenses and tell us where she's hiding, but if that isn't needed anymore..."

"Unfortunately, none of my spies have located her yet. However, the Golden Beacon has now been discovered missing by the Emperor—with evidence of fae magic at the scene."

"Oh, darkness." Groaning, Saskia shut her eyes for a long moment. "Lorelei, *why?*"

"She did promise to 'deal' with him as a problem," Ailana reminded her. "She never actually told us how."

"So she decided to restart the godsdamned war just when we'd managed to postpone it? *Argh!*" Saskia felt her crows rousing worriedly around the castle, responding to her rising emotions; she forced herself to send a feeling of calm reassurance to settle all of them, but the cushions on the couch around her lifted from their positions, twirling in tight, anxious circles to let out her anxious energy.

Ironically, just as Saskia's own peace was shattered, Ailana looked to be regaining her composure. "The situation isn't quite so dire, yet, as it could be. There was no evidence of Lorelei, in particular, to anyone who doesn't know her as well as we do. So they'll mount a manhunt within the Empire to begin with. After all, it could have been any fae who took him—and they haven't managed to expel *every* fae citizen from their vast borders yet."

"We don't want any innocent fae put in danger," Saskia said. "Nor would Lorelei." Despite her maddening volatility, the Queen of Balravia had more than proven her loyalty to her fellow queens *and* to all of the magical denizens of the continent who were under threat from Emperor Otto.

"She would not," Ailana agreed, "and that is what most concerns me. If she'd heard this news herself, she certainly would have made a public appearance by now to shower glitter on everyone's faces and claim full credit for his abduction. For all Lorelei's quirks, she has never tried to shift the blame for her own actions."

"But if she hasn't even heard the news . . . oh, *no*." Saskia winced as the obvious explanation slid into place. "No wonder none of our spells have found her yet! We're not only fighting her own magical shields—if she's in the fae realm, none of us can reach her."

"And if she's carried him there with her, there may be no salvaging this situation . . . in more ways than one." Ailana's lovely face tightened. "Without General de Moireul taking his place in the Emperor's private councils, there are no advisors left who dare even *try* to rein in Otto's hubris. The last Imperial high priest is currently awaiting trial for so-called treason, which will carry a sentence of death—and according to my spies, the new Imperial high priestess never speaks at all. She only sits in smiling silence to lend divine blessing to every one of his plans."

"Ugh." Saskia's nostrils flared with distaste. "So much for piety! No, wait, I remember—isn't she Otto's own sister?"

"She is," Ailana said tightly, "and all the other advisors in his council chamber now are unscrupulous toadies competing to enable his every whim. General de Moireul is the only one left with both the power and the courage to stand against Otto when he finally informs them all of his plan to adopt Purification as Imperial policy."

"I still hate that name for it," Saskia muttered.

Bigotry would have been a better title for that growing movement fueled by hatred. Most archduchies in the Empire had already expelled their magical residents, leaving them to take refuge in the various independent kingdoms scattered around the Empire's borders—but Purification, a cruel fanatic's cause, called for magical creatures no longer to be allowed to survive at *all*. If Otto had his way, he'd use it as his guiding beacon to spread his empire all the rest of the way across the continent, leaving death and destruction in his wake.

"How long do you think we have until they discover who was behind the Golden Beacon's disappearance?" Saskia asked. "Or until they decide to use it as an excuse to start the war regardless?"

"If we're lucky? I'd say a week. If we aren't . . ." Ailana's nostrils flared as she took a slow, deep breath. "Perhaps two days, given the circumstances."

"Two days," Saskia repeated and made it a vow. They had two days left to track down their incorrigible friend and save all three kingdoms; between them, she and Felix would find a way to do it. "Very well. It's time to get to work."

9

Despite all the illusions and magical creatures around him, it felt surprisingly easy for Gerard to fall into the familiar rhythms of combat and rest. It was at challenge days like this that he'd first proven himself at the academy, years ago—and when he and Lorelei stepped off the tournament field after their first trial, they were greeted by a buoying roar of applause.

Of course, he knew it wasn't aimed at him, the mortal stranger in their midst. Lorelei, for all that she ruled a mortal realm, was clearly still considered one of them and, even more clearly, had been missed. He shifted out of the way without regret as a winged and clawed crowd of her admirers surged towards her on the sidelines of the field, every fae attendee eager to greet and congratulate her for this first triumph.

Gerard came to a halt far enough away not to be trampled but close enough to keep a wary eye on his mischievous captor—and a hard, flat-handed blow hit the back of his bare left shoulder. Instinct dropped his hand towards the hilt of his waiting sword. Discipline curled his fingers together before they could clasp that hilt and start him down the path towards a rash new battle.

Keeping his expression unperturbed, he turned without haste and found an eight-foot-tall creature from a fairy tale beaming down at him with unmistakable goodwill. The broad antlers of a stag speared out from the fae male's tawny, shoulder-length curls, polished hooves poked out beneath his dramatically billowing purple trousers, and the furred hand he'd clapped against Gerard's shoulder in congratulations now pulled back in a friendly, beckoning gesture. "Well done with that basilisk!" he boomed deafeningly. "But you'll need to dress yourself for your next trial. Come over to my stand, and we'll see what I can do to cover you!"

With the autumn air prickling against his sweat-laced skin, it was a tempting offer—but Gerard cast a quick glance at the crowd that surrounded Lorelei and stayed firmly in place. "I appreciate the offer, but I had better wait for my partner."

"Oh, she won't mind. See?" The antlered vendor waved cheerfully above the heads of the crowd to catch Lorelei's attention. "Princess! May I have the honor of clothing your partner, please?"

"Aw. Only if you insist on taking away *all* my fun." Even without being able to see Lorelei's face, Gerard could hear her theatrical pout in that teasing voice. "Put the cost on my account, please, and do help him find us drinks while you're at it. Gerard, darling, don't panic," she caroled. "I'll join you soon, I promise!"

With an effort, Gerard resisted the temptation to roll his eyes. "I'll do my best not to panic too much in the meantime," he said—and allowed his new, antlered companion to lead him into a scene of magical chaos.

Apparently, while he had been fighting his first trial, every vendor at the court of Efaelen had been busy creating a whole village-worth of small wooden stalls with an eyewatering assortment of goods on offer. Banners for each stand danced in the air above them without any visible support, while flashy illusions reached temptingly towards attendees from every side.

The actual payments changing hands made little sense to Gerard's human eyes—could a simple acorn or a small brown leaf truly purchase a rich velvet cloak?—but with Lorelei as his promised sponsor, he was thankfully spared the challenge of working out any more dangerous fae bargains on his own. Within minutes, he had settled on the least garish tunic he was offered, belted it securely into place over his woolen trousers, and set out to find food and drink. He would need it to fuel all the trials to come...

And there were plenty of them.

Of course, time passed differently in the fae realm; Gerard had known that much for years. Even so, it was a shock to realize, several hours later, that the bright sun *still* hadn't shifted in its arc across the sky.

The beautifully carved mug he'd been given after his first trial by a leaf-haired, bark-skinned dryad refilled itself again and again across the day with a sparkling, transparent juice that tasted of fresh pears and ginger. It tingled against Gerard's tongue, filling him with newfound energy every time. Its taste perfectly complemented the hot strips of earthy venison, fried with mushrooms and onions and richly flavored with savory herbs, that he and Lorelei scooped up together after their fourth trial.

By that point, the large mass of competitors who had all started together earlier had been split into a series of separate trials, half of them competing on the field each time while the other half rested and awaited their next turns. Lorelei's admirers were all busy in the stands now, leaving the two of them alone for the first time since the tournament had begun. Food had been their first joint goal—but then, in an agreement made by nods and glances through the chaos of the noisy vendors' village, they made their way to a quieter spot where they could eat and watch the ongoing trials.

Gerard's fixed intention was to analyze the tactics and skills of their competitors, the better to prepare to face them later. Even so, as they stood together, it was impossible not to take any note of his captor, more unguarded than he'd ever seen her before.

Leaning against the trunk of an oak tree with her fine gown spattered in mud, her long, blonde hair in wild tangles, and a smudge of dirt covering her left cheek, Lorelei looked nothing like the sophisticated, sultry royal whose scandals had inspired salacious plays and songs for the past decade. As she studied the field before them, her blue eyes were bright with interest, enjoyment, and unshielded calculation.

For once, the rapid workings of her brain weren't hidden behind her usual guise of gay, careless frivolity . . . and as he watched her track the progress of all fifteen simultaneous trials on the field with ease, Gerard's lower body tightened against his will.

Heedless of his covert gaze, Lorelei popped another rustic strip of venison into her mouth with her small, bare fingers, letting the juices slip carelessly down her palm. Shadows from the leafy, trailing branches above her dappled her fair skin, while a light, autumnal breeze played with her tangled curls.

Gerard would never know how it felt to touch those curls and discover just how soft they might feel against his own calloused fingers.

. . . And it shouldn't have even occurred to him to wonder. That idea was so outrageous, it should have been *unthinkable*—but Jovar knew, this whole day had been beyond his conception. First, he'd been transplanted from the icy depths of a mortal winter afternoon to a comparatively warm fae autumn morning, and now he was surrounded by impossibilities on all sides. No wonder his mind and body were both straining at his leash!

Finishing the last of her snacks, Lorelei slipped one finger into her mouth to suck off the last of the juices . . .

And Gerard swiftly averted his gaze, lifting his cup to his lips for a long, refreshing swallow.

Ahhh. His shoulders relaxed as magical energy tingled through him once again, gifting the strength that he needed to force his rebellious attention back to the action on the field instead of the enemy beside him.

"There!" Four minutes later, Lorelei pointed decisively at the second pair to win a trial, ignoring the official results being announced by a herald at the top of the field. "Those two will be our most dangerous competitors. Did you see how they took out that final troll in their obstacle race?"

Gerard's eyes narrowed in consideration as he followed the path of her finger to a partnership of hobgoblins. He'd taken note of that particular pair, too, but until now, he hadn't sensed her paying them any special attention. "They weren't the fastest at completing their trial," he said, leadingly.

"But they were *clever* about it—and that's what'll count in the next rounds," she told him. "Everything we've been called upon to do so far"—defeating the basilisk, escaping a seven-headed hydra, shattering illusions, harnessing a wild wyvern, and more—"has been based on simple feats of physical or magical strength. Once the first mass of contestants is winnowed away, though, everything will become much harder. Then we'll need cunning as well."

Excellent. The word rose through Gerard's throat with such force, he had to snap his jaw shut to contain the telltale utterance before it could escape into the air and reveal too much to her... and to himself.

In the names of all seven of Jovar's holy sentinels, what was wrong with him?

He *was* still a prisoner, despite his captor's earlier teasing; no bribes, however delicious or enticing, could possibly change that grim truth. He knew better than to allow himself any traitorous *enjoyment.*

But, damn it, it had been years since he'd last had the opportunity to pit his wits and strength against such satisfying challenges... and as the bells rang to summon them for their next round, he couldn't deny the simmering anticipation in his gut.

He ought to fight against every lifelong instinct and make himself lose to shame his captor. He *ought* to want this whole venture to explode in Lorelei's face, to make her the laughingstock of the fae and force her to regret ever daring to abduct him.

And yet...

If he did forfeit these trials and put on a show of utter helplessness, how would that reflect upon his own emperor, who had granted him so many great honors in the first place?

How would it reflect upon the Serafin Empire itself if any mischievous fae observer were to spread the news of the pitiful display they'd witnessed to their friends in the mortal world?

He imagined Emperor Otto—whose towering ego had always been so paradoxically fragile—hearing any such stories spread about the might of *his* Imperial high general...

...And Gerard's shoulders relaxed as certainty filled him.

Setting aside his mug, he brushed his hands briskly against his trousers to remove the last of the venison's grease. Then he strode towards his starting position by Lorelei's side with the same focused determination that had transformed him from the weakest member of his boarding school to the head of the Serafin Empire's armies.

This time, he and Lorelei were directed to line up on the field beside four other partnerships who had successfully completed all of their own earlier challenges. The pair of hobgoblins wasn't there, but the others—ranging from tall and haughty fae archers to red-capped gnomes with long, curving dark claws and dagger-like teeth—would all be worthy opponents.

Gerard lowered his chin in a respectful nod to his competitors, and even the high fae gravely returned the action as their glinting green gazes swept across him in speculation.

Lorelei, of course, gave them all a jaunty wave, scattering colorful glitter through the air with her usual abandon. "Good luck, darlings! We will truly hate to beat you."

At that, the closest gnome snorted, her leathery lips pulling back into a grin of amusement. "Good luck, Princess."

"You'll need it!" added her partner with cheerful malice.

Lorelei's bright expression dimmed. "'Queen,'" she corrected them softly. "Not 'princess' here anymore."

Gerard's eyebrows rose at the echo of old pain in her voice.

A high, haunting hunting horn sounded in the air before he could ask any questions. The world whirled around him and the grassy field fell away beneath him for a moment that felt endless . . .

And then sticks and leaves crunched under his feet with the force of his landing. Head spinning, he straightened slowly from his first, instinctive crouch, inspecting the thick forest that now surrounded them. Beside him, he sensed Lorelei doing the same, her figure turned tense and wary.

The others were all gone . . . and this felt nothing like the forest he and Lorelei had walked through earlier on their way to the tournament.

Here, the trees loomed over them with knotted trunks and tangled branches. The leaves that formed a choking canopy above were so dark that they looked nearly black, and they glistened with an unpleasant-looking moisture. The knots in the trees merely looked misshapen when inspected full-on, but from the corners of Gerard's eyes, they seemed to take on nearly human faces with sinister, gloating expressions.

No birdsong or buzz of insects cheered this ominous silence. It hung around them like a shroud. *Waiting.*

Turning, he met Lorelei's gaze. She pressed her lips firmly together. He nodded in perfect understanding.

Neither of them would speak out loud to alert whatever menace awaited them.

Wordlessly, he gestured at the scene around them and raised his eyebrows. She shook her head.

Unlike some of their earlier trials, this was no simple illusion meant only to be broken—at least, not until they had first successfully completed the challenge that lay within.

But as for what that might be...

Without any instructions, they would have to use their wits to divine what was expected of them. Lorelei was already scanning the thick canopy overhead, her eyebrows furrowed with concentration. Gerard turned his attention to the twisted trunks of the trees nearby, and to those oddly shaped knots along their sides, which looked like no natural configuration.

His first instinct had been to wince away from the sight of them when viewed sidelong—as any human would if they glimpsed a shadowy hint of impossible faces leering at them in the dark. They would reassure themselves that it was only their imaginations at work.

But Gerard was standing in a world where his own imagination couldn't compare to fae reality—and he had learned as a child never to cower away from nightmares. Holding himself perfectly still, he focused all of his attention on the bulbous knots in the trees to either side of him, allowing those sinister faces to take on clearly defined shapes and detail in the corners of his vision.

Noses twitched. Teeth gnashed with threat. Long, black tongues licked out as if to taste his scent. A whole variety of furious, intimidating expressions played out across all the different lurking faces...

But as he kept himself still and unmoving, every one of their eerie gazes swiveled in the same direction.

Gerard turned as carefully and as quietly as he could.

A giant, twisted old oak splayed its massive trunk—at least twice the width of Gerard's own substantial shoulders—across the forest floor before him. It was closely flanked by two smaller trees that leaned heavily against it, both of them wound about in chains of poison ivy.

In the trunk of that great oak, centered at the level of his heart, was a large, ominously gaping hole. Inside it, all he could glimpse was utter blackness.

Who knew what kind of venomous creature might be lurking inside, only waiting to lunge when disturbed?

Scooping up a long, fallen stick from the ground, Gerard crossed the space with two careful, quiet strides, and—bracing himself—levered the tip of the stick cautiously into the hole.

No resistance met his movement. Even as he stepped forward, closer and closer until he was peering directly into it, he couldn't see a single hint of life within the darkness—and the stick moved easily through it until only his own hand remained safe outside. The back of the tree was nowhere to be found.

Turning back, he gestured to catch Lorelei's attention.

She had been kneeling down, inspecting a pile of fallen acorns, but her eyes widened as he pointed to the oak, and she jumped to her feet to hurry over. Tipping her head close against the tree's bark, she inhaled deeply . . . and then she grinned in a sudden, delighted flash of mischief that seemed to light up the whole gloomy clearing. Lifting her chin with perfect confidence, she stepped directly into the trunk of the tree.

As her bare foot hit bark, she disappeared from view.

With a fierce grin of his own, Gerard followed.

The supposed oak melted around him like a dream, leaving him standing behind Lorelei on a narrow footpath lined by thick, towering hedges and blanketed in late twilight. The first stars already glittered in unfamiliar patterns high overhead.

How long had they spent in that dark forest?

Lorelei half-turned to arch an expectant eyebrow at him. Gerard nodded, pointedly compressing his lips.

These new surroundings might not—yet—feel quite so ominous, but the same expectant silence held sway here. It would be foolish to break it now.

It would be even more foolish to let himself reflect on how

shockingly easy it felt to communicate without words with his greatest nemesis.

. . . Or, worse yet, on how treacherously *natural* it felt to do so.

No. Setting his jaw, Gerard wrenched his malfunctioning thoughts firmly back under control.

He was Queen Lorelei's *prisoner*, not her partner . . . and he would win this challenge purely for the honor of his empire.

With that mission once more in mind, he tilted his head meaningfully. His beautiful—no, *wicked*, impossible—captor gave a graceful shrug in answer and then started forward, leading the way along the path towards the next stage of their challenge.

10

Long, sharp-thorned brambles trailed through the hedges on each side of the narrow path like clawed and questing fingers. Lorelei gave them an indulgent smile and then dismissed them with a flick of her hand. They curled swiftly out of the way, leaving her to walk freely, all her senses alive to the night around her.

The whisper-soft sounds that followed behind a moment later made her wince, as those same brambles scraped audibly against her human partner. At least the Golden Beacon was no longer half-naked; surely thorns couldn't damage his skin *too* badly now that he was fully dressed.

It had been a mingled disappointment and relief when his lost shirt and belt had been replaced by that helpful vendor after their first challenge.

Unfortunately, his new top was a silky red tunic that emphasized his absurdly broad shoulders and looked far too soft and touchable for Lorelei's liking. He should have appeared ridiculous with that vivid, dramatic fae tunic clasped into place over the plain blue woolen trousers of a stodgy Imperial officer. Instead, the snarling silver fox head of his belt buckle accentuated the uncomfortable truth:

High General Gerard de Moireul looked *even better* when he finally let himself go a little wild.

Sylvana save me! Lorelei bit back a wistful sigh. *No seductions allowed.*

He might have shown himself to be a better man than she would have admitted a few days ago, but Lorelei only played her games with *safe* men nowadays. From dreamy opera composers to self-important counts and princes, she traded pleasure with ease but never trusted any of them with anything that mattered.

Gerard de Moireul—far more principled, more intelligent, and more damnably compelling than any of her past lovers—was the epitome of *unsafe*. Even if he did ever experience a change of heart when it came to his appalling political allegiance, the man would be gods-driven in everything he did. Whenever he finally let down his iron shields, he would commit with ferocious intensity to his chosen partner—and she would end up revealing everything to him.

So Lorelei shifted her focus from the tantalizing challenge close behind her to the lethal challenge surrounding them both. They had escaped the first stage of this trial without setting off the lurking menace that they'd both sensed, but they still hadn't discovered their ultimate goal. So far, she hadn't even glimpsed any helpful hints . . . and as she turned a corner of the winding path, she found herself at a branching fork with both paths leading into pitch darkness.

Of course it had to be a maze. Nothing in this tournament would ever be easy—and apparently, they'd be navigating this part without any light to guide them. Fortunately, Lorelei had always had her own ways of orienting herself in Efaelen.

Tipping her head back, she gazed up at the constellations forming high overhead, where the purple of late twilight had shifted into full black. She'd learned the names of all those stars when she was a child, along with the epic stories of how each of their formations had come to be; by the time she was five, she'd known how to find the ones that would lead her safely home at this time of year.

Unfortunately, as she gazed upwards now with mounting confusion, she realized that everything looked wrong—jumbled up, *unfamiliar*—and her heart gave a sickening lurch of panic. Was Oberon right about her after all? Had she really spent so many years away that she'd forgotten her first sky?

The cool breeze that rippled through the hedge path seemed to pass directly through her bones, as if she'd gone hollow.

Then Gerard stepped up to join her, and the tingling warmth of his body looming behind her brought her back to herself with a start.

Regardless of any secret failures, she was *still on stage*—and damn it, she was the infamous Fae Queen of Balravia. A thousand vicious gossips and a hundred songs and plays had already tried and failed to drag her down. She would *not* fall apart now in front of her partner—*prisoner*—or their unseen watchers in the stands.

Wouldn't Oberon love to see me crumple?

Lorelei arranged her face into bright interest as she turned and gestured questioningly between the branching paths. The Golden Beacon was famously, inexorably methodical in all he did—and he *had* been the first to spot that camouflaged fae portal in the first part of this challenge. In this single, particular context, Lorelei could bear to let him take the lead . . . at least until she'd sorted out her malfunctioning memories and wasn't feeling so unforgivably *weak* anymore.

He looked over her head from one side to another, his shadowed eyes narrowing. No sounds emanated from either direction except the quiet, steady rustling of the breeze through the thick hedges ... and the underlying, heavy silence of this challenge's mysterious guardian, still *listening* and lying in wait for anyone careless enough to speak aloud.

Still frowning thoughtfully, Gerard took hold of one of the nearest hedge branches—and Lorelei realized with sudden horror what he meant to do.

Biting back a cry, she flung herself forward and wrapped both of her hands around his big fingers where they rested in the branches, poised to rip and break. *No greenery here could be harmed without terrible consequences!* She shook her head frantically—and he nodded in acceptance, his fingers loosening beneath hers.

Her whole body sagged in relief ... until she realized, a moment later, that she was still holding his left hand in both of hers, no longer in the firm grip of a captor but in a near-cuddle, her thumbs stroking thoughtlessly along the lightly haired back of his hand. It felt so strong and so deeply appealing, his warm skin tingling against hers, trying to draw her even closer—

Not your toy, Lorelei! Let the nice man go. With a grimace she couldn't quite repress, she dropped his hand and hastily stepped backwards, brushing her palms against her gown to wipe away that moment of temptation.

Still, it hadn't been for naught. He'd had a good idea, when it came down to essentials. All she needed to do, to enact it without any unnecessary risk, was ... *aha.*

She *had* been clever after all to ferret away those two acorns in her bodice, back in that dark forest! She'd taken them with the vague idea of planting them later—most of those trees had been real, and she wouldn't mind a twisting dark oak or two to lend atmosphere to her palace gardens—but just now, she had a far more pressing need for *bait.*

And what would be the point of having a partner famous for his physical prowess if she didn't give him a chance to show off? Scooping out the hoarded acorns with a quick shimmy and rearrangement of her bosom, she presented them to Gerard with a cheerful grin and wink, ready to be entertained.

For a long moment, he did nothing but study the offerings on her palm in the growing darkness, his face tightening as if in pain. Finally, he took a deep breath—which did *astonishing* things to his broad chest, she couldn't help but note—and took the acorns from her, his rough fingertips brushing lightly against her palm.

Goddess help me. Lorelei bit down hard on her lower lip and stepped out of his way, giving him space to throw.

It *wasn't* a retreat.

He tossed the first acorn to the left, into that impermeable blackness. Lorelei held her breath as she listened for its landing.

No sound emerged. After a long moment, they traded a glance and then turned to face the right-hand path. Gerard tossed the second acorn in a smooth, underarm swing . . .

And a roar of rage sounded from that second darkness, emerging from the beast who'd hidden there.

They moved in tandem, with no need for any signals. Lorelei lunged down the left-hand path with Gerard close behind. This path was broad enough for them to run side by side, but as pitch blackness fell over them, Lorelei took the lead without question, her senses sharper than those of any full human. She could *feel* the tall hedges growing on each side, knew where to turn and when to stop before she ran into a sudden green, growing barrier that screamed, to her heightened awareness, a warning of poison. She grabbed Gerard's hand just in time to hold him back, and his fingers closed firmly around hers as he let her lead him away from the waiting danger.

In the distance, through the darkness, Lorelei could hear more noises now—the unmistakable sounds of fumbling movement. Were their competitors lost along with them in this maze? The others must have found their way here from their own separate sections of the shared trial—which meant that whoever found the maze's center first would win the entire challenge.

Lorelei felt Gerard's fingers tighten around hers with the same realization—and determination—and she bit back a laugh of intoxicated delight. Did anyone else *really* imagine they could beat Balravia's Fae Queen and the Empire's Golden Beacon, working together at long last?

Keeping his hand safely in hers, she nearly flew down the next path, light and free in the utter darkness. She *did* still belong here after all! Princess or not, this land *was* still hers, she could feel it in her bones...

And then bright moonlight splashed, sudden and unwelcome, over them both as they arrived at a final turning with six different branching paths.

Six paths? *Really?*

Blinking and dazed by moonlight, she turned in place to study their options. All of them were identical to her vision and to every other sense—and above them, that same damnably mismatched jumble of stars embroidered the sky once again, like a taunt meant to puncture all her confidence.

Every other fae competitor would be able to use those stars for orientation. But Lorelei...

Gritting her teeth, she turned her attention to the ground beneath their feet, now visible in the moonlight. It was covered only by soft grass, and there were no acorns left in her bodice to be tossed down any of those paths.

She lifted her gaze to Gerard and found him waiting expectantly for her direction.

Oh, goddess. He finally, actually trusted her, for the first time since they'd met. But she...

Lorelei swallowed a groan as light footsteps sounded behind them, closing in far too quickly. It was an awful, telltale sign of weakness, but she couldn't help flicking a quick glance at the two fae archers who tumbled into place beside them in the broad mouth of the branching paths. These two had emerged, somehow, from a different direction than Lorelei and Gerard had used, but they both stumbled to a halt just as she had, blinking and dazzled by moonlight, staring out at the stars spread above them . . .

And she recognized the expression that flickered across their faces:

Confusion. The others didn't recognize this night sky either!

She could have wept or danced with the intensity of her relief—but no, she hadn't time for celebration. She was here to *win*, and in that moment, she knew she could, no matter how badly her own self-doubt had slowed her progress.

If this *wasn't* the same sky she'd once known, then she hadn't forgotten anything after all, no matter what Oberon had made her fear. But if this particular skyscape had been laid out for the trial, then there must be a guiding purpose behind it.

Half-slitting her eyes, she let her searching gaze pass once again over that jumbled mass of stars. If she set aside everything she'd once known about their positions in the sky and focused only on their shapes, then—yes!

She *did* know those constellations, even now, when they'd been jumbled up into a wildly unfamiliar order. She knew their stories, too. Murmured into her hair as a child, they had never left her—and *there*, sitting neatly above the fourth branching path, three constellations were lined up like an arrow pointing downwards:

The Older Sister, Sylvana beckoning Her people home.

The Key, unlocking every secret.

And *the Crown*, ready to reward victory.

She leapt forward without a second thought.

This time, Gerard didn't follow her onto the path.

An arrow whistled above her head as she ran, followed by a muffled but powerful expulsion of human breath. She jerked to a halt and turned back. Gerard's broad shoulders blocked the mouth of her path as he stood, strong legs planted firmly, grappling with one of the taller fae.

Immediately, she started back to help—

But the impatient jerk of his head spoke louder than any shout.

Curse the man! Of course he would believe he could take on two high fae without her help—but then, he was a master of military strategy, wasn't he? And he was right: The other two fae did have longer legs than Lorelei. Set on the same path, they'd overtake her in moments. Her only chance now lay in the others being slowed—and Lorelei and Gerard had been partners all the way. She could hardly refuse to trust him just when he'd won them both a real chance at victory.

Sylvana keep him safe! Some emotion that felt sickeningly like real, personal fear rose within her—but Lorelei whirled back into the darkness and *ran*.

She was here to win. When she did, every fae—including her mother—would understand exactly how well she still fit here.

Hedges rose around her in zigzagging formations, but she took every corner without a stumble. Tangling whips of thorns lashed out to block her. She leapt high over them, took the final curve—and stumbled to a halt just before she could run into a dead end.

A wall of leaves rose high before her, rustling a warning.

There was nowhere else to turn.

She stared in open-mouthed shock. She'd been so certain of her path! She hadn't even sensed this final part of the hedge waiting for her as she'd neared it. What had she done wrong?

Tipping her head back, she gazed up once again at that night sky...

And then her lips curved into a smirk of satisfaction as she took in, once more, those three guiding constellations. *Of course.*

To follow the Older Sister home and claim the crown, she would have to turn the key.

Lorelei knew exactly why she hadn't sensed this final hedge. It wasn't a green, growing wall, after all. It was a *door* cloaked in illusion.

Which means... Stepping forward, she lifted her chin and reached into the rustling hedge with perfect confidence. *Let's turn that key.*

Her hands moved through the perfect simulation of branches . . . and a quiet but definite *click* sounded in the darkness.

The applause of the crowd broke over her in a roaring wave as she stepped through the glamoured door onto the end of the field, only a few feet before the throne where Oberon sat with a false smile fixed on his deceitful face and a feather of shining silver laid across a pillow of orange leaves on his lap.

"We have a winner for this challenge," he drawled. "How . . . delightful to see you so pleased with yourself, Sister. I take it you'll be wearing this feather in your hair to show off among the mortals you've always preferred?"

"Oh, Oberon. So wrong, as usual, about so many things." Lorelei lifted a hand, smiling for the crowds of applauding fae; she didn't spare Oberon a second glance. "I *could* explain it to you, but I don't care enough for your opinion, so . . . *yes!*"

She had left the door from the maze hanging wide open when she'd run through it—and she'd known, oh she had *known* who would be the next to emerge through it, despite all the odds.

Transported into an unfamiliar realm, forced to fight from the weakest possible position against multiple fae opponents, Gerard de Moireul was *still* ready to conquer any battlefield. He strode out onto the field with the air of a man who knew it.

The billowing sleeves of his silky red tunic had been shredded by thorns.

Dirt and bruises covered the hard lines of his face.

As he stepped onto the grass of the field, the last of the true day's light hit his thick, golden hair and made it glow . . . and his amber gaze moved straight to her, with a gleam in his eyes she'd never seen before.

"This reward is for both of us," she announced to the watching crowd, and she scooped the silver feather from Oberon's lap to hand it herself to her prisoner-turned-partner. "We won it *together*."

11

Gerard had built a reputation as a patient man but a relentless opponent. At the close of the first day of trials in the Tournament of Leaves, he had to exercise every ounce of his patience to wait through the hours of celebratory feasting that were apparently deemed necessary. As massive bonfires shot hot orange sparks impossibly high into the darkness, he ate delectable new food with methodical precision, watched the flying, dancing, and celebrating fae all around him with courteous attention, and *refused* to acknowledge any of the deeply disturbing feelings trying to riot underneath his skin.

When the feasting did finally come to a close, it was followed by a full hour of matchless singing from eerily beautiful fae voices and then a demonstration of new magics from younger members of the court. Illusion followed upon staggering illusion; wonder eclipsed breathtaking wonder; and he took it all in with the air of impenetrable calm he'd perfected decades earlier. Only inside were his emotions heating to a boiling point.

After every disorienting turn of this day, he had questions that needed answers. Patient or not, he *would not* wait forever to claim solid ground once more!

Lorelei had been flitting from one bonfire to another all night long, shining and gay and carefree in the leaping light of the flames, like a colorful butterfly that could never be pinned down. Everywhere she went, she was greeted by cries of welcome from creatures of all shapes and descriptions; everyone she spoke to was the glad recipient of her glowing, vibrant warmth.

. . . Everyone except the lord of this tournament, who lounged in his seat of honor at the top bonfire, surrounded by sycophants but with his brooding gaze turned all too often upon Lorelei.

At long last, the bonfires were subdued. At Oberon's drawled command, the surrounding trees withdrew in a splendidly slow and grand procession to reveal a second field laid out beyond. This one was already covered in spacious silk tents, each dimly lit from within by flickering lights and tethered to the ground with gold and silver ropes. Lorelei appeared by Gerard's side as he stood at one corner of the field to study them.

"Shall we, darling?" Casually linking one small arm with his, she started forward with a confident bounce. "Of course, we *can* take separate tents if you prefer, but—"

"No." His voice was hard as he allowed her to pull him forward. "We'll take the same tent," he told her flatly.

"Really?" She blinked, sending rainbows sparkling between them in the darkness. "I mean, how terribly sensible of you! So, you've finally realized I'm irresistible?" With a feigned sigh—and her tongue clearly firmly in cheek—she shook her head. "My beauty *can* be a true curse, I confess, but of course I understand. You've been so tightly laced for so very long, you must have an *enormous* amount of energy to work off. You poor man! We should probably get *some* sleep before tomorrow's challenges, but if you really must insist on being ravished first, I'm sure I could force myself to—"

Gerard cut off her teasing without the slightest compunction. "We need to talk." He lifted the silk door of the closest empty tent and gazed over her head at the field they'd left behind. In the distance, he found Lord Oberon watching, as he'd expected. "... *Alone*," he finished grimly and followed Lorelei inside.

As the door fell closed once more behind him, the shifting lights within the tent were revealed to be dancing streaks of blue flame that swirled through the air in a sinuous circle beneath the peak of the pointed silk roof. Despite their odd color, they cast more than enough light to illuminate a giant, bed-shaped pile of autumn leaves and blankets that covered most of the floor, like a wild creature's nest.

"Oh, how lovely! This really *will* be cozy." Lorelei collapsed onto the makeshift bed with a sigh of delight, splaying her limbs wide across the piled blankets and wriggling luxuriantly to create a hollow within them.

Gerard, on the other hand, was all too pricklingly aware that their forms must be perfectly outlined for any hostile observer to see through the walls of the tent. He remained stiffly standing on the empty patch of floor, his hands tightly linked behind his back and his gaze fixed on her face with an intense effort of will. "Is there any way to shut off those lights?"

"The will-o'-the-wisps, you mean?" Lorelei turned to blink up at him, loose blonde curls falling over her cheek as she nestled among the blankets and leaves, looking perfectly relaxed ... and far too inviting. "Why would you want even *more* darkness? Darling, if *you* feel self-conscious about the way you look, I can't begin to imagine—"

"*Lorelei*." It was the first time he'd ever called her by her name without its title, and it snapped out without his conscious intention. He barely even took in the startled widening of her eyes as he fought to regain control over his surging temper—and other, more disturbingly physical sensations. "Enough teasing," he gritted. "You can't avoid a serious conversation any longer."

"Oh, very well." Rolling her eyes, she lifted herself up on one elbow and waved her other hand in a flowing, beckoning motion.

The ground shuddered underneath Gerard's feet. An instant later, shadows shot up every side of the tent, new leaves rustling noisily against the silk, and solid branches clamping tightly into place to form an impenetrable lattice all around it.

It was an awe-inspiring demonstration of her power—and he clenched down hard against the flare of arousal that *could not* be allowed in response.

"There," said Lorelei. "Now no one can see inside to know what we're doing . . . or *not* doing, as the case may be." There was a distinctly mocking light in her expression as she tsk'd up at him in the dim light of the still-dancing will-o'-the-wisps. "And here I thought you were always so careful to maintain your perfect reputation above all. Are you finally ready to join me in the joys of scandal?"

Jovar preserve me! All arousal disappeared as Gerard's spine snapped tight, old panic rising to clog his throat with unrelenting force.

Scandal and ruin and the price of weakness . . .

He had also learned long ago, though, how to resist being baited into falling apart for anyone else's entertainment. Setting his jaw, Gerard waited until he could be assured of full control over his voice. Then he said, with perfect calm, "I thought we should avoid any onlookers—or eavesdroppers—sharing in our discussion of today's events and tomorrow's strategy."

That much was true and reasonable. The fact that he'd felt the weight of Lord Oberon's gaze on his captor like a burning brand, impossible either to ignore or to accept, could have nothing to do with it . . . nor with the fact that, until Lorelei's reminder, he hadn't even *considered* the propriety of enclosing himself in a small, intimate space with the woman whose actions supplied the most scandalous stories to circulate across the continent each year.

... Oh, damn it, no. He might be able to fool her, but he would not pretend to fool himself.

He'd spent *decades* operating with perfect caution and propriety, but tonight, all he'd cared about in that moment of choice was shielding *her*, his outrageous abductress and longtime nemesis, from that fae lord's bitter and hungry observation.

Everything was off-kilter ... especially the inexplicable emotions that kept trying to pierce his shield of self-control whenever he looked at her now, after all the trials they'd completed together.

And when he remembered the way *she'd* looked earlier, bright joy lighting up her face as she'd handed him that silver feather ...!

They truly had shared a shining victory, and it had felt ...

It had felt ...

Gerard winced as the weight of unacceptable truth crashed through him. Jovar forgive him, it had all felt *right* for one impossibly perfect moment that had shaken all his foundations.

Queen Lorelei of Balravia, as he'd been reminding himself every day of the past seven years, was widely known to be selfish and fickle, ruled by her own vanity and any passing moment's whim. She wasn't meant to be the loyal friend he'd witnessed in action at the Kitvarian border, standing strong by the sides of her fellow Queens of Villainy and defending the gentle Estarian Archduke.

Nor was she meant to be warm and generous in victory—much less the best partner ever to fight at his side, catching his every strategic intent without a word and following it up with her own brilliant flashes of inspiration. He'd already known that she could read him far too well; until today, he'd never expected to take pleasure from that fact.

He could never have expected the intoxicating, illicit, *unforgivable* thrill that he would feel when they worked in tandem.

Perhaps it was only due to her skills at illusion-spinning. He'd been telling himself that all night long . . . but the need to know for certain was so intense now that he had to stiffen the muscles in his legs to keep safely to his position, standing upright and steadfastly away from the bed where she lounged so decadently before him, like a painting of temptation.

"Ugh, you and your endless *strategies*." She sank back into a fully prone position, stretching her arms above her head and sighing. "We did well enough today without planning ahead of time, didn't we?"

"Did we?" He arched his eyebrows meaningfully. "As I recall, you hadn't expected to see Lord Oberon—and you didn't seem best pleased that he forced you into entering the tournament after all."

"*Nothing* about Oberon has ever pleased me," she muttered. "But we're in the top twenty pairs of the tournament now, aren't we? *There's* something anyone could take pleasure in, even you."

Even him? Gerard's eyes narrowed, but he didn't allow himself to be drawn off track. "Haven't any of your past partners wished to talk strategy?"

"'Past partners'?" Letting out a snort-laugh, she rolled over to face him, propping her head on the deliciously rounded curve of her left arm. "Darling, I may have *watched* the tournaments take place many times, but this part is new to me as well. Who could I ever have partnered with until now?"

"Lord Oberon might have volunteered himself," Gerard suggested through gritted teeth.

"*Eww!*" She gave a dramatic shudder in response. "Here's a word of advice for you, High General: Never fight with an untrustworthy partner at your side. It isn't worth the risk."

And yet, she'd fought by *his* side all day long . . . and Gerard had to admit that even in the fiercest heat of combat today, he'd never suffered a single doubt that she would shield his back in battle, too.

He would have to think more about it later . . . but for now, he shelved that disturbing realization to dig down deeper, past her bright, superficial façade. "Why not partner with your cousin Katrin, then? She seems a worthy warrior. Wouldn't you trust her at your back?"

"I would trust Katrin with everything I cherish." All the humor was suddenly gone from Lorelei's voice, leaving weariness behind. "But I never could, because she is my mother's niece. If she ever played and won at the Tournament of Leaves, the court would claim it was unjustly earned from royal or family preference."

Gerard blinked. "But you don't think the same will be said of you, now?"

"How could it be?" She gave a careless shrug of her right shoulder, her eyelids drooping as her lips curved. "Darling, my mother cast me off *decades* ago. It's ancient history! When she gave me up to the mortal realm, she made it clear to all and sundry that I no longer held any place in the family tree. I have no claim to the line of Efaelen's succession anymore, nor any position in its court except as an occasional diplomatic visitor of state."

Her tone was light; as Gerard listened to her words, he considered that perfect smile. "How old were you at the time?"

"Really, who could bother to remember such inconsequential details?" Laughing scornfully, she waved the question away.

Gerard de Moireul had never gambled in his life. In that moment, though, he would have confidently risked everything on the certainty that Lorelei remembered that detail with vivid and unchanging clarity . . .

Just as he would never forget the moment when his own life had imploded at eight years old. Then, he had lost everything he knew and everyone he loved and been sent to a school where all of the students and teachers were prepared to loathe him from the start.

How welcoming had the human court of Balravia been to a young, transplanted, and only half-human princess?

Unsettled by the question, he sought for a safer topic on which to goad her. "So, when it comes to the list of those you trust with your life, from your cousin to your second handmaiden... I presume the Balravian Chancelloress... and your two royal allies in Kitvaria and Nornne... is there a single man you would name?"

"A man?" Her eyes narrowed, a snap of temper finally entering her tone. "Well, General, let me think a moment. My *father* tried to murder me when I was a child. Then my first lover, upon my ascension to the throne, chose to celebrate the occasion by slipping me poison on behalf of my *dearest* cousin, Johann. After that, my second lover sold my closest secrets to the highest political bidders for a tidy profit. When I discovered the truth and cut him loose, he responded by making me the subject of his most famous and most libelous song, which has been applauded across the continent ever since... and, oh, yes, the last time I visited Efaelen, my *almost* stepbrother, Lord Oberon, tried to trick me into drinking a love potion in an attempt to seduce me against my will, after I had refused all of his advances."

"He did *what?*" Gerard's voice lowered to a growl of fury as he took an involuntary step forward.

"Oh, it was a political move, no more. He wanted a queen of his own, you see, even if I was a second-best option in his view." Her tone was as bright and as brittle as a frozen rose petal. "I can promise you, I did *not* leave him heartbroken, no matter what all the songs and stories about me suggest."

"Did you at least leave any of his bones broken?" The tips of his boots were brushing against the edge of the bed, but he couldn't bring himself to step back. The thought of vibrant, incorrigible Lorelei assaulted in such an intimate way, robbed of her free will and all choice over her own body and mind...

"Ha!" The startled laugh she let out in response to his words sounded far more real than her earlier feigned amusement. "No, although I should have loved to. If he weren't the son of my mother's consort, I might have given in to that temptation—but have no fear, I dealt with the problem in my own way. The court of Efaelen was laughing at him for *months* afterwards, according to my sources."

"And that is why he hates you," Gerard finished with a sigh. "Of course." That kind of vicious weakling would always blame his own attempted victims for any acts of self-defense...

And Gerard himself had been shamefully wrong in his own assumptions about that past relationship. Worse yet, even after his own experience with the lies and smears spread by scandal, he had still been more than willing to believe the worst of her, based on the reputation built and spread over the years.

What other false assumptions had he made about his nemesis?

He lowered himself heavily to the silken floor, crossing his legs and resting his hands on his knees. "I don't suppose you ever considered trying to publicly prove that first, libelous song incorrect and put forward your own side of the story to the world?"

It had taken him years of work and brutal determination to overcome the damage done to his own reputation by his parents' actions, but he had managed it in the end. Surely, if Lorelei put the force of her brilliant, unpredictable mind to the matter, she would succeed one day, as well.

"Why on earth would I want to?" Her nostrils flared as she finally pushed herself up into a sitting position, her face drawing into haughty lines. "Darling, I don't have to prove myself to *anyone*—and it's all the better for my kingdom that everyone else thinks me a shameless flibbertigibbet without brains *or* any resistance to an attractive set of shoulders. Unlike some people, I quite like being underestimated by my enemies."

And by your friends, too? He thought the question but didn't ask it, his mind filtering carefully back through everything she'd said—or not said—tonight.

Queen Lorelei might be famous for her glamorous lifestyle and endless public stream of lovers, but it was becoming increasingly clear to him that there were few true friends in her inner circle, and perhaps even fewer who were allowed ever to glimpse much of her inner truth behind that sparkling mask.

He'd always known that a dangerous intelligence lurked behind her carefully crafted demeanor, but he had never before allowed himself to wonder what more vulnerable—or even more compellingly admirable—traits might be hidden there, too.

The thought of finding out felt as dangerous as if he were teetering atop a precipice with no safe landing beyond.

"Well?" she prompted after a long moment of silence. "Isn't there anything more you need to ask in this *serious conversation* before we can finally go to sleep?"

"... No." Gerard let out the word on a heavily expelled breath. "No, that's all for tonight."

Earlier, he'd been certain that getting answers to his questions would sort his turbulent emotions neatly back into order. Now, though, as he stretched out on the plain cloth floor to spend the rest of the night in the haven she'd created for them, he felt even more perilously unsettled than before.

12

In the grand, sprawling Imperial winter palace in Fiora, there was one particular room into which almost no one was allowed to enter. It was small and octagonal, without any windows but with thick and soundproof walls on every side, and it was reserved for the Emperor's most private meetings. Not even the most trusted servants were ever allowed to enter, and guards were kept carefully on watch outside at all times to prevent any secretive intrusions.

Even the notorious spymistress Queen Ailana of Nornne had never found any way to slip inside that private chamber. Fortunately, she had her own employees in that palace, including one long-serving, senior palace maid who took care, every time a new council was summoned, to discreetly set a small, transparent shard of ice in just the right position to witness each rare and privileged visitor on their way inside.

Of course, no shard of ice could last forever so far away from Ailana's magic. Far sooner than she'd like, every one of them did melt. But until they did...

Many hundreds of miles to the north, alone in her office, Ailana leaned over the sheet of ice on a silver tray, her eyes narrowing with focused attention as the first council member came into view.

That inner circle had shifted only subtly in the first five years of Otto II's reign, as various long-trusted advisors of his father were gradually eased into retirement and replaced by new courtiers eager to make their mark. By the beginning of this year, though, the differences had become impossible to ignore. They'd been reflected in Otto's shift in public policy to the expansionist agenda he'd always dreamed of—and just this week, both his private council and the Serafin Empire as a whole had been rocked by a politically seismic event.

Soft-spoken but powerful and stubbornly peace-loving, Imperial High Priest Bohdan had wielded a gentle authority in the Empire for decades... until this week, when he'd found himself arrested in the middle of the night by members of Otto's own private Imperial guard. The charges trumpeted in every newspaper the next morning shouted of high treason and corruption—and that very afternoon, as the continent reacted with shock to that unprecedented news, another announcement had been dispatched from the winter palace.

Apparently, every other recalcitrant member of the previous generation who'd remained in Otto's council until then had chosen that same day, entirely coincidentally, to submit their regretful resignations. As the Imperial recorder noted with carefully tempered regret, they were "ready to lay down their work at last and enjoy the fruits of their well-earned retirement."

In other words, Ailana surmised wryly, *they were ready to surrender their principles to save their heads.*

There would be no such internal battles between principle and survival for most of Otto's new council members. Unlike his late father, Otto II chose his political favorites based on their abilities to flatter, to fawn, and to slavishly follow his every lead even when he leapt from one extreme stance to another. Today, no doubt, every council member would be eager to prove their fealty to Otto's aims by agreeing with every aggressive new plan he proposed and seconding every vicious claim he made about his enemies.

But as for what had drawn him to call them all in today...

Damn it, if only they would talk a little louder! Sound filtered *so* unsatisfactorily through that tiny piece of ice lodged so far away from any of them.

As Ailana leaned even closer, straining to make out any individual words, her breath fogged the ice in her silver tray, blurring her view of the gorgeously dressed sycophants who paraded in all their overblown glory down the small private corridor that led to the council chamber. Pressing her lips together in self-chastisement, she flared her nostrils and sucked back all warmth and moisture from the room, leaving the ice before her cold and clear to showcase all of her most dangerous new enemies.

Dukes with diamond-studded cravats followed counts with foot-high, polished top hats and ruby-topped walking sticks, one by one in colorful procession...

Until the final pair paced their way into view.

Aha. The Emperor, of course, must always be last to arrive as a matter of consequence. Only his sister, the new Imperial high priestess, was allowed the signal honor of sharing that stately journey. Today, she'd laid one fair hand across his arm as they walked step by step together. As she tipped her head attentively to listen to whatever self-aggrandizing nonsense was spouting now from his ever-moving lips, she smiled with perfect, unchanging tranquility.

... And at the edges of the table that held the silver tray, Ailana's fingers tightened with frustration.

That thick red hair was still every bit as fiery as she'd remembered, but only a few carefully tidied strands were allowed to gleam around the edges of Imperial High Priestess Clothilde's giant new gold headdress. Beautifully full-figured and utterly confident, the new high priestess was unusually young for the position, still only in her early thirties. However, she projected an air of palpable strength and looked every inch the serene and ultimate holy authority for the Serafin Empire, personally responsible for millions of souls ...

And as Otto talked and talked in her ear, she never uttered a single word of protest or discouragement.

Otto, at least, *always* spoke loudly enough to be heard in fragments, through the ice. "... Said he'd never *seen* any man handle ... so impressively! And ... *I* said ... how they all laughed!"

Ailana's teeth clenched at the inanity, but she couldn't look away. For the sake of her own people and her allies, she couldn't afford to miss a single telltale detail.

So she caught the fleeting instant when the Imperial high priestess tilted her head and slipped a swift, sidelong, oddly *knowing* look at—

Wait! Ailana's eyes flared with alarm.

Was Clothilde actually looking at *her*, through her shard of ice?

It wasn't possible. That had to be a coincidence, no more.

The Imperial high priestess's smile never faltered as she turned back to her brother, but Ailana remained seated by her silver tray, skin prickling with tension, for a long time after the Imperial siblings disappeared from view.

13

Lorelei was hardly unaccustomed to sharing her bed with a man. It was, after all, one of her favorite pastimes. Sharing her *sleep*, on the other hand, she hadn't done in years... and sharing not a bed but a bed*chamber*—offering easy access to attack without giving herself the chance to feel any subtle movements that might warn her in time to wake and save herself?

Now, *that* was entirely unprecedented...

As was the fact that, with Gerard de Moireul lying scarcely three feet away from her, she had somehow, absurdly, fallen into the deepest and most satisfying sleep she'd experienced in weeks. It was as if her misbehaving body, in its deeply weary state, had somehow interpreted the presence of the Serafin Empire's most dangerous general—still openly loyal to his appalling master—as *protection* for her.

It was a potentially lethal mistake and an unsettling truth to awaken to—especially when she realized, half a minute later, that she hadn't even been the first to open her eyes. Behind her, she could hear soft, repetitive movements against silk and the sound of steady but effortful breathing. Not only was her prisoner apparently awake, he was already in action, and she hadn't even noticed. Apparently, he could have done anything while she'd slept on and on. He could even have *left*!

At that thought, she surged upright on a wave of panic...

And found herself presented with one more unprecedented experience for her morning:

Gerard de Moireul, the Empire's famously chaste and noble Golden Beacon, was stripped to the waist and doing one-handed push-ups on the floor of her tent with silent, focused concentration.

Oh, my! Lorelei's eyes flared wide. With his gaze still studiously trained on the floor, she was free to look her fill—and there were just *so many* different muscles on display for her delectation, running all along his broad shoulders and down his back.

Ohhhh, and his closest upper arm—!

Lorelei's breath shortened, but she couldn't look away from those flexing muscles. Of course she'd seen plenty of well-built men before—but this was different. This wasn't just another random bedmate.

This was *Gerard de Moireul*, whom she'd been studying and teasing and battling for years without any long-term satisfaction. *This was the one impossible man who challenged her in every way*... and even the scratches left on his arms by last night's thorns added an extra layer of animalistic appeal, tugging at something deep inside her. As she watched him steadily rise and fall, again and again, with relentless purpose, she swept the tip of her tongue over her upper lip, fighting to contain the blaze mounting within her.

She felt like a cat preparing to pounce on the most delicious, irresistible bowl of cream she'd ever witnessed...

Cream that was *off-limits* and entirely forbidden!

Ugh, this was entirely unacceptable.

She couldn't even stop a noisy huff of frustration from escaping her lips, because apparently, all of her poise and self-control had utterly failed to wake up with the rest of her today.

At her uncontrolled sound, Gerard finally turned. Holding himself effortlessly still mid-push-up, he raised his eyebrows questioningly. His keen amber gaze passed over her face . . . and then, to her horror, she saw his lips twitch. "Not a fan of early mornings, I take it, Your Majesty?"

Oh, *gah*. Her long, sleep-tangled curls were an absolute disaster, weren't they? She hadn't even realized until now that they were rumpled in all the wrong directions. And there, that sticky feeling just to the left of her lips—Sylvana save her, had she *drooled* while she was sleeping?

Fortunately, it was not actually possible to die of mortification, as Lorelei had learned from experience many years ago. Sucking in a deep breath, she beamed at him as she shook back her hair and swept a quick, sparkling glamour over her face to hide every imperfection. "Why, darling, whatever do you mean? I'll start loving mornings most of all from now on, if I'm to be greeted by a show like this each time I wake."

"Mm." As he completed his last push-up, Gerard turned his face away, but not quite quickly enough to hide his expression.

Had that been a *smirk* pulling at the lips of a man whose face ordinarily rivaled stone for its rigidity?

Even phoenixes could burn with mortification. Lorelei made a furious mental note *not* to allow General de Moireul to share her tent ever again. Last night had been a rare lapse in judgement, brought on by how raw she'd felt after sharing too many painful old secrets . . .

And by how foolishly—childishly—she'd wanted the security of his sleeping presence there beside her, where she could see for herself that he was safe.

She would not allow it to happen again.

Ready to conquer the day and be rid of all such weaknesses for good, she gave him a firmly expectant look. "Now, *if* you wouldn't mind giving me a moment of privacy to ready myself?"

"Of course." Moving unhurriedly, he raised himself to his feet in a rolling stretch, and Lorelei did her best *not* to drool in waking life to complete her humiliation. As he pulled yesterday's half-shredded fae tunic back over his head, his muffled voice emerged from underneath. "If you wouldn't mind lowering the gates first? I'd prefer not to battle any more thorns until today's official challenges begin."

Gates—? *Oh, yes.* Lorelei gave a gracious wave of one hand and released the lattice of branches and thorn-stemmed roses that had surrounded them all night long, along with the lingering spell of silence that had kept them safe from any eavesdroppers. "If you insist."

With the withdrawal of all her shields, the tent was abruptly flooded by the full clamor of the waking camp outside. Any ordinary human man would have flinched at that sudden shift, but of course, General de Moireul refused to give her any such satisfaction. Instead, he responded with a small, approving nod, as if it were exactly what he'd expected from her.

Was she becoming *boringly predictable?*

Smiling brightly and full of rage, Lorelei watched him step through the raised flap of the tent door. Holding perfectly still, she watched the door fall closed behind him.

Then she exploded into action.

The portal she drew in the air was shamefully basic, but she didn't have time for any ornamentation. She dived through that rough hole in the world like a salmon lunging upstream, and she landed in the gas-lamp-lit burgundy evening parlor of her Balravian hunting lodge, where she could finally let out all of her feelings.

"Arrgggh!"

"So, it's *still* going that well with the Golden Beacon, is it?" Snorting, Lorelei's cousin Katrin released the hilt of her sword and turned away from her watchful stance by the darkened window.

Snowflakes brushed softly at the glass outside, while a warm fire crackled in the fireplace. Two glasses of red wine sat on a curving side table by a deck of cards, but both of them looked untouched.

From the nearby couch, Ilse gave Lorelei a sweet smile. "That was quick. Have the two of you won the tournament already?"

"No, we have at least two days left. But—Ilse?" Lorelei blinked, distracted by the pile of lacy napkins being sorted on her second lady-in-waiting's lap. "Are you preparing to host a party here while I'm gone?"

"No, silly. I'm just getting the lodge ready for when your friends arrive."

"My *friends?*" Lorelei's eyebrows shot up in disbelief. "Darling, you aren't tipsy on frog spit right now, are you? You must know I haven't invited anyone."

"Well, *someone's* battering at the spells that hide this lodge," Katrin said flatly, "and for all of our sakes, the two of us hope it's one of your fellow Queens of Villainy, not a corps of the Emperor's Gilded Wizards."

"Ugh." Sagging, Lorelei grimaced at both of those equally daunting options. "It can't be Imperial Gilded Wizards. They're only called in under the command of the high general—and Gerard isn't there to do it."

"So it's 'Gerard' now, is it? Already?" Katrin turned to Ilse's couch with a sigh.

"I told you!" Ilse gave her a mischievous look from under her lashes. "I win. That means another swordfighting lesson for me."

"Really?" Katrin asked with heavy meaning, leaning closer. "After *everything* that happened last time?"

"Save your flirtation for later," Lorelei commanded. "Right now, I need help urgently." Yes, time passed differently in the fae world, but she still ran a fine balance when it came to how long she could afford to remain here.

"Of course." Katrin straightened immediately. "Only tell us what to do."

When Lorelei landed back in her tent ten human minutes later, she found it still empty, to her relief, but the clamor and commotion in the camp outside had lessened to a worrying extent. Luckily, it hadn't yet disappeared entirely—so she hadn't lost *all* of her sense in the past day. When she sailed out the door, clad in a shimmering rose-pink and gold concoction made of scandalously layered strips that combined eroticism with comfortable ease of movement, she met Gerard waiting just outside, his strong back turned to the door, his legs planted in a guarding position, and his watchful gaze scanning their rapidly emptying surroundings.

"*Very* impressive," she said warmly as she eyed him up and down. "But oh, dear, that poor, ruined tunic does rather lessen the effect, doesn't it? Fortunately, we should have at least ten more minutes before the first trial begins. Why don't you take your turn changing outfits now?"

His eyebrows rose at the suggestion—perhaps due to the lack of any spare clothing in the tent when he had left it—but he was wise enough not to waste time with questions. Instead, he ducked back under the tent flap and then emerged, less than five minutes later, clad in a clean new set of uniform trousers, shirt, cravat, and stiffly buttoned-up military jacket. He looked every inch an Imperial commanding officer once more . . . and Lorelei bit back a sigh as she absorbed that depressing transformation.

"I take it you abducted my travel trunk at the same time you abducted me?" he asked wryly.

"It was the only polite option," she assured him. "You see, none of the men's clothing left with me across the years would have been nearly large enough to fit. You wouldn't have cared for it at all."

His expression was skeptical. "And you were, of course, terribly concerned about my preferences when you chose to abduct me."

"Of course!" Lorelei said piously. "I might be wicked, darling, but it's never necessary to be *cruel*."

Even more important, putting him back into uniform was a desperately needed shield to erect between them. This way, she would have a visual reminder of exactly why she'd brought him here in the first place . . . *and* why she needed to keep her hands off him.

That shredded fae tunic had simply offered too much temptation to resist.

As he sighed and stepped towards her, he began to offer his arm with the automatic courtesy of any Imperial officer to a lady—and then hesitated, apparently catching himself in the act. A rare flush rose on Gerard's cheekbones as he looked from her to the arm he still held half-raised between them; for the first time that she could remember, he looked uncharacteristically and delightfully awkward.

Had he actually forgotten for a moment that he was her prisoner and begun to believe she was his true partner? That realization was enough to send her mood shooting skywards. She *was* winning this battle, after all, no matter how often she might stumble along the way!

Wincing, Gerard cleared his throat. "I beg your pardon."

"Never mind." Lorelei risked a quick pat on his safely covered arm, feeling so much better than before that she only *barely* noticed his muscles shift, through all those layers of cloth, in reaction to her touch. "Far better for both of us to keep our hands free as we prepare for the next challenge."

Not all of the dangers at this tournament would politely wait for the trials to begin.

They arrived at the top of the field, where the rest of the day's contestants were assembling, as Oberon's herald crossed the grass with her horn held ready. Lorelei smiled graciously at the scowling lord of the tournament—poor, dear Oberon must be *so* disappointed she hadn't been a few seconds later, to give him the perfect excuse to declare her entry forfeit!—and tipped him a perfectly gauged nod of condescension before she turned to warmly greet her competitors.

The other nineteen pairs had all survived yesterday's challenges and won against impressive opponents; not one of them could be dismissed as a potential threat. Still, with the Golden Beacon towering at her side, Lorelei couldn't summon up any nerves about her prospects.

True, she had allowed herself to be drawn into sharing far more vulnerability with her captive than she'd intended. She certainly wouldn't claim not to have made *any* missteps, especially when it came to this morning's mortifying awakening. But Lorelei knew how to learn from her mistakes. From now on, she would simply take care *never* to let Gerard see deeper than was comfortable or safe—and as long as the two of them continued to fight side by side, they would surely be unstoppable.

The herald's horn rang out, high and haunting, and silenced every conversation. A thick hush of excitement hung over the field as Oberon—no longer scowling—rose gracefully to his feet.

His lips curved into a smile as he swept the crowd with his gaze . . . and as his eyes lingered first upon Lorelei's face, and then upon Gerard's, that smile widened ominously.

"It is time," he announced, "to begin the most entertaining segment of this year's games—one newly added late last night for the court's particular enjoyment. I promise you all, by the end of today's trials, less than half of our competitors will remain in play . . . and many others may be lost to us forever."

Lost forever? Lorelei's eyes narrowed as Oberon's smile morphed into a sneer of satisfaction. What was that weasel planning to make him look so giddy? And what did that mealy-mouthed warning mean?

Every trial in the Tournament of Leaves ran the risk of death. What made this one any different?

Looking directly at her, Oberon gave a nod of taunting condescension that mirrored her own earlier move *far* too well for comfort. Then he turned to the rest of their audience and dramatically raised his arms. "Let Day Two of the tournament begin!"

14

Gerard might be out of place on this fae field and unfamiliar with local customs, but there was one truth that all of his instincts shouted as he readied for today's challenges:

Lorelei was hiding from him.

Oh, she stood physically beside him in the autumnal morning light, along with their fellow competitors, but from the moment she'd sent him out of their tent that morning, she had withdrawn more tightly behind her veil of illusions than ever before . . . and the disconcerting glamour that she'd cast over her face was the least of it.

He would never forget the sight of her that morning when she'd first awoken, her hair streaming around her in sensual abandon and her expression open, warm, and vulnerable.

The tip of her tongue had swept out to lick her upper lip as she'd gazed at him with unmistakable hunger . . .

And he'd nearly doubled over, mid-calisthenics, with the force of his own sudden, piercing *need*.

It was the first time he'd glimpsed the Balravian queen entirely unshielded. Her usual sophisticated flirtation was all too tempting, but that open vulnerability had been nigh-on *irresistible*. It had taken every ounce of his own willpower to breathe through the moment and maintain an unaffected demeanor . . .

And her disgruntlement, only a moment later, had been *adorable*. There was no other word for it. Rarely in his life had he felt so disappointed as when she'd cast that unsettling glamour over her features as a mask, smoothing over every touchable inch with chilling perfection.

On a deeper level, though, a new, hot spark of challenge had lit within him at that sight. If ever-confident Lorelei actually felt any need to hide from him, that meant he'd finally caught the incorrigible queen wrong-footed. In this obsessive, unstoppable competition that they'd been privately enacting for years, she had taken a seemingly insurmountable lead when she'd abducted him. Now, though, *he* suddenly held the advantage.

He didn't intend to let it slip from his hands again.

Had Lorelei exposed more of her true self last night than she'd intended? Enough to make her this nervous now? Then he would hunt down *all* of her secrets while he was here. Gerard wasn't known as relentless for nothing . . . and the sharp tug in his chest to learn even *more*, to know all of his contradictory captor's deepest truths, was undeniable.

Besides, it made perfect political sense. Without any fae blood of his own to guide him through the veil between worlds, he couldn't mount any escape plans from the fae realm. Therefore, his clear Imperial duty as well as his personal compulsion demanded that he turn around the trap she'd closed upon him and use it to ferret out every secret he could for his empire's advantage.

Oddly, that rationalization felt more dampening than uplifting . . . but he shifted his emotional response aside. The only thing that could matter in this situation—or any other—was his duty. That was *his* deepest truth. Nothing could ever matter more.

So, with his hands clasped behind his back, Gerard listened calmly and attentively to all of Lord Oberon's self-important pronouncements, and he waited with carefully hidden impatience to tackle the day's official challenges . . . *and* his own unofficial hunt.

"Let Day Two of the tournament begin!" Lord Oberon finally declared with the over-the-top grandeur of an insecure man who'd been dying for real power for years.

Gerard braced himself for the inevitable, dizzying shift through a new fae portal into a new illusory setting.

Instead, he found himself suddenly standing alone on the tournament field as everyone else disappeared. Lorelei was gone, along with their competitors. Lord Oberon and all of the onlookers were missing, too.

A deep and strangely peaceful hush filled the air as Gerard turned slowly in place, looking warily upon the vast green field and the forest of orange-leafed trees beyond it that hid the tent where he had slept last night. Every stand erected for the tournament's audience was empty.

Not a single threat was in sight. He couldn't hear any sound, not even the soft whispering of the autumn breeze that had drifted across him only a moment ago.

Was this a new illusion that he was meant to break? Lorelei had handled all of the magical challenges for their partnership thus far, but perhaps, if he put his mind to it . . .

"CAREFUL." It was a vast, sighing breath through the trees and across the field, so strong that it bent those distant branches and made the hair on his wrists and the back of his neck stand up. Goose bumps broke out all across his skin.

That was no mere illusion ... and had it been a woman's voice?

Slowly and carefully, Gerard slipped one hand to the hilt of his sword, but he didn't draw it.

"Hello?" he called out. "I mean you no harm, madam."

Were fae crowds still watching him from those empty stands? This didn't *feel* like any of the challenges he'd faced yesterday.

Perhaps it was one of those more difficult trials that Lorelei had promised would arrive on the second day. Was he about to be posed an enigmatic riddle? Or set upon some sort of quest?

The trees beyond the field began to ripple even before that sighing voice reached him once more, sounding both massive and impossibly distant. Its power resonated through his body but forced his ears to strain after every word. "WE ONLY HAVE ... MOMENT ... TOGETHER," that impossible voice sighed out. "YOU ... NOT OF MINE, BUT STILL ... WARNING:

"BE CAREFUL WITH HER!"

With the force of that final, urgent command, a blast of cool air swept from the forest across the field, nearly knocking Gerard off his feet. Staggering, he squeezed his eyes shut against the painful, stinging force of it—and breathed in the sudden, overpowering scent of fresh greenery mingled with sweet-smelling rose blossoms.

"Lorelei?" he whispered, his voice caught in the unnatural wind.

A storm of sound erupted around him in answer. Opening his eyes, he found himself transplanted into a new setting after all, standing—heart still pounding and skin hotly prickling—in the middle of a lushly crowded greenhouse with a high, rounded ceiling. The warm, moist air was filled with cheeping, singing, and squabbling birds who strutted proudly along the pathways and flew over his head, their wings flashing bright shades of blue, yellow, and green. The floor itself was lined with rows of tall green plants. Colorful flowers bloomed all around, and several of Gerard's opponents stood braced for action nearby, looking as startled as if they, too, had only just arrived ... but not nearly as shocked as they ought to if they'd experienced anything like his unnerving interaction beforehand.

Had any time passed for the rest of them since Lord Oberon's announcement? Gerard couldn't help the irrational but powerful conviction that time had somehow held still for him alone on that field, as if he'd been scooped out from the ordinary turning of the day by someone—or some*thing?*—to receive that enigmatic warning.

But why? Gerard, of all people, hardly needed any magical intercessions to warn him against his own abductor.

. . . Who, he realized abruptly, was nowhere to be seen.

Lorelei wasn't the only one who was missing. As Gerard swiftly catalogued the competitors around him, he realized that everyone here had been separated from their partners for the first time since the tournament's opening trial.

That challenge had been designed to prove that each partner had the strength to fight on their own, without their partner's help. What was this new trial meant to test?

A deep and ominous bell chimed in one corner of the greenhouse, and Gerard's gaze snapped to the face of the tall clock that stood there, surrounded by glistening yellow flowers. His brows lowered as he watched the thin second hand move steadily in the wrong direction.

Fae time might not match up with the mortal world, but he'd never heard of it ticking backwards . . .

Aha. This wasn't a real clock at all. It was a visual countdown device. Judging by the pace of those slow ticks, Gerard judged that he had less than ten minutes to complete the full trial before failure would be declared. As so many of this morning's competitors had been planted in the same room together, he must be in competition to complete it before anyone else.

And in order to complete it . . .

Of course. Letting out a controlled breath, Gerard finally wrenched the last of his scattered thoughts out of that empty field he'd just left and squarely into the moment of this challenge.

What else could the goal be? There was just one thing everyone here was missing... and oh, how the fae did love their illusions!

Every sense alert for clues—and danger—Gerard began to slowly pace the rows of the greenhouse, searching for his missing partner.

Around him, other fae were calling out to their own partners without any luck. This had to be a true spell in action, not just an illusion, if it had taken away the volition of all those lost competitors as well as disguising them. Lorelei wouldn't be able to come to Gerard herself or offer him any helpful hints.

He would have to hunt her down on his own, regardless of her disguise. Otherwise...

What was it that Oberon had said to everyone at the beginning of this challenge? *"Many others may be lost to us forever."*

A chill formed at the base of Gerard's spine, spreading rapidly upwards. What *would* happen if he didn't find Lorelei in time? Regardless of whether or not they won this challenge, would she be set free at the end of it? Or would she remain trapped in her spelled shape in this lush greenhouse forever?

He thought back to the self-satisfied smirk on Oberon's face and knew the answer.

"Forever..."

Gerard's chest tightened with a surging, uncomfortable sensation that felt far too close to fear. He shut it down immediately.

Emotions never helped him. What he needed was *strategy*.

Years ago, alone in his school library, he had read that the fae were bound by tradition and honor to the rules of any game they agreed to play. Gerard didn't know all of this tournament's rules, nor exactly how Oberon had exploited them to force Lorelei into participating when she'd tried to slip away on their first arrival. Still, he'd seen for himself how the individual trials worked.

Each challenge might be intimidatingly difficult, but none of them could be genuinely impossible, for the sake of their eager audience as well as the contestants. Even if Lord Oberon was confident that Gerard—human, ignorant, and nonmagical—wouldn't be able to complete this trial, a method for completion must exist.

All he had to do was think through it.

How *would* he recognize Lorelei in any form? What was her true essence?

Slowly, his head tipped back to examine those bright, colorful birds who'd been flitting back and forth above him all along.

On the floor around him, competitors hurried past his still body and swore at the various small, drab, brown birds who obstructed the path. Time ticked down on the clock of flowers, but Gerard's gaze remained fixed on the bright plumage of the birds loudly squabbling above.

Was one of them more colorful than the others? More extravagant in her beauty? More likely to win this aggressive, nonstop battle over territory that they were all fighting? Or . . .

Wait. Everything inside him stilled as he suddenly remembered that vast, impossible voice from the field whispering to him, *"Be careful with her."*

He'd taken it as a warning against Lorelei. What if it had actually been the opposite: a reminder to him *not* to make any more careless mistakes in judging her based on false gossip and his own preconceptions?

To the world at large, Lorelei did indeed present a fabulous show full of color and light. But when it came to her private *essence*, behind every mask and illusion . . .

What had he been missing all along?

"Curse you, get out of my *way!*" a male voice snarled. A soft thud sounded in the air an instant later, followed by a chirp of pain. "I don't have time for this!"

Gerard's gaze snapped downwards. Farther down the path, one of the fae noblemen had just kicked aside a small, drab, brown bird . . . who had apparently been trying to shield two other birds on their way across the path.

As the nobleman stalked off, the injured bird picked herself up, scornfully shook off her feathers, and strutted over to take up her shielding position once again for a full family of birds about to cross the path, including three fluffy hatchlings. As Gerard watched, she puffed up her brown feathers, lifted her beak, and caroled a high and noisy taunt to all the large and dangerous threats currently clomping through the glasshouse.

...Just as Lorelei had taunted Gerard a few days ago as she'd stood beside her allies.

"Two minutes!" That was a dryad, her voice high with panic. "Gods above, there's only two minutes left! Silverthorn, *find me*, damn your eyes!"

Calmly, Gerard took note of the announced time. Then he strode two steps closer to the slowly crossing family of birds and raised one booted foot as if to step downwards.

The family's self-appointed guardian ran directly at him, hopping and flapping and shrieking unmistakable bird taunts. As usual, she was doing everything she could to be so outrageous that she kept all the world's eyes fixed firmly on her—and away from those she was determined to protect.

Gerard's lips curved as he reached down to scoop her up in his palms, ignoring every irate squawk and peck of her small, sharp beak against his skin. "Of course I won't hurt them," he murmured. "Lorelei, I *see* you."

Whether she was feathered or not, for the first time in seven years, that statement felt *true*.

Light shimmered in his cupped hands, far too bright to bear. He had to press his eyes shut against its blinding force, but he never turned away or released his grip as the shape in his hands shifted from a small, round bird into a beautifully rounded woman...a woman he'd misjudged in so many ways. He was still holding her shoulders—now covered in layers of silk and shivering with convulsive tremors of reaction—when the light finally died down and he opened his eyes again.

Her blue eyes looked wide and lost, darting from side to side in confusion—and then they fixed on his and steadied.

Still holding his gaze, she took a long, deep breath. He tightened his grip, steadying her as her shivers gradually eased.

"I see you, Lorelei," he murmured once again.

He'd meant his words as reassurance, but she reacted as if she'd been slapped, head jerking backwards. Her eyes flared with panic as she started to wrench herself free from his grip . . .

And the countdown clock in the corner chimed a low, resounding knell.

The trial had ended.

15

The morning of Lorelei's nineteenth birthday, she had woken from her first-ever poisoning, her fever having finally subsided, to find that the world around her had turned far too loud and bright while she had been ill. As she'd lain in the bed she'd shared with her poisoner only two nights earlier, absorbing everything that had happened since then, she had felt as fragile as a crystal ballerina riddled with hairline cracks, ready to shatter at the lightest of touches.

But, oh, how she had danced that night at the glittering ball she'd hosted for the nobles of her court and every visiting foreign dignitary. Two hours after the public executions of her cousin and his co-conspirator, her lover, she'd been perfectly glamoured to hide her sickly pallor and the deep bruises beneath her eyes. Flanked by her ladies-in-waiting, she had laughed and danced for hours with fierce vivacity, sending a message to her court and to all the men greedy to steal her new kingdom from her:

I will never be defeated.

Lorelei had a goddess-gifted purpose for her life. She *would* fulfil it, no matter how many cracks formed beneath her surface.

... And no matter how terrifyingly clearly one man had finally seen beneath it.

She pushed all of that away as the tournament field took shape around them, leaving her and Gerard standing on soft grass, surrounded by *far* too few of their earlier competitors.

For once, there was no roar of applause from the watching crowd—only a deep, shocked silence as they all absorbed the unprecedented results of this trial.

Every year, one or two competitors did lose their lives in this tournament. But no challenge-based enchantments had *ever* been made permanent after a trial's ending. Enchanted combatants had always been returned to the field to accept their defeat and join the audience for the rest of the tournament.

... Until now.

Including Lorelei and Gerard, six partnerships had survived from the original twenty pairs. That was all.

One no-longer-partnered dryad knelt, weeping helplessly, on the grass, her nails elongating into roots that tethered her to the ground as she shook, heedless of her audience. The other thirteen un-partnered competitors stood rigidly to attention before the tournament's throne, as was proper, but their expressions were dazed and hollowed out by grief.

Oberon sat with his pale, long-fingered hands clenched tightly around the elaborately decorated arms of the throne, his eyes burning with rage.

Lorelei's upper lip curled as she looked at him. "My, my, you poor dear. All that time you must have spent last night to come up with that nasty new trial, all for naught. You aren't rid of me after all. What a terrible nuisance for you! And *such* a shame you had to torture so many innocents to do it."

At her final words, there was a ripple of audible unrest from the watching crowd. Beside her, she felt Gerard's big figure shift. She didn't have to look to know that he was bracing for a fight . . . to defend her.

She put that thought away for later, too. For now, she shook her head pityingly at Oberon. "No doubt you forgot this tiny point of protocol in all the time you spent expelled from court for bad behavior, but it's not a good idea to end the tournament too soon, before your audience is satisfied."

"*I'm* not the one who's forgotten the ways of this court," Oberon snarled. "I am lord of this tournament!"

"Oh, I know," Lorelei purred. "My mother named *you* lord of the Tournament of Leaves to represent her in her absence. She trusted you to ensure a fine entertainment for her court and kingdom, to turn the seasons properly in order . . . which is how *I* know that—regardless of any misunderstandings or deceptive appearances"—she waved at the far-too-empty field around her—"you would *never* truly be so cruel as to leave all those failed ones imprisoned in that greenhouse, enspelled and lost to us forevermore.

"You *wouldn't* choose to disappoint my mother and our audience so badly for no reason but to spite me. Would you?"

His lean jaw worked as he glared at her. Her bright, confident smile only widened.

On the grass nearby, the dryad looked up with sudden, desperate hope. A vibrating silence hung over the field as hundreds of fae held their breath, waiting for his answer.

No one else here could speak to him so freely. No one else had the right or even the ability to try in this court full of ancient and magically bound hierarchies.

But Lorelei had lost her own place here long ago and gained a different kind of freedom. So she kept her expectant smile on her face... and beamed the silent message with all her might: *Don't make me kill you after all.*

The temptation had never before felt quite so strong.

Lord Oberon had always been a fool in every way that mattered, but even he could apparently read the mood of the watching crowd. Slowly, reluctantly, he inclined his head. "How very perceptive of you, Sister. I am glad you were not deceived by *appearances.*" Releasing the right arm of his throne, he snapped his fingers impatiently at the line of nervously watching fae spellcasters. "It is, of course, my deepest pleasure to return our lost ones despite their disappointing failures, as a token of *my* personal mercy and appreciation for their hard work in the tournament thus far."

Behind the other contestants, every lost partner shimmered into place on the grass, one by one. They were all shivering and shocked—Lorelei had to repress a shudder of her own, remembering that horrible, disorienting sensation—but at least they were *there* once more, back in their own natural forms.

Resounding cheers broke out from the watching crowd, ferocious with the intensity of relief. That mass jubilation roared over the tournament field as separated partners lunged to embrace each other, weeping and laughing.

Still, Oberon's venomous focus remained on Lorelei. "Of course, everyone here understands that no such mercy would be expected or even *desired* for a warrior so proud as yourself. Isn't that right?"

"Oh, Oberon," she sighed. "When has *anyone* in my life ever pretended otherwise?"

Gerard's searching gaze felt like a torch held much too close to her skin, uncomfortably hot and bright. Keeping her own gaze fixed on the less dangerous enemy before her, Lorelei tilted her head and batted her eyelashes sweetly. "So? When may we begin our next trial, please? Or had you not actually thought that far ahead, dear?"

It was exactly the right goad to choose. Within minutes, she was satisfyingly enmeshed in a nonstop whirl of action, solving riddles and outwitting opponents on the field. Today, on Lord

Oberon's gritted command, *no* breaks were to be allowed between challenges—which exactly suited her purposes.

Safely back in her own body and free from the sickening fog that had trapped her in that morning's spell, Lorelei kept every sense tinglingly alert and every mental shield raised, *especially* against her own partner.

Alas, she and Gerard hadn't won that first trial—a pair of kobold twins and one long-married couple of sprites had been quicker at solving it—but with eight partnerships allowed to remain in the competition after all, due to Oberon's concessions, they were still well positioned to take the lead by the end of the day.

... *If* they kept all of their focus on the competition and didn't converse about anything else.

"Duck!" she announced triumphantly midway through the afternoon, solving their latest riddle—and as if in answer, elfshot whistled close enough to ruffle her hair with its passing.

"A bit late for that warning." Gerard's words were dry, but his movements were fluid as he whirled to shelter them both behind the silver shield he'd won in combat against a troll an hour earlier.

More elfshot battered helplessly against that shield, and Lorelei reached out with her magic to tug at the gorgeously scented rosebushes nearby. They climbed up a huge nearby arbor that would have made her eyes widen at its size only this morning—but in the elaborately landscaped gardens they'd been questing through for the past hour, *everything* was sized at least five to ten times larger than usual. It was child's play now to send one of those massive rose stems lashing out like a whip to knock the whistle from the hands of the goblin who'd shot at her—and then bind him and his taller partner to the ground.

They were the second pair who'd tried to pick off Lorelei and Gerard in the past hour; there was one more pair lurking somewhere behind them, but she would deal with them later.

Gerard calmly lowered his shield. "... Or were you not referring to our latest attack?"

"See for yourself." Lorelei pointed to the riddle she'd found etched into a small silver leaf that hung from the branch of a gargantuan oak tree, their fifth stopping point so far.

At home in air and water's flow; with me you'll avoid any blow.

"It *could* conceivably have served as a warning," he said, "but I doubt Lord Oberon could have predicted the timing of our opponents quite so well."

Lorelei snorted. "I wouldn't trust Oberon to predict *anyone's* actions, much less try to warn us against them." Lorelei turned in place to survey the majestic lines of greenery around them. "At any rate, he's not clever enough to design this trial by himself."

Oh, he had definitely been the mastermind behind their first trial today—*that* had had his malicious fingerprints all over it with its grasping overreach and disregard for consequences—but this one was far too elaborate and detailed to have been designed in the few days that had passed since her mother had named him her proxy. No, it must have been carefully crafted across the past year by the same team of powerful spellcasters who'd been running this tournament behind the scenes for centuries.

... Which made it all the more intriguing.

For the last hour, she and Gerard had been moving steadily through the different stages of this vast garden as if they were curling around the curves of a huge snail's shell, letting four other partnerships speed ahead of them. Each section was distinct in landscaping theme and carefully separated from its neighbors by elegantly shaped topiaries of implausible proportions—and in the center of it all, still at least half a mile distant, towered an impossibly tall castle made of rough and weathered stone, where their final goal must await them.

Lorelei did not care for the look of that castle at all.

Fortunately, she had a partner who understood the need for thoroughness. Unlike most of their rivals, when first let loose in the farthest section of the outer gardens, he had insisted on taking the time to inspect every detail of the space where they'd landed, rather than leaping to the conclusion that this challenge was a race. That methodical care had paid off for both of them in the discovery of a series of cleverly hidden riddles, each solution leading them on to the next step of the puzzle.

But as for what they would find at the end...

"Tell me," Gerard said, his voice perfectly mild, "why *did* your mother cast you out from her court so long ago?"

Caught off guard, Lorelei twitched. Then she sneered magnificently. "Really, darling. Are you *that* hard up for gossip, after only a few days away from Otto's court? This is decades-old news and entirely uninteresting."

"Not to me."

"Well, it will have to wait until after we've finished today's challenges." *And I'll make sure you forget about it by then.* The last thing she needed was for Gerard de Moireul—not yet even *pretending* to have committed to Lorelei's cause—to discover that she'd been chosen for that very cause by the wild, quicksilver Sylvana, the single goddess most *unlike* Gerard's own humorless patron god of war and justice. "Now," she said briskly as she strode towards the next break in the thick walls of topiary, "have you spotted any sign of ducks flying overhead?"

Gerard's steps were steady behind her. "Judging by everything else we've found so far, any duck that flew over this garden would have been the size of a dragon and unmissable."

"Good lord, are you nearly making *jokes* now? I knew a holiday would be good for you!" Smirking, Lorelei stepped through the arched green passageway. Her eyebrows rose. "Ah. Speaking of unmissable..."

No one could describe what spread before them now as a mere duck pond. Waves lapped at the long, shell-lined shore from a lake-sized body of glittering blue water that spread from where Lorelei stood to the castle's massive doorstep on its other side, with no bridge or boat in sight... and with who-knew-what hiding underneath the water in between.

There had been four partnerships ahead of them earlier; now, she spotted only three questing towards the castle along the lakeshore's curve. An ominous bubbling of water in the center of the lake indicated volumes about that last pair's fate.

Swimming had not been a good choice for them.

The only other option for approach was to walk all the way along the curving shoreline, adding at least an extra mile to the journey. The three leading partnerships were doing just that, jostling for position along the way; as Lorelei squinted, she saw the fastest pair start to rappel up the weathered castle wall amidst a shower of attacks from their closest competitors.

"I *think*," she said, "that we may wish to hurry."

"Ah." Gerard's gaze followed hers as he stepped up beside her. "I see."

Grim understanding passed between them without any need for words.

When that lead pair found their way inside the castle, whatever final menace lurked within would be awakened . . .

And without having solved the full series of riddles beforehand, there would be no way for *anyone* to defeat it.

16

Naturally, there were at least two dozen ducks swimming in the lake, all of them damned near identical. Gerard blew out his breath as he gave up the idea of spotting their next target from a distance.

Apparently, nothing about these trials could be simple—especially not his own partner, who felt more elusive than ever as she stood beside him now, clad in that scandalously revealing gown that offered mouthwatering glimpses of bare skin with every movement. All day, she'd been emoting the bright, high-strung effervescence of a hummingbird ready to dart out of reach at any instant . . . or be crushed within his grasp if he tried to seize firm hold.

Queen Lorelei might have kidnapped him for her own mysterious purposes, but he'd recognized the panic in her eyes after that morning's first trial. Despite all of the notorious displays she put on, Gerard had never known anyone so desperate not to be truly *seen*. If archaic fae rules hadn't bound her to complete this tournament, he was certain he would have found himself returned to his cold tent in the mortal world, *alone*, immediately afterwards, expelled from her presence for the unforgivable crime of perceiving her too deeply.

He had no intention of allowing that to happen—which meant he couldn't afford to fail this challenge and be knocked out from the Tournament of Leaves, no matter how many ducks might be scattered across the water in hopeful distraction. Fortunately, he didn't imagine that any test of cunning would involve swimming out to inspect every individual, flapping bird for clues . . . and run afoul of whatever underwater monster had already devoured two earlier competitors.

Gerard turned away from the obvious lure on the lake's surface to focus on the wide pathway that ran alongside it, punctuated halfway around the lake by an elegant fountain that shot an endless arc of sparkling water into a large, bowl-shaped pool of veined marble without any helpful duck occupants. Pale and glittering in the low autumn light, the path itself was made of crushed shells that crunched beneath his feet, none of them large enough to take on any recognizably avian shapes. To the right of the path was the lake; on the left stood a deep-green wall made up of massive topiary figures just like those which had framed every other themed section of the garden thus far.

In the first section of the garden, every tree and bush had been cut into the shapes of leaping stags; the sections since then had been lined by wolves, hares, gryphons, and boars, respectively.

Here, Gerard's gaze passed over a line of elegant green swans in a row, one after another . . .

With just one exception. His lips curved with satisfaction as he crossed to the single bush that stood shorter than the rest, shaped into the distinctive bill and body of a different kind of bird.

"'Duck' indeed." Lorelei's throaty laugh sounded behind him as he peered into the thick greenery. "And with more than one meaning after all!"

Slipping past him, she ducked down to wriggle underneath the main body of the bush, heedless of her silk gown. As her front half disappeared underneath the greenery, strips of pink and gold cloth spread outwards from her round, raised bottom. Under Gerard's fixed gaze, one strip slipped free from its place and began to slide down . . . down . . . until he could almost glimpse—

No! Gerard jerked his gaze upwards, breathing hard.

Lorelei was a longtime master of her weaponry when it came to fashion, but he understood her tactics by now. He *would not* be distracted by the irrelevant question of just how much smooth, bare skin might be revealed to his view if he only looked back down.

A slippery strip of fabric brushed against his uniform trousers as she shifted forward, wriggling farther underneath the bush. His skin burned as if with fever.

He had to force himself to go on the attack to save himself from dropping to his knees and surrendering everything. "Surely, if your expulsion from your mother's court is such tedious old news to you, it should be simple enough to relate the story while you search."

Her figure stilled. He held his breath, excruciatingly aware of the strip of cloth trailing over the toe of his left boot.

Then she said brightly, "*I'd* rather gossip about something far more interesting. When did you start supporting the cause of Purification, General?"

"*What?*" He let out a startled half laugh. "Of course I don't support Purification. Why would you ever imagine that I would? It's a tiny fringe movement formed by dangerous extremists and bigots and led by a charlatan. No one with a brain thinks any more of it."

"Oh, dear." Lorelei's voice was muffled by the greenery but still all too clear. "Hasn't Otto shared the good news with you yet, darling?

He's about to adopt it as the guiding principle of your precious empire."

Relaxing at the sheer absurdity of this new strategy—was she struggling with distraction, too?—Gerard shook his head. "That is patently ludicrous." *No one* who knew anything about the history of their continent and its various peoples could possibly support the idea of expunging all nonhuman magical creatures within it. "You, of all people, should know better than to listen to rumors."

"Oh, but I do love the power of rumors, don't you? They can be *so* useful! And this isn't mere gossip, I'm afraid. I happen to know for a fact that Otto's been holding private meetings with members of that little group . . . and he's found them to be *very* persuasive."

Gerard shouldn't listen to anything she said about the ruler to whom he'd sworn his loyalty—and yet he found his shoulders shifting restlessly as if to dislodge her implausible claims. "You couldn't possibly know any such thing if *I've* never heard of it. Remember, I am a member of his privy council."

"Oh, darling." She clucked her tongue at him with fauxsympathy as she wriggled backwards, emerging from beneath the bush on her hands and knees with one hand closed around whatever she'd found there. "Did you actually believe that Otto was fool enough to share *everything* with you? He may have appointed you for the sake of your glorious exploits and lovely, shiny reputation—our poor Otto does *so* yearn to feel popular with his people, if only by association!—but he's canny enough *not* to offer you the chance to disagree with him."

"In point of fact, I disagree with him *frequently*." Gerard clipped out the words, his spine stiffening. After all their years of circling, did Lorelei truly think so little of him? "Regardless of what you may imagine, I have *never* withheld my true opinion in any of our meetings since my first appointment. It is an essential part of my role as high general to brave even His Majesty's deepest displeasure with my honest consideration."

"Of course it is—and he knows that you believe it." Lorelei

bounced cheerfully to her feet. "That's why he didn't invite *you* to any of those secret meetings with his new favorite Purifiers!"

This was outrageous, libelous nonsense. There could be no other possible explanation.

But when Gerard thought back to a few seemingly idle comments that Otto had made over a late supper only a week or so ago, comments that Gerard had assumed—or had he merely hoped?—were no more than appallingly tasteless jests . . .

Damn it, they *had* been jests. What else could they have been? Otto himself had laughed heartily when Gerard had remained still and silent in shock for too long, having actually imagined his emperor to be serious about them.

Better yet, rather than lingering on that offensive moment of humor, Otto had immediately switched to a different, far-more-palatable topic, to Gerard's vast relief. They had said no more about it.

Why had Lorelei chosen *this* particular line of nonsense as her latest attempt to turn Gerard from his duty? Had someone else overheard their conversation that night and misunderstood what was happening between them?

"Lorelei . . ." he began.

A massive crash sounded behind them, followed by a deafening, animalistic roar of rage that shook the ground beneath their feet. Both partners spun around in unison, Gerard's free hand falling instinctively to the hilt of his sword.

Massive grey stones the size of boulders hurtled outwards from a gaping new hole in the castle's front wall, showering with lethal force across the wide expanse of water and sending ducks shrieking and flapping to escape. One pair of competitors was still clinging frantically to the bumpy side wall they'd been in the middle of climbing; neither of the other two pairs was visible until Gerard spotted two bodies floating limply in the water amidst the scattered debris. Whether unconscious or dead, that leading pair must have been thrown through the wall as punishment for disturbing the castle's occupant—and he didn't seem inclined to go back to sleep now he was rid of them.

As Gerard glimpsed ominous flashes of the massive creature behind that gap in the wall—and heard the screams of the second pair, still trapped somewhere within that building—his fingers clenched around the hilt of his sword. Still, he kept his voice steady. "Did you happen to find our next clue beneath that topiary?"

"Oh, *now* you want to focus and stop chatting?" Lorelei's voice was sharp, but she held out the silver leaf she'd been clutching. "It was too dark to read under there, so I still haven't seen it myself."

Gerard shifted closer, until her shoulder brushed against his chest. "We'll read it together." Tantalizingly soft hair wafted against his cheek as he leaned closer, but he didn't allow himself to flinch away.

A house built in spring but empty by fall;
I hold hopes and dreams but have no wall.

Curse the fae's endless love of riddles! Half of Gerard's mind was already busy working through defensive tactics; he didn't have time to parse out clever wording, too.

His sword would do nothing in a situation like this except irritate the castle's owner on the way to devouring them. Both pairs of competitors ahead of them had carried bows and arrows as weaponry, but none of those seemed to be slowing the creature down. Unless this final clue (Jovar help him, this had *better* be the final clue!) led them to a trebuchet of monumental size . . .

"*Aha.*" Lorelei's announcement came out in a gust of relief. "Of course. Keeping with the theme!"

"Which is?" he prompted, one eye still on the castle ahead of them.

"Waterfowl, of course." Shaking her head, she prowled forward along the lakeshore. "Apparently we're looking for a nest."

. . . Something *far* too small—even in this oversized setting—to hold any useful siege engines! Gerard bit back a growl of frustration. In any other situation where he was faced with an impossible threat with another soul at risk, he'd be ordering his partner to retreat for their own safety—but on this type of battlefield, Lorelei was the expert, and she'd only laugh if he ordered her to shelter behind him.

He *had* been hungry for a new type of challenge, hadn't he? All those petty border skirmishes he'd been sent to quash over the years, none of them requiring any real thought or insight...

All those hours trapped in endless meetings of the privy council, listening to Otto's self-aggrandizing monologues go on and on and fighting with all his might to maintain his patience, to remain a voice of reason *without* igniting the Emperor's notorious temper so badly that Otto would dig in his feet and insist on having his way regardless of logic or common sense...

Jovar save him, Gerard would just have to find a damned nest.

Like the rest of this oversized garden, the curving line of the lakeshore was beautifully tended, with neatly trimmed grass leading from the water to the shell-lined pathway and from the other side of that pathway to the topiary border beyond. It should have been a simple matter to spot a nest perched anywhere along that shore... but as he scanned it, he saw nothing but green grass and the pale, empty path, studded by that arcing fountain.

Lorelei was already darting from one topiary bush to the next, ducking beneath each one to search within its shadows. He started forward automatically to join that exercise—but as another, even louder roar sounded from the castle, followed by a third flung body, Gerard's whole body stiffened in place with a resistance borne from well-honed instinct.

Wrong strategy. Checking underneath every single bush would take time they didn't have—and they hadn't found the answer to their last clue by inspecting every duck on the lake.

So, what else in this pristine landscape could hide—or symbolize—a nest?

This time, when he scanned the path with a hunter's gaze, he wasn't searching for an actual nest of sticks, but for the *shape* of a nest... and his gaze landed, halfway along that path, on the large, veined-marble bowl of the fountain.

More catastrophic crashes sounded to his right as even more of the castle wall exploded outwards. With no time left for hesitation, Gerard lunged forward into a run. Lorelei made a startled sound behind him, but he didn't pause his thundering race down the path. Small pieces of shell crunched and sprayed from beneath his feet; he didn't allow himself to trip or slide.

He had achieved every improbable target he had fought for in his life. He *would not* fail now, with Lorelei's life at stake.

The mounting chaos to his right turned into a dull visual and aural blur as all of his attention narrowed in on that stone bowl, closer and closer to his reach with every running step. At first, all he could see was the sun-dappled surface of the fountain, kept at a continuous ripple by the steady arc of water soaring out and back into it. As he neared it, though, more and more of the water beneath the surface came into view, along with glimpses of sloping calligraphy etched within the inner bowl.

Not another gods-damned riddle!

He grabbed hold of the bowl's rim as he finally reached it. Deep within the transparent pool of water, he could see a plain white egg lying still at the bottom of the bowl.

Above it, running along the bowl's inner surface, he read with intense irritation:

I can be stolen, given, lost, and broken; know me as true love's token.

"What does it say?" Lorelei was only an instant behind him, panting for breath.

"See for yourself." Turning away, he planted himself like a wall between her and the nightmarish scene beyond the lake, where an immense and terrible figure was pushing its way out through the crumbling wall, roaring all the while. "Perhaps we need to find a ring?"

"I'm not sure—oh. *Oh.*" The sudden horror in her voice was enough to make him flick her a quick, wary glance, despite the danger. She looked suddenly pale and sick as she stared down into the depths of the water at the egg that lay on the marble bottom. "I've heard of this, but I've never seen it before. What a horribly cruel and stupid bargain to have made."

Gerard's brows knitted together. "What do you mean?"

Fae bargains were notorious for their dangers. Bound by deep magic, once made, they could never be willingly broken by either of the participants. He'd read numerous warnings even before he'd felt the weight of them himself yesterday, when he and Lorelei had committed to their own bargain and scorching magic had sealed their agreement. Still, as he gazed at the horrifying figure now emerging from the remnants of the broken castle, Gerard couldn't imagine anyone forcing that monumental creature into *anything*.

An actual giant out of legend, the castle's owner stood at least twenty feet tall, with unkempt long brown hair, a filthy, trailing beard, and only a tattered loincloth to preserve any final shreds of modesty. Excrement and blood covered his body, while mad, feral rage contorted his massive face.

Arrows soared towards the giant from one side of the broken castle, where the third partnership still crouched, but they scattered off his skin without leaving any marks.

What Gerard wouldn't give for a whole array of cannons at his command!

Lorelei's voice, though, was laced with what sounded bizarrely like sympathy. "The giant exchanged his heart for immunity to all other dangers. *That's* the bargain that he made."

"His *heart*?" Gerard's eyebrows shot upwards, but this time, he didn't turn. The giant was already stomping into the lake to splash furiously towards them, the detritus-filled water reaching no higher than his broad, filthy waist. Gerard's chest tightened as he drew his sword, already knowing that it wouldn't be enough. "Do you mean his actual, literal heart? Or—"

"Oh, yes," Lorelei said softly. "It's right here, trapped in that egg. All we have to do is crush it."

17

"*Right.*" The Golden Beacon's whole body had already been drawn into taut lines of anticipation. The moment Lorelei finished speaking, he dropped his sword and plunged his right hand into the pool, ready to crush the giant's hidden heart on her direction.

"Wait!" Lorelei latched onto his big arm with both hands, so driven by panic and instinct that she barely even noticed the muscles flexing against her grip. "Not yet."

"Not *yet*?" His eyebrows soared as he stared down at her, but he was too much of a gentleman, even now, to shake her off. "You want to wait for him to arrive and crush you instead?"

"Crush *us*," she said impatiently, "but, Gerard . . ." Desperately, she cast about for a reason, *any* reason that made sense. "Don't you remember that basilisk, the first day? You spared its life. Can't you do that again?"

He let out a huff of disbelieving laughter as the loud splashing sounded closer, the giant already almost halfway across the lake. "That basilisk was rendered utterly harmless. Killing it would have been cruel and unnecessary. This time, it's a matter of self-defense. He will *kill you* if I don't stop him—and apparently, this is the only way in which he *can* be fought."

"But—"

"Lorelei," he bit out, "take one look at that creature's expression, and you'll know it to be true. He *cannot* be reasoned with."

The giant's next wordless roar was so powerful that it buffeted the hair on her head, even from halfway across the lake; she gritted her teeth as she waited for the sound to end so she could finally answer. "Of course he can't, because of *this*!" Still restraining Gerard with both hands, she jerked her head towards the egg lying at the bottom of the pool between them. "He traded away everything soft and compassionate inside him because he thought he *had* to, to stay safe. Doesn't that remind you of anything—or any*one*?"

Gerard's amber eyes widened. "Good gods. Do you actually imagine this creature to be anything like you? I'm sure you must have had to harden your own heart to become an effective queen, but—"

"Don't be ridiculous! I was talking about *you*." Her heartbeat thundered in her ears as the giant splashed towards them, ready to trample all over everything—just as the man before her would trample over everything she loved in this coming year if she didn't find a way to stop him.

There *had* to be a better way than killing him—killing *either* of them!

Gerard was still staring at her in disbelief as flecks of spray landed on his hair from the giant's path. "You think of me as a wordless, feral monster driven by rage?"

"Of course not. But I do think you'll follow Otto's orders, no matter how terrible they may be, because you don't think you're allowed to have real feelings of your own anymore—much less *listen* to them when they contradict your orders!"

His arm stiffened into the solidity of rock between her hands as he bit out his response. "Not everyone can or should allow their *feelings* to drive them wherever their latest whim takes them, *Your Majesty*. Some of us are sworn to serve a higher duty than our own personal desires."

"And you think I'm *not*?" She could have laughed at the sheer irony of that statement—but an incoming tide of cold lake water splashed over them both, leaving her dripping wet, coughing, and glaring at him with her hands still clenched around his arm. The giant's next roar sounded so close, it shook through her body, but she didn't let go or drop Gerard's furious gaze as she waited for her opportunity to speak again. "Come now, you're meant to be the most brilliant strategist the Empire has ever seen. Can you *really* not think of any way to defend us without killing him?"

More water cascaded over them. In the corner of her eyes, she could see the giant's outline . . .

And Gerard wrenched his arm free of her grasp to scoop the egg from the bottom of the pool.

Lorelei cried out in protest, but the sound was lost in the din as the giant surged towards them, his shadow casting darkness over both of them. Water surged over their heads.

Spinning around to face their opponent, Gerard pulled back his right arm and hurled the egg through the air to crash hard against the giant's massive, bare, blood- and excrement-smeared chest.

The shell of the egg split.

A blinding red glow filled the air . . .

And the giant's roar abruptly ceased.

In the shock of that sudden cessation, Lorelei stumbled back a step, her own harsh breaths suddenly shockingly loud in her ears. Blinking lake water from her eyes, she watched the giant reel backwards in open-mouthed silence.

Shattered pieces of eggshell fell to mix in the water with all the other debris...

But that red glow remained fixed on the left side of the giant's chest for a long moment.

At last, it faded away. The giant shook himself hard, scattering even more water across the lakeshore.

Lorelei braced herself, casting out her senses to hunt for any useful strands of pondweed in the lake beneath him that she could use to trip him up. Beside her, Gerard set his hand on the hilt of his sword.

Neither of them would be able to slow that huge creature for long—but at least anything they did *could* potentially affect him, now that his heart was back in its rightful place.

Lorelei held her breath.

The giant's face contorted in horror as he stared down at his own bare stomach, covered in filth. One massive hand splashed water at his skin in a desperate attempt at cleaning; the other clapped against his head and tangled in the foul mess he found there.

He let out a moan of pure despair, backing slowly away from the lakeshore.

... And Gerard's voice snapped through the air with cold command: "*Hold!*"

Even the giant stilled for an instant at the force of that command—but it hadn't been aimed at him.

The last partnership of competitors, the same pair of hobgoblins Lorelei had taken note of yesterday, had crept stealthily along the grass behind them and aimed their sharp throwing knives directly at that retreating figure, while the archers at the other side of the lake had drawn their bows.

Amateurs! Lorelei might have struggled to contain a giant with mere pondweed, but her competitors were no challenge at all. Both sets of bows and arrows across the lake withered into limp husks of wood and twine at her command. At the same moment, roots from deep underground lashed up through the dirt to fasten around the hobgoblins' ankles and yank them waist-deep into the earth, knives falling hopelessly out of their reach.

"Apologies, darling!" Lorelei called out to the giant, stepping forward. His bloodshot gaze had widened with new outrage at the sight of that failed assassination attempt, but she waved gaily to distract his attention from the hobgoblins scrambling uselessly to get free. "This was all due to a terrible misunderstanding. You see, you actually attacked several of our companions here only a few minutes ago, when you weren't yourself."

"I . . . ?" The giant's voice was a low, hoarse rumble that sounded horribly pained. *Of course.* Poor thing—no doubt his throat was raw from all that earlier roaring. He shook his massive head in confusion, his matted beard and hair scattering gore with every move.

"Behind you?" Lorelei pointed helpfully at the bodies floating limply in the water behind him . . . or, at least, those bodies that were left. The first partnership had been snapped up by the time they'd arrived, but truthfully, she was relieved to see four bodies left on the water's surface. The lake beast must be a slow eater.

Following her gesture, the giant swiveled around—and let out a hauntingly mournful groan at the sight of the remaining floating bodies and the broken castle behind them. His gigantic body hunched over as if he had been struck a mortal blow at last. "I . . . Did I—?"

"You don't even remember, do you?" Sighing, Lorelei gave up on negotiating from a distance and waded into the water towards him.

"*Lorelei!*" Gerard's voice was a furious snap, but she ignored it as she hurried forward, letting the strips of her dress rise to float around her in the dirty water.

"It's all right," she said softly as she approached the giant's hunched figure from behind. The water was nearly as high as her chin by now, but she didn't allow that to slow her down. "We all know you didn't intend any of this."

He didn't answer in words, only in a choked sob that sent a responsive pang through her chest.

"It's *not your fault*." Carefully, she set one gentle palm against the smeared blood and filth of his skin just above the waterline, as high as she could reach.

He gave a convulsive jerk at her touch.

"That's it," Gerard growled behind her. "I'm coming in to get you."

"Don't you dare." Lorelei kept her voice calm and her hand held out in offering as the giant lurched back around, sending another wave cascading over her. Swallowing and blinking more water from her eyes, she tipped her drenched head back all the way to meet his anguished gaze, so high above her. The stench that surrounded him was nigh-on overwhelming, but she refused to allow her nose to crinkle. "This is the fault of the one who tricked you," she said steadily. "You did not choose any of it."

No, *that* fault lay with whichever fae noble in her mother's court had taken this innocent creature and turned him into their pet monster for their own malicious entertainment.

In that moment, Lorelei made a vow not to her own patron goddess, Sylvana, but to Divine Elva, the mother of all wild and magical nonhuman creatures: she *would* find out who had mistreated this one so badly . . . and she would exact revenge.

But she kept her fury locked safely inside as she crooned, "You have your heart back now, my dear. You're finally free. You can let all of this go, I promise. You are not to blame."

For a long moment, silence hung over the lakeshore. Even the hobgoblins trapped in the dirt behind her stopped struggling as they, too, waited for the outcome.

Then a giant, open mouth erupted up through the water's surface just beside her, rows upon rows of teeth wide and waiting for Lorelei as a dozen thick tentacles lashed out to drag her down.

She didn't even have to shift out of its way. The giant grabbed the lake beast before it could touch her, holding it back like a nobleman restraining an overeager hunting hound.

"No," he growled. "No more. Never again."

Shoving the creature back into its watery domain, he turned his big back on Lorelei and strode across the lake with determined, splashing steps. He didn't aim for the shattered castle walls. Instead, he moved from one floating body to another, gathering them all up in a pile in his arms before bringing them back to lay them all gently—apologetically—on the lakeshore where Gerard stood.

"*Free,*" the giant rumbled.

The ground shook as he stepped out onto dry land beside them. Water spattered like a sudden storm as he shook himself.

Then he strode away, trampling elegant topiary with every step as he left the prison in which he had been trapped.

Lorelei could have wept with the force of her emotions. Instead, she tipped her head back to smile triumphantly at Gerard as she emerged from the lake, too. "You see? I *knew* we could work out a better way together. Are you ready to praise my wisdom and good sense now, partner?"

He shook his head at her with what looked more like furious disbelief than the wonder she certainly deserved. "*You . . . !*"

Before he could say what he thought of her brilliant actions, the air rippled around them.

The lake and the broken garden disappeared.

Lorelei and Gerard stood on the tournament field once more, surrounded by their surviving competitors . . . and for the second time that day, there was no applause for the end of the trial. A tense, watchful silence filled the open air, prickling with warning.

Oberon didn't even try to hide the hatred that twisted his face as he glared at her from the autumn throne. "How *very* disappointing."

18

Gerard was not in control of his emotions. From the moment he had found himself rashly throwing that egg at the giant's chest instead of listening to reason and crushing it, he had been hanging by a thread. Watching Lorelei splash directly towards that blood-soaked, murderous creature and then, in an act of inconceivable recklessness, start *petting it*—as if her own safety meant nothing!—had ripped that final thread to pieces.

For seven years, this woman had haunted his life and his dreams with her incorrigible teasing and their circling, joint obsession. The possibility of watching her be killed before him now—just as his parents had been, so long ago!—had whited out every thought in his head and left behind only furious, panicking denial in their place.

He *could not* bear a world without his nemesis in it. All of his most unacceptable, desperately-repressed-until-now feelings were focused on *her*.

And when he saw that giant—whom Lorelei had actually compared to Gerard!—break free of his own bindings . . .

Gerard couldn't name every overwhelming, tumultuous feeling rioting through him in answer. All he knew was that their concatenation was deafening. *Overwhelming.*

He couldn't think clearly over their racket—but when he landed back on the fae field, instinct drove him to take a swift step to Lorelei's side to face the tournament's lord together.

The sight of Lord Oberon's expression, directed at Gerard's partner, was a metaphorical splash of water colder than the lake they had left behind.

The man who sat before them was no longer simply angry. No, the man Gerard was looking at now was a petty, vicious weakling who had lost all control and was about to break the last remaining social rules that bound him . . . unless someone broke his concentration first.

"I assume you are about to crown us the victors, my lord Oberon?" It took every ounce of Gerard's willpower to make his words a calm inquiry.

Still, Lord Oberon jerked with surprise when he spoke, as if Gerard had been invisible to the fae lord until then. Oberon's snarl deepened, but his gaze shifted from Gerard to the silent, watchful field of observers around them, and his throat worked soundlessly for several swallows in a row. When he finally replied, his voice was once again pitched to reach their full audience. "Sadly, you have *all* failed this challenge."

"What absolute nonsense." Lorelei shook back her long, wet curls over the shoulder of her drenched gown, and Gerard fought back the impulse to shift protectively in front of her too-exposed form. "As everyone here has clearly seen, we solved every riddle *and* defeated the giant, too."

"'Defeated'?" Oberon's hands clenched around the arms of his throne as he half-rose from his seat, his body taut. "That beast still lives! The bargain I set him seven years ago has been broken, and now you've released him to rampage over your mother's people. Do you care *nothing* about the world you chose to abandon?"

Chose? Gerard made careful note of that word.

But Lorelei was already snapping back, "That so-called beast *is* one of my mother's people, and the bargain you tricked him into was unforgivable! A queen owes her protection to every member of her nation, not only to those who happen to look like her. If you knew anything about true governance beyond the glory and the stage setting of it—"

"If you knew anything of your own *people*, you'd be able to distinguish between us and our enemies!"

The words lashed out like a whip, and Gerard saw them hit true as Lorelei physically flinched. Not a single fae in the gathering of advisors behind the throne, the surviving competitors on the field, or the audience members in the stands beyond raised a voice in disagreement.

. . . And as Gerard watched, he saw *that* hit her, too.

Lorelei was a queen in her own right, his most inveterate nemesis, and an unrelenting political intriguer who openly loathed Gerard's emperor. No matter how deep his previously denied feelings might be, if she refused to stop her scheming and back down from the oncoming international battlefield, his vows of loyalty would eventually force him to wield Imperial troops against her nation.

But at this moment, all the willpower in the world couldn't have stopped Gerard from taking his final step to close the inches of distance between them until his arm brushed firmly against her small shoulder.

Her startled blue gaze flashed up to meet his. He held it steadily, his message unhidden:

Partners. At least for now.

For a long moment, there was silence.

Then Lorelei blazed her most triumphant smile, and high-summer heat suddenly erupted all around them, vibrant red and yellow lilies shooting up from the grass in a circle around their feet and a hot, dry breeze sweeping across the field to dry their wet clothes, hair, and skin in an instant.

An audible ripple of wonder passed through the stands. Even the advisors behind the throne were wide-eyed as they bent together to whisper frantically. Behind where Gerard stood, the sounds of mumbles and groans emerged from the contestants who'd been unconscious when they'd arrived. He didn't need to turn around to understand that they'd been awakened, now, by Lorelei's magic.

He also didn't need to be an expert in fae culture to see the way Oberon's lips twisted and know that Lorelei's display had been far more powerful than anything the other man could ever summon . . . and *everyone* on this field knew it.

"Enough!" Oberon snapped. "This day's trials are officially *over*." With a whirl of silken red and orange robes, he stalked away from the throne and towards the thick woods beyond, leaving his lackeys to scurry after him.

No heralds signaled the end of this day's challenges with glorious peals of their hunting horns as they had the day before. There was no smooth shift into an easy, scheduled celebration. Instead, uncertainty seemed to hold the field in a state of suspended animation, everyone waiting tensely for someone else to take charge . . .

Until Lorelei turned to wave at them all with graceful—and entirely false—gaiety. "Well! What an entertaining day it has been, darlings, hasn't it? And don't you fret about a thing. I'll leave you all to enjoy a lovely gossip without having to worry about me listening in!"

Still wearing that wide and brittle smile, she drew one forefinger in a swift, circular motion and opened a shimmering portal into darkness just before her. The circular portal was already starting to close as she stepped through it, showering colorful glitter in her wake—

But Gerard was braced and ready for his partner's flight. He threw himself through that narrowing gap and felt it snap shut just behind him.

He landed in a controlled forward roll, not in utter darkness as he'd expected, but atop a bed of soft grass in dim, shifting light. As he pulled himself up, dusting dirt and glitter from his jacket sleeves, he met Lorelei's startled gaze once more under a canopy of gold-and-red-leafed branches, with no other sound but distant bird calls and the humming of insects.

Still, something about the sharp, vibrant taste of the air and the deep humming of the earth beneath his feet . . .

"This isn't Balravia, is it?"

Lorelei turned away as she replied, but she didn't quite manage to conceal the swift wiping of her eyes. "Ah, no. This is an even older spot of mine, actually." Eyes dry once more, she shifted back to him and waved with casual grace at the small clearing where they stood, surrounded on all sides by wild woodland with no paths or markers. "My trees formed this clearing for me when I was a child."

Before she'd been expelled to the mortal realm, then—or, in Oberon's version of events, before she had made the choice herself to go there. That was a contradiction that required answers, but Gerard was in no mood to patiently dig them out.

In the past hour, he had been challenged, baffled, enraged, disturbed, awestruck, and, for the first time in years, terrified all the way down to his bones. Every bit of it was due to the actions of this small woman who stood before him now, her blue eyes seemingly guileless and all of her true emotions hidden, pretending that she hadn't a care in the world.

For seven long years, she had tried to drive him mad. Deep down, he must have always known that she would eventually succeed.

Right now, reckless madness felt like freedom.

"It's not Balravia," he repeated evenly. "We're not in the mortal realm. Here, in the fae realm, you're not the queen, and Otto isn't an emperor."

"No . . . ?" She tilted her head, watching him with dawning suspicion.

"That means," he continued inexorably, "that in this realm we are not enemies."

And if they finally weren't . . .

"Well, of course we're not!" Relaxing, she rolled her eyes at him with all of her usual impudence. "Had you already forgotten, darling? We're *partners* as long as we're here—we *both* agreed to that yesterday, remember? That's why—"

"That is why I can finally do this." Every moment in the last few days—no, the last seven years—had led him here, now, taking a single purposeful step across the grass with all the weight of worlds behind it. Coming to a halt just before her, he raised both hands until they hovered by her shoulders.

She tipped her head back, golden curls sliding over her shoulders, to watch him with wide eyes.

The palms of his hands already burned with the light and energy she gave off even from half an inch away. What would it feel like to finally close his hands around her?

For years, he'd sworn that he would never know. But now . . .

"Lorelei," Gerard said hoarsely. "May I kiss you? Please?"

The breath stopped in Lorelei's throat as his words sank through her.

Gerard de Moireul—the Emperor's own godsdamned Golden Beacon, famously noble, stoic, and brave, heart-wrenchingly soft-hearted and *wrong* for her in every possible way—was holding his big hands cupped in the air around her shoulders as if she, of all people, were too delicate to touch. His amber eyes gazed down at her with unconcealed, devouring hunger, as if he'd been starving for years and she was his final meal.

Gods, but she understood that feeling! Lorelei flung herself at him with a moan of pure, undiluted need. She had yearned for this man in her arms, in her bed, in her *life*, for so long now!

Something about that thought set distant warning bells chiming in her ears, but she couldn't stop to listen to them now.

Lorelei braced her hands on his broad shoulders as she leapt, and his arms closed firmly around her, warm bands of strength holding her safe and close as she wrapped her legs around his waist and finally, *finally* kissed Gerard de Moireul in waking life, just as she had in so many hot, frustrating dreams over the last seven years.

Ohhh but real life was so much better! No bubbling champagne could ever taste as intoxicating as his lips, no longer held firm in resistance against her but soft and welcoming her touch. She nibbled at them until they opened, savoring his harshly indrawn breath, and then she drew his tongue into her mouth and nearly swooned at the gorgeous taste of him.

He might not be an experienced kisser, but as she'd already known, Gerard de Moireul was determined to win every new challenge he was set. Within moments, he had learned to wield that tongue as a weapon, stoking the heat inside her into flame. Within another minute, he was scraping his teeth against her bottom lip, and she was horrified to hear a helpless, mewling sound fall from the back of her throat as she writhed desperately against him, nearly ready to explode.

Sylvana save her! She was *notoriously* experienced. She couldn't let him take her apart so easily!

Lorelei had never before kissed *him*, though. When she drove her fingers into his thick, short-cropped hair and scraped her nails lightly against his scalp, she wasn't only enjoying one more beautiful man; she was exploring Gerard, the infuriating, impossible opponent who'd consumed far too many of her thoughts and plans over the past seven years. When her sensitive breasts rubbed against his hard, muscular chest, it was *Gerard* setting all of her senses alight through their layers of interfering clothing, that unstoppable mountain of a man turning all of his focused energy and determination upon the challenge of *her* pleasure.

It was everything she'd secretly longed for without fully confessing it to herself until this moment, and it felt *glorious*. No, more than that: It felt *life-changing*. It went far beyond the pleasure of mere satisfied attraction, unthinkably far beyond anything she had experienced in years, until it almost felt like . . .

"*No!*" She wrenched herself back, panting for air, as ice-cold realization flooded through her.

She couldn't do this. She *would not!* She'd learned her lesson too many times.

Never again.

Gerard's arms still supported her full body with unbending strength as he stared at her from mere inches away, his broad chest heaving with effort and his golden hair standing out in wild hanks, disordered from her desperate finger-work. His massive body pulsed against her, and she bit down hard on her lower lip to swallow down a groan.

"*Lorelei.*" Her name rumbled like crushed stone from deep within his chest, at least half an octave lower than his usual speaking voice. The sound sent a shiver of pure need coursing through her, instinctively tightening her legs around his waist.

No more! Forcing her recalcitrant legs apart, she pushed the flats of her hands against his chest to shove herself free before she could dissolve back into him and lose everything.

Without a hint of resistance, he released her and helped her leap safely to the ground.

Of course he did. Gerard de Moireul, damn his eyes, was a gentleman, and that was *exactly* what made him so dangerous. Unlike Lorelei, he was noble and high-minded and everything else that she'd once dreamed a man could be: the kind of man who could become a true partner in life, one she could safely put her faith in forever.

Lorelei was a grown queen now, not a child to indulge in

self-destructive fantasies. She knew exactly what happened whenever she let down her guard and allowed emotions to overcome her common sense with any man in the real world.

So she backed swiftly away from his deliciously looming figure and felt his tingling, hungry gaze track her every fleeing step. She couldn't stop her hands from trembling, but she locked them behind her waist as she pinned a careless, carefree smile to her face, as if he were any other would-be lover and she were as unaffected as she should be. "Well! What an eventful day it has been. Shall we rejoin the feast now that we've worked off a bit of spare energy?"

His gaze rested on her, shifting before her eyes from raw hunger to cool calculation.

He had always been the worst sort of enemy: the kind who could think clearly in any situation and who never missed a single false step on her part.

"As you wish." He lowered his head in a nod that was not surrender but concession: He would give her time to gather herself, but he wouldn't forget this moment.

Nor would she. As she turned her back on him to draw an impatient portal back to the safety of gathered crowds, Lorelei swore never to give in to temptation and touch Gerard de Moireul again.

She had a nation to defend and her people's future to save. She couldn't afford to risk her heart on any man . . . especially not this one.

19

Stepping back onto the sunlit tournament field after the soft, shadowy intimacy of Lorelei's wooded clearing felt like a brutal assault on Gerard's senses. His skin felt too tight for his body, prickling and raw; the bright light and sounds and colors of the crowd broke over him in harsh attack.

Only a moment ago, he'd held Lorelei in his arms. His fingers flexed at his sides, reliving those unforgettable sensations.

The vibrant, glowing warmth of her body twining around him as if she would never let him go; those *sounds* she'd made in response to his touch as they'd devoured one another . . . !

Dragging a deep breath through his chest, he blinked hard, fighting to clear his vision and his mind of those too-vivid memories. When he finally came back to himself, he found Lord Oberon gazing directly at him, narrow-eyed and focused, from a nearby group of fae.

In the immeasurable period of time that had passed since Gerard and Lorelei had first left the tournament field, it had been reclaimed and fully covered by vendors, musicians, and members of the day's audience, all mingling now in bright array. Lorelei was already dancing lightly forward, weaving her path through the crowd so gracefully that no one except Gerard would know how urgently she was fleeing him and everything that she had just revealed.

His first, driving instinct was to follow, but logic and strategy clamped down hard to hold him back.

Here on the field, surrounded by observers, Lorelei would be safe from any physical attacks. She didn't need him to act as a shield by her side, and she certainly wouldn't let down any of her own shields for him in public.

But in the focused intent of their host's gaze, Gerard sensed a sidelong, treacherous attack on its way. Decades of experience turned him to face it full-on.

"My lord Oberon." It took just two long steps to cross the grass to where Oberon stood surrounded by a small group of gossiping sycophants. Gerard scanned their faces in an instant and, just as quickly, dismissed them. He'd met far too many like them in Otto's Imperial court, desperately clinging to the coattails of anyone who stood close to real power. Looking past them, he nodded—but did not bow—to Oberon. "You wished to speak to me?"

"Ah . . ." Oberon's gaze slid shiftily to his followers, then away. "I do indeed. Will you walk with me? I'm sure you and I will have much to share with each other. After all, I so rarely meet visitors of your . . . sort at our traditional festivities."

"My sort?" Gerard gave the fae lord a look of mild interest. "Soldiers, you mean?"

Oberon's upper lip curled, and a huff of low, contemptuous

laughter sounded from the tall, smirking fae woman beside him. "Not quite." Waving dismissal to his entourage, Oberon turned in a ripple of orange and red silk. The autumnal crown shone on his smooth brown hair as he gestured to Gerard with haughty grace. "Come. This way is best."

Standing in the next group over, the antlered vendor who'd found Gerard a tunic yesterday widened his eyes . . . and then, safely out of the fae lord's sight, grimaced in unmistakable warning. Gerard fractionally lowered his chin in a discreet nod of appreciation.

If he'd ever needed proof that the Purifiers' claims were rancid nonsense—that the fae, as a people, possessed every bit as much heart and soul as their human counterparts—he'd found it again and again in the assortment he'd met here . . . just as he had discovered, in this tournament's host, another all-too-familiar type.

Lacing his hands behind his back, Gerard followed agreeably as Oberon stalked his way through the crowd, waiting at almost every step for his temporary subjects to clear the way before him. They did so with haste every time they noticed him, but Gerard took note of the way Oberon's high cheekbones colored deeper every time he had to let out an authoritative clearing of his throat to catch their attention.

Oh, yes. Gerard had met plenty of men like him, first at military academy, where they'd made the most of their limited power, and again once he took his place in the army. There, they had only been truly dangerous until he had been promoted past them; then, they had become mere nuisances to endure.

Stopping at the edge of the forest, some twenty feet past the last of the crowds, Gerard ignored Oberon's attempt to lead him farther into the trees, braced his booted feet on the sunlit grass, and set himself to endure this nuisance, too.

. . . A nuisance that had nearly done real harm to Lorelei more than once—and tried to use Gerard to do it, too, in this morning's first challenge. His fingers tightened behind his back at that memory, but he kept his expression unmoved.

"Well, then." Apparently giving up on leading him any farther, Oberon fell back and rearranged his features into a smooth smile. "Now that we have some privacy to talk... I don't believe you've shared your name with anyone here yet."

"No," said Gerard calmly, "I haven't."

Thank all the gods, Lorelei had apparently kept that detail private even in the letter she had sent to her mother before their arrival—the letter Oberon had intercepted. For centuries, mortals had whispered about the ability of some high fae to control them with the use of their true names if ever they dared step into the fae realm, where they were vulnerable. To her credit, Lorelei hadn't made use of that particular poisoned gift since their arrival, but then, her own father had been mortal as well. By now, it had become clear to Gerard that, for all of her remarkable powers, there were a number of traditional traits that she did not share with her more inbred immortal brethren.

On the other hand, those immortals apparently had weaknesses of their own when it came to contemporary mortal cultures. Any member of the Serafin Empire or its surrounding mortal kingdoms would have guessed Gerard's rank, if not his name, by the uniform he wore; Oberon's face only tightened with barely restrained frustration as he scanned Gerard's bigger, bulkier figure.

"She's entirely covered you in glitter, you know." The words were a petulant slap.

Gerard's lips quirked as he glanced down at his jacket. "So she has." There was a scattering of rainbow glitter along his shoulders and the edges of his uniform trousers, left over from the gaudy portals she had drawn, but also, covering the front of his jacket where she had pressed herself so intoxicatingly close against him, a light coating of golden glitter sparkled in the sunlight. Was there some distinction to be drawn between the colors that Lorelei shed by instinct versus those she chose for performance? Or...

"*Well?*" Oberon snapped. "Aren't you going to wipe it off now, before everyone on that field sees you and knows exactly what you've been doing with her?"

Gerard's muscles stiffened with instinctive panic—Jovar save him if *that* story reached the mortal world, after all the years he'd spent building an irreproachable reputation!—but he forced himself to breathe through the moment and not alert his opponent to the glaring weakness in his defenses. "I can't see any particular reason why I should want to hide it," he said at last, "unless . . . ?"

He glanced idly at the man who stood before him. "Would you, by any chance, prefer your fellow courtiers *not* to witness Queen Lorelei's choice, after your own failed earlier attempts?"

"You have no idea what you're talking about." Oberon's lips pulled into a snarl as his voice lowered. "You're nothing more than an ignorant, mortal animal dropped into an immortal world of which you know *nothing*. You may currently be enchanted by her wiles, but I assure you, Lorelei sees you as a mere pawn in her games. You will never survive them if you refuse to take good advice when it's offered!"

"Hmm." Gerard allowed his expression to become thoughtful. "It is an interesting puzzle, then, that my partner and I are managing so well in the competition thus far. Based on the number of remaining competitors, I assume we have only one day remaining before the final decision must be made?" He waited for Oberon's reluctant nod before continuing, "In which case, her games seem to be surprisingly helpful for both of us."

Oberon hissed out a breath through his teeth. "You—mortal—*soldier*! I am attempting to help you *survive* that decision, as a favor to *you*."

"Indeed?" It was always fascinating to see a man so convinced of his own superiority. Gerard had learned a long time ago that his build and military bearing, to a particular type of aristocrat, implied a concurrent lack of ability to think outside a battlefield.

Diplomacy *was* another type of warfare, though, and one he'd had to master in order to rise through the ranks. So he didn't allow amusement to bleed through into his voice as he asked, "In your far more elevated opinion, what would you advise me to do?"

"Go home, of course. Now! To the mortal realm. Save yourself!" Oberon waved one hand with fluid fae grace and firm dismissal. "Let this all become a distant dream to you of which you can brag to your friends and commanders—the week in which you, alone of all magicless mortals, were allowed to join in one of Efaelen's most honored traditions as a near-equal."

"Tempting." Gerard tilted his head, studying the other man's expression. "However, you may not realize that it is anything but simple for a ... mere mortal to travel between realms. Even our witches and wizards can't manage that feat, so how would you advise that I do it without, as you observed, any magic of my own?"

"Never fear." Oberon's face relaxed into a smugly condescending smile. "You may rely upon my assistance for that part. I assume you work for one of the many mortal kings in your own realm?"

"Something of the sort," Gerard agreed easily. Was Oberon, he wondered, even aware of the Serafin Empire's existence? Led by Otto II's grandfather, it had devoured most of the continent's individual kingdoms decades before Gerard's own birth—but of course, the other man, despite his youthful appearance, was immortal and clearly considered human cultures unworthy of his attention.

Gerard made a careful mental note of that weakness, in case it should prove useful in the future.

"Well, then." Oberon's smile broadened. "You may inform your ruler that I chose to help you as a gesture of renewed friendship from Efaelen."

Gerard's eyebrows twitched upwards. "And are you now authorized to speak for the Queen of Efaelen in *all* things, not only this tournament?"

The angry flare of the other man's eyes was an answer in itself. "We haven't time to quibble over details," Oberon snarled, "and you wouldn't understand them anyway. Just hear me, soldier, when I say to you in truth: Regardless of any other bargains you've sworn, if you only hold out your hand to me now, I vow to the trees and rivers that I *shall* deliver you, safe and sound, back to your mortal realm, free to return to your own petty concerns. All you need do is take my hand in agreement, and this long and perilous dream of yours will be ended."

"All you need do is take my hand in agreement..."

Lorelei was already fully cloaked in illusion, invisible and inaudible to Oberon and Gerard. Still, her breath instinctively stopped in her throat at Oberon's offer, as if her body itself, lanced by shock, feared giving her away to the two men who stood only a few feet away from her.

She had followed them from the moment she'd first seen Oberon lead Gerard from the field, but she'd done it with the pure intention of protecting her partner. She'd known Oberon must be up to some new, malicious scheme; she'd feared what he might do to her partner to harm her... and yet, it still hadn't hit her until this moment what Oberon could *offer* Gerard, instead, to steal him from her.

Curses, she *knew* she should have taken the time to hammer out a better bargain with her new partner yesterday! True, he had sworn to fight by her side in every trial he was called to—but he *couldn't* be called to any of them from the mortal realm, so Oberon's bargain would count him free from their agreement.

At the time, she'd let that loophole go unfilled rather than risk him noticing the even larger loophole he'd left her in return... when he'd failed to insist that she return him to the mortal realm *alive, unharmed,* or even *freed from her captivity.* Unlike the fae, humans weren't trained to gauge every word in the bargains that they swore, with no magic to act as a firm binding. So, she'd judged it a risk worth taking, as he couldn't leave the realm without her anyway...

But of course Oberon could transport him between the mortal and fae realms with ease. Anyone with fae blood could do it, apart from Lorelei's own contractually bound mother. Even more persuasively, Oberon would have to do it without pulling any nasty tricks along the way, to fulfil that binding vow he'd just spoken.

And when Gerard did abandon her...

Unlike any of the other men she'd trusted, he wouldn't even consider it a betrayal. Blinded by her own dazzlement, had Lorelei actually forgotten that he still considered himself her prisoner? *Of course* he would leap at the chance to return to his ordinary life, blindly serving the emperor she hated and trampling over everything she loved!

Once he was safely returned to his Imperial home, he would probably never sleep again without cold iron lining his bed to guard against her entry. After this, she would only ever see him on the opposite side of a bloody battlefield, forced to either kill him or be killed herself. He would never again fight by her side or hold her or kiss her as if...

Gerard spoke over her spiraling thoughts, his tone as mild as if he were discussing the fucking *autumn weather* instead of his entire future and hers, as well. "A generous offer indeed, my lord, but I won't trouble you to fulfil it."

"*What?*" Oberon's mouth dropped as both he and—invisibly—Lorelei gaped at Gerard in joint astonishment.

"Was I unclear?" Gerard rolled his big shoulders in an indifferent shrug. "Much as I appreciate the offer, I've already committed to fighting this tournament at my partner's side. I may be a mere mortal, but I do not break my vows, Lord Oberon."

Oh, gods... Lorelei stuffed her right fist into her mouth to hold back what felt uncomfortably like a sob as tremors of relief rocked through her body. *Of course.* The magic of her bargain might not bind him, but his rigid sense of duty had kicked in, despite every other contradictory concern. It was everything that she both hated and loved about—

No. No love was involved in her feelings for the Golden Beacon. It was just so very *him*.

"However," Gerard continued, "as we're speaking of fae magic . . . a moment ago, I seem to recall you accusing Queen Lorelei of using enchantments to take away my good sense, which brought up an interesting question. May I ask whether her mother, *your* queen, knew of your own attempt to make a similar assault on Lorelei by means of an illicit potion?"

Lorelei abruptly stiffened. *Oh, Sylvana . . .* She didn't want to hear the answer to that question.

She'd never told her mother herself, but Morgana had eyes and ears everywhere in Efaelen's court. Lorelei couldn't bear to see Gerard's reaction when he learned how little her own mother cared for her welfare anymore.

However, it was Oberon's face that blotched with color. "I am the chosen proxy for Queen Morgana at this tournament!"

"Which doesn't answer my question," Gerard observed, "but it does bring up another issue I've wondered about ever since your status was first announced to us. You've been intriguingly careful with your phrasing every time you've stated that you *were* chosen . . . but you've never said by whom. *Did* Queen Morgana herself actually choose you? Or was it someone else entirely?"

Oh . . . Lorelei leaned closer, her skin prickling with new tension and an excruciatingly painful, childish hope.

If her mother *hadn't* really chosen to treat Oberon as her favored successor, after everything he'd done . . .

Oberon's gaze flicked rapidly back and forth around Gerard's big figure, as if searching for any helpful distractions on the empty field around them.

Apparently failing in that quest, he stepped back, his thin

nostrils flaring in a sneer. "Enough questions! You've made your own choice, *soldier*, so you'll endure mine in return. Before tomorrow's games are over, I wager you'll *wish* you'd been wise enough to take my offered friendship."

Oberon shook his head in bitter condemnation. "Enjoy your final evening of celebration, mortal. You *will not* have another one."

20

It might not be magic, but Gerard still found it impressive that Lorelei could orbit him with such precision all across the long evening of feasts and musical performances while managing to appear entirely unaware of his presence. Not for an instant did she ever come close enough to touch—or even attempt conversation—through the shifting crowds. Yet, every time he turned around, from the moment he first returned from his private discussion with Lord Oberon, he glimpsed her in the crowd close by, seeming fully focused on her various companions . . . but always keeping him within her view.

Had she noticed him talking privately with the tournament's host in her absence? Perhaps she was watching him so closely now in order to prevent any attempts at escape or betrayal.

If so... how very little she understood the seismic shifts that had altered his perspective since she'd swept him away to Efaelen and overturned all of his preconceptions.

Luckily, he knew exactly how to take advantage of an opponent's mistake.

Gerard was used to being on guard against observers, after so many years of public life. But he'd never before *enjoyed* the sensation of being stealthily studied—nor had he ever so keenly anticipated flipping the hunt around. By the end of the night, his body was humming with awareness, and he was more than ready to set his trap.

Tonight, just like the night before, a ceremonial gesture from Lord Oberon sent majestic lines of trees marching in retreat to reveal the same extravagant array of waiting silken tents, each lit from within by dancing will-o'-the-wisps; unlike the preceding evening, Lorelei made no move to join Gerard or take him with her to the tent they had previously shared.

Despite all those teasing overtures she had made in the past, it seemed he wasn't, after all, the only one who'd been internally battling their yearslong attraction... and like any wily opponent, she was ready to withdraw from her current position of weakness and focus on rebuilding her defenses. No doubt she planned to wait for him to choose a tent and then claim the one beside it, all the better to keep an eye on him without actually *talking* with him and thereby risking the loss of any more of her secrets.

Gerard had quite a different plan for the night ahead. Nodding a polite farewell to the fae gathered around him and setting down the half-full mug that he'd been holding all night long, he turned and began to stroll unhurriedly away from the waiting village of tents, towards the darkness of the trees on the other side of the tournament field. For a moment, he considered whistling an easy tune as he walked, to increase the effect—but no, that would be excessive.

It took less than a minute before Lorelei's voice sounded behind him, slightly breathless from exertion but still wryly amused. "Have you lost your way, General? In case you hadn't noticed, the festivities have ended for the night."

Aha. The first skirmish was officially his. "You astound me." Turning politely, Gerard tilted his head in question. "Shouldn't you be finding your own rest for the night, then?"

Studying him in silence, she bit down on her lush lower lip.

Gerard's stomach tightened in primitive response. He breathed through it.

"If you're in need of even *more* vigorous exercise," Lorelei finally said, "you'd be better off taking it inside a tent."

Vigorous exercise... in a tent? What exactly was she offering? Caught off guard by the unexpected—and dangerously tempting—images her suggestion had summoned, he stared at her wordlessly, his eyebrows soaring upwards. She stared back. Then, for the first time in their seven-year acquaintance, he saw something he would never have imagined possible: the scandal-loving Lorelei of Balravia wincing in pink-cheeked mortification.

"That's not—I only meant that you could do your—your—*whatever* that was this morning in our tent!" she cried, gesturing desperately. "That thing, with your shirt off, on the ground—I mean—"

"My calisthenics. Naturally." As a deep, almost irrepressible laugh rose unexpectedly through his chest, Gerard realized that he was enjoying himself now even more than he had during any of the tournament's official challenges. Gravely, he asked, "What else could anyone have imagined?"

Lorelei's blue eyes narrowed in deep suspicion. He kept his lips in a straight line and tamped down the laugh that wanted to escape.

Gerard was not a man known for breaking into laughter. But with Lorelei in this liminal, magical realm, with soft darkness wrapping around them both... all of a sudden, extraordinary developments felt tantalizingly possible. The Queen of Balravia, after all her years of determined flirtation, could blush at an unintentional insinuation; Gerard, if he allowed himself, could laugh with her as if she were a friend—the *best* friend he had ever had; and together . . .

She let out a gusty sigh before his improbable fantasy could spool out any further. "I am thinking of your *safety*." From the ground-glass tone of her voice, it was a painful—perhaps even embarrassing—admission. "I would *prefer* you not to go wandering on your own at night, without me to keep an eye on you."

His eyebrows rose. "If you think I'm plotting an escape . . ."

"I know you're not," she said impatiently, "but I'm not the only one here with magic, remember? It isn't sensible for you to walk anywhere alone without witnesses."

Was Lorelei actually concerned about his welfare, or was this just another scheme on her part? He studied her expression, searching for any hints of deeper strategy.

"Oh, don't give me that look." She shook her head at him pityingly. "We all know you're a terrifyingly impressive warrior—everyone who's watched the tournament so far is well aware! But you *still* don't have any magic of your own, and it's hardly an insult to say that you're vulnerable to a magical attack."

"Clearly," Gerard agreed. "After all, a powerful magic-worker abducted me from my bed only two nights ago, as I recall."

"*Ugh!*" Spinning around, Lorelei started to stalk away from him but then stopped, only a few feet from where he stood, her back braced with tension and her hands clenching by her sides as if she were fighting an internal battle.

As he ran everything she'd said through his head, pieces clicked into place with satisfying exactness. "Just how did you know I wasn't plotting an escape?" he asked, already certain of the answer.

Her shoulders barely twitched in reaction. But Gerard was watching her closely—Jovar forgive him, when had he *not*, across the last seven years of this growing obsession?—and he knew every one of Lorelei's tells, even as she turned to smirk back at him with perfectly played condescension. "Really, General. You don't think I know your stodgy ways by now?"

"No," he said, "I think you were listening to my private conversation with Lord Oberon, and that explains why you've been stalking me ever since."

"I have not—!" Crossing her arms, Lorelei scowled up at him, looking—although he wasn't self-destructive enough to say it—as ferociously adorable as an enraged kitten. "I've been *trying* to protect you, not that you've made it easy for me. You are *my* prisoner. It's my job to keep you safe!"

"Really?" Gerard gave an unimpressed shrug. "It would be an easier task if you didn't feel a need to hide from me as you went about it."

Her eyes narrowed into slits of hot blue flame. "I *do not* hide from anyone, much less from you."

"But you're afraid to be alone in a tent with me tonight." Gerard stepped closer, all his muscles bracing for any sudden appearances of magical thorn whips or throttling vines. Still, he kept his gaze fearlessly locked on hers as he leaned down to speak directly to her, close enough for their breaths to mingle. "You didn't dare even talk to me all evening until I finally tricked you into it."

"*You*—!" From the look of fierce turmoil on her face, he could have equally well believed she was about to drag him the rest of the way down for a kiss or stab a sword of thorns through his heart.

Instead, she gritted through her teeth, "*I am not afraid of you,*" and then turned to stalk, barefoot as always, across the darkened field, back towards the tents beyond.

"And yet you're still running away," Gerard called after her.

"No," Lorelei snapped without looking back, "I'm *leading* you, because you seem to have lost your sense of direction along with all of your sense. *I'm* not afraid of sharing a tent or hearing any of your questions. But if *you* want to talk, you'd better be prepared for what I'll ask you in return."

"Understood." Following behind her through the darkness, Gerard stretched his lips into a grin of keen anticipation.

Challenge accepted.

The moment she stepped into the tent—the exact *same* tent they had shared last night, curse it, with all of its unsettling memories hanging in the air like prickling warnings of danger and bad decisions—Lorelei scooped out the sealed jug of fae wine that she'd been hiding all evening in a bag cloaked by illusion. At the time, she hadn't dared drink anything that might dampen her senses, but she'd planned to indulge herself once she had surrounded Gerard's separate tent in a protective shield of thorns.

Now she sat cross-legged on the silken floor of her own tent and plunked down the jug as an act of war. "It's time for a game of truth," she announced.

Gerard's gaze shifted from her to the jug and back again as the flap of the tent fell closed behind him and Lorelei's rustling shield of thorns and magic grew around the silk to cage them in together. This tent was perfectly spacious, but even so, his big figure seemed to draw all the energy in the room as he loomed over her, bringing back hot, perilous memories from hours ago. "A drinking game?"

She shrugged, yanking the cap off the jug with more violence than it required. Sometimes it *hurt* to resist temptation! "You must have played plenty of those at military academy, judging by the stories I've heard."

"Stories of other men's experiences, perhaps." He lowered himself to the floor to sit across from her, cross-legged, in the soft light of the will-o'-the-wisps. "My time there was far less festive than you might imagine."

His voice was perfectly steady and uninflected, but as she looked up from the newly opened bottle to meet his eyes, she caught sight of something in his expression that made her first response—*"Even then, you were determined to make yourself a saint?"*—die upon her lips, unspoken.

"Do you *not* drink?" she asked instead. Of course, she knew he would never drink to excess. Still, she could swear that she had seen him sipping glasses of wine at various events across the years. Or had he only been pretending? Sighing, she sat back, leaving the wine untouched between them. "Never mind. We don't need to—"

"Explain the game," Gerard said firmly, cutting off her retreat. "The alcohol wasn't what I was referring to."

Aha. He'd meant the games themselves, then. Lorelei's mind flashed back to what he had revealed the day before about his time spent alone in his school library.

Gods, but children could be vicious to anyone who didn't fit in! Biting down an entirely inappropriate wave of protective anger, she picked up the open jug and said, "Well, then. Consider this your *initiation*."

The words came out in a throatier tone than she'd planned, and his eyes darkened in response. Damn it, how was she supposed to stop flirting with him now, after so many years of practice? Fighting the urge to inch closer, Lorelei continued as if she hadn't sensed the erotic charging of the air around them. "This is the simplest possible game to begin with. We'll take turns, each of us asking a question. In response, you may either answer honestly or drink. But no lies may be spoken in the game. We both swear to it."

"Is that an official fae bargain?" Gerard's voice was low and smooth, and it curled deep inside her.

Sylvana help me. "Yes it is," Lorelei said firmly, and with her words, she felt the weight of old magic thicken the air above them, waiting to descend. "Do you agree to it as well?"

"I do," Gerard said without hesitation.

The bargain was struck. Lorelei felt it land at all of her binding points—wrists, throat, heart—and fasten there, pinning her down with him in the soft light of the tent, with darkness gathered all around them.

"My turn first." There were too many questions all jostling for precedence; the least important of all was the first to break free. "Why didn't you accept Oberon's offer?"

Pressure built in the air around them, waiting for his answer. The weight of the bargain pressed against them both.

Gerard didn't even glance at the open jug between them. His steady gaze was fixed on her. "I wouldn't leave you without a partner for this tournament, especially not to benefit him."

"I . . ." The words *thank you* hovered, waiting to be spoken. Lorelei licked her lips, suddenly wishing that she had taken a sip of that wine.

"My turn," said Gerard. "Why was it impossible to back out of the tournament in the first place, when you realized Lord Oberon was its host?"

Oh, *that*. Lorelei snorted out a humorless laugh. "Can't you guess? If I broke my sworn word in public, I'd lose my entry to the fae realm forever." It was the single unforgivable sin in fae culture. "You ought to approve of that rule, with your famous principles."

"Mm." His eyebrows compressed. "Your turn."

Right. Time to borrow some of his skill at strategy and start thinking through her questions. "What drove you to build such an unblemished reputation in the first place?" His fellow students might have shunned him at the academy, but the gods all knew he must have had more chances since then. With his impressive figure and the even more impressive chain of military victories to his credit, offers must have been flung at him nonstop—and not only by her at their first meeting.

She was watching him closely enough to see his gaze slip down to the open jug . . . but then it shifted back to her, and he said evenly, "It was my only option."

"That isn't an answer." Even the bargain itself agreed with her statement, pushing down hard against her skin and lifting the light golden hairs on his wrist with visible contact.

"No, I suppose not." He drew a slow, deep breath before continuing. "When I was eight, my parents were executed for treason against the Empire."

Really? She'd known there was some ancient scandal associated with them; she'd never guessed at that one. Holding her breath, she waited for him to continue.

"Their deeds were . . . scandalous. Corrupt. Conscienceless. And . . . infamous." Each word dropped heavily into the charged air. "The details were kept out of the newspapers at the time, for reasons of state security, but everyone knew the general idea, and I . . . very quickly was made to recognize that I, too, would be closely watched forever after, in case I should follow their example."

Made to recognize? Lorelei frowned, leaning closer. "By the newspapers?"

"By them, too." He hesitated, his jaw setting. "The only reason I was allowed to survive was to fulfil the single mission I'd been left: to prove my family name was worth saving after all. To prove myself and my loyalty true to the Empire, no false steps would ever be allowed. My actions must always be above reproach."

Oh. Oh, the implications of that were . . . well, they were far too much for her to take in at this moment when it came to all of her hopeful plans for the future. But for this one instant in time, she let herself forget all about strategy or planning as she said thickly, "You were *eight years old* when you were 'made to understand' that?"

He didn't have to answer that second question; the bargain wouldn't insist upon it. But his hard jaw lowered in a fractional nod, and breath billowed out of her.

She knew the weight of a lifelong mission at that age. She felt it more than ever as she gazed at the powerful, driven man before her and *saw* the young boy still inside him who had lost everything he'd loved and counted on and been left with an unbearable burden . . . just like her.

So much like her. How could they be so devastatingly twinned when the outside world had fated them to be enemies? When she looked at him now, every instinct she'd ever trusted fought to push her even closer—and insisted that was the only option that was *right*.

But if she followed her own sacred mission, without blinking...

"My turn," Gerard said. "Why did you run from our kiss today?"

Lorelei's hand shot out to grab the jug and lift it to her mouth without an instant's hesitation. Sparkling fae wine cascaded down her throat, warmth prickled through her skin, and she cast a prayer to Sylvana that it would give her the strength to survive the rest of this dangerous game.

In the back of her mind, in ominous response, she heard the echo of a goddess's low, pitying laughter.

21

By the light of the will-o'-the-wisps that danced in the tent above them, Gerard watched Lorelei's cheeks pinken with her long, luxuriant sip of fae wine. The exacting fae bargain *might* have allowed a mere drop in her throat to suffice—but of course, Lorelei would never do anything by half-measures. Gerard felt something twist deep inside his stomach as she lowered the jug at last and her eyes reopened, silver glitter sparkling decadently on the tips of her long eyelashes.

Gods. Had it been self-destructive madness, after all, to insist upon sharing a tent tonight?

No. This was the best chance he would ever have of working out her most elusive truths. He couldn't walk away now.

"My turn," Lorelei announced, and smiled dangerously as she leaned towards him. "What do you *really* think of our dear little Otto as your emperor?"

"I . . . think he deserves my allegiance." It was the truth; the bargain surely couldn't question that. But its eerie, invisible force tugged once more at his skin, raising goose bumps and the fine hairs on his wrists once more; in other words, his answer hadn't gone deep enough to suffice. Breathing deeply, Gerard added with firm conviction, "He is my emperor by right of law, as sanctified by the Imperial high priest."

"That sweet, pacifistic old man he just had arrested for so-called corruption and treason, you mean?" Lorelei's voice was perilously dry. "Or were you referring to the *new* Imperial high priestess Otto appointed from his own family so the Empire wouldn't have any mitigating counterforce to stand against him any longer?"

Thank Jovar, the bargain required no answer to that second question. Instead, with finality, Gerard said, "I swore vows of loyalty."

The shock and horror that he'd felt at High Priest Bohdan's arrest would not soon subside, but he knew—he was *certain*—that the Emperor could be persuaded into leniency with the man's final sentence, if only for the sake of appeasing general opinion. It was one of the many reasons Gerard had to return to Fiora soon—to make that argument and hold to it long enough to shape Otto's fluctuating opinions.

"Hmph." Lorelei narrowed her eyes at him. "Well, if you can't share your *true* feelings about him, you had better take a sip of wine."

The bargain plucked at him even harder in agreement. Resigned, Gerard picked up the jug that she had set down between them and raised it to his lips. The sparkling, effervescent concoction lit up his senses like fireworks as he swallowed.

No wonder Lorelei had flushed when she'd drunk it! He had taken the smallest possible sip, but even so, as he returned the jug to the ground, Gerard's cheeks prickled with a new, much-too-pleasurable warmth. This was no ordinary, mortal wine... and this game might well prove to be more perilous than he'd realized.

Still, her question led to the one he'd been wanting—and fearing—to ask ever since their argument earlier that day.

Could he bear the answer?

Bracing himself, Gerard said, "Do you really believe that Otto is a secret supporter of the Purifiers, or was that only a ruse?"

The fae bargain wouldn't allow Lorelei to lie; of that much, he was certain. Still, he half expected her to scoop up the jug once more, only to torment him with uncertainty.

Instead, she let out a sigh that sounded genuinely weary. "Darling, if it were up to me, I'd never give those pathetic would-be villains another thought—but Ailana's spies report that he's met secretly, many times now, with a whole assortment of Purifiers, including their leader, that foul Feodor Rapenthe. No one knows, yet, exactly which promises have been made, but Ailana is *certain* that Otto's planning to use their cause as his banner and rationale to conquer the rest of the continent, just as he's been yearning to do all along."

Hoping to conquer the full continent—that much, Gerard could not deny. It had been Otto's most passionately expressed dream for as long as Gerard had been a member of the Emperor's rarefied private council. As far as he knew, though, Otto didn't *have* any higher rationale but the goal of reclaiming all the lands of the legendary *first* Serafin Empire, which had ruled uncontested for nearly a thousand years before its destruction five centuries ago. Otto's grandfather and namesake, Otto I, had formed the new, less-all-encompassing Serafin Empire in its memory, and Otto II had grown up with the firm conviction that it was divinely ordained for him to finish the job... regardless of all the innocents who would be killed in that expansion for no reason but his own personal glory.

Still, Otto had never once claimed in any council meetings, not even the most private, to have any specks of fondness for the extremist bigots who screamed about "Purification" and drunkenly assaulted harmless nonhumans at any opportunity.

"*Ailana* is certain," Gerard repeated carefully. "So, in other words, you're basing your conviction on the Queen of Nornne's spy network and her claims."

It was a second question, uncompelled by their bargain, but Lorelei answered anyway. "I would trust Ailana with my life."

The bargain might not judge this answer, but Gerard didn't need magical confirmation to believe the loyalty that rang through it. It was the same strong, protective emotion she'd shown to both of her fellow Queens of Villainy at the border of Kitvaria, days ago. Back then, it had startled him and seemed uncharacteristic, but he was coming to understand that it was just as essential a part of her nature as her incorrigible mischief.

Like him, Lorelei kept most of her true feelings buried in public most of the time. Her own outer façade might be the opposite of his, but underneath . . .

What actually hid beneath that mask of frivolity felt unsettlingly—compellingly—irresistible.

"My turn," she said. "If you believed me about Otto's plans, would you listen to your conscience and abandon your post to fight against the Empire?"

Gerard's breath stopped as his vision whited out.

He was back at the military academy again, covered in bruises and walking into the dining hall under the gaze of all the other students.

"Little traitor . . ."

"There's the traitors' son . . ."

"Bad blood runs true . . ."

"Did your parents wail like cowards while you watched?"

"Gerard?" Lorelei's voice broke through. "Are you unwell?"

If only the bargain would accept *that* question as the one he had to answer!

Gerard swallowed hard and met her gaze as panic roiled sickeningly within his gut. "I would never willingly abandon my post," he said, "but I *will* listen to my conscience."

"Oh, for—!" Sitting back, Lorelei flung up her hands in disgust as the weight of the fae bargain lifted. "How could that answer have been allowed? It's utter nonsense."

"It is the truth," Gerard repeated steadily. "As Imperial high general, it is my duty to make use of my position and advise His Imperial Majesty against any choices whose consequences he might not fully comprehend."

"He *comprehends* them perfectly well," Lorelei muttered. "That's not the problem! But what will happen when he orders you to carry out Purification anyway and makes it into a law you think you don't have the right to break, because it's your godsdamned *duty*?"

That was a nightmare beyond imagining. Fortunately, it was his turn to ask the questions. "Why did your mother send you away from the Efaelen court as a child?"

Glowering, Lorelei reached for the jug—and then stopped, her hand hovering in midair, as Gerard raised his eyebrows pointedly.

"*Fine.*" She drew in a deep, put-upon breath and directed her gaze to her hand as she lowered it to the silken floor. "I had a more important mission to fulfil."

Pressure mounted around them, and strands of her long, curling hair lifted from around her face with the force of the fae bargain tugging at her. "It was *foretold*," she gritted finally. "I couldn't stay at my mother's court forever. I had to inherit the Balravian throne, no matter what."

"Or else . . . ?" he prompted.

When she looked up to meet his gaze, her expression was stark. "You must know the answer to that yourself, by now."

Gerard frowned. As he recalled, the other candidates for that throne had been an assortment of useless human cousins only known for their inept turns in military service and sloppy drinking parties. He couldn't imagine any of them—unlike Lorelei—having the sheer drive or conviction to force Balravia into *any* great political movements, so . . .

Aha. They couldn't have resisted those movements, either. The answer settled into place. "You think you were put on the throne to save Balravia from being enfolded into the Serafin Empire."

"Not only Balravia." She shook her head slowly, her voice unyielding. "And I'm not fighting only to preserve political independence. Ailana isn't wrong about Purification, Gerard. No matter what you need to believe to comfort yourself for working for a villain . . . if we don't win this war, *no* fae will be left in the mortal realm in fifty years' time. My mother was shown that truth. THIS FIGHT IS FOR MY PEOPLE'S FUTURE."

As she spoke, her voice deepened and echoed with skin-prickling effect. It was as if someone else—no, *Someone* else—was speaking in divine chorus.

Gerard abruptly remembered that vast, sighing voice that had rippled the trees with its force when it warned him this morning to protect Lorelei, in that impossible frozen moment out of time.

In all their years of enmity, he had never imagined flighty, flirty Lorelei as the avatar of an actual goddess.

But as he looked into her eyes now—their blue irises sheened over with an impossibly bright, forest green—he finally understood.

More than that: He *believed*.

"You are goddess-touched," he breathed. There was a strange, tight feeling in his chest: mingled wonder, awe, and . . .

Was that regret? No: *pain*. Aching pain for the child who had been torn much too early from her home and sent into a realm that hated her to take on a task with impossible weight.

He knew that feeling all too well.

"Who do you think set my mission in the first place?" As her eye color returned and that impossible echo vanished, Lorelei's lips curved ruefully. "Only my mother and her closest handmaidens know—even her consort has never been told, for fear the news might spread and panic lead to disaster—but Sylvana came to my mother long before I was born. *That* was why Queen Morgana was able to let me go so easily and forget me so quickly: She'd been waiting to give me up from the very beginning."

Her smile faltered, but her voice did not. "One daughter is hardly too high a price to pay in order to save an entire people . . . from the armies that *you'll* be leading."

"Lorelei . . ." It hurt to breathe through the constriction in his chest. Still, Gerard leaned forward, ignoring the ache, and reached out to take her smaller hand in his. Light tremors shivered through it as he closed his fingers firmly around hers.

He wouldn't break his sworn word and betray his empire even for her sake—but this was a wholly different matter. "I will not let the fae be eradicated from the mortal world," he told her. "I *will not* allow my troops to carry out any orders of Purification."

Lorelei left her hand in his, but her lips wavered into a bitter smile. "Fine words, General," she murmured, "but can you actually carry them out?"

"It is a *promise*," he said firmly. "I swear it to you, now—and you know I honor all of my commitments."

No, he couldn't simply walk away from his post and all of his responsibilities, the way she had apparently imagined. But what stronger position could he hold at this profound turning point than the right hand of the Emperor himself? As Imperial high general, Gerard could and would fight with every political and diplomatic lever he held to change Otto's mind before it was too late. Now that he knew the imminent danger, Gerard could convince his emperor of just how unforgivable such a course would be and how harshly the history books would judge Otto's reign if he gave in to that temptation.

Gerard had the miraculous opportunity to end this forewarned madness before it could ever take effect. *That* was his new mission. That was a goal he could wholeheartedly believe in.

Thank the gods Lorelei had kidnapped him, after all! If she'd tried to tell him any of this two days ago, he wouldn't—couldn't—have believed her. But it wasn't only the magic of the fae bargain, preventing all lies, that proved the truth of her words to him now.

It was the trust and respect they had gained for each other across the last two days of trials. It was the compassion she'd shown, again and again, to everyone with less power than herself, and the strength and the heart that shone through all her illusions.

Now that he'd finally been allowed to see behind them, he would never look away again.

"Trust me, Lorelei," he said, tightening his grip on her hand. "I won't betray my vows to the Empire—but I won't betray *you*, either."

"Ohhh . . . !" Lorelei shook her head, tears glistening in her eyes. Then, with a muffled sound of despair, she shoved the jug of wine aside and launched herself at him.

22

It was useless, and Lorelei knew it even as she cast aside all the restraints that had bound her.

She would never have this beautiful, kind, strong, and honorable man to keep by her side forever. That had always been an impossible dream—she'd known it even as she'd indulged herself by abducting him—but she hadn't been able to resist the doomed attempt.

Tomorrow, the Tournament of Leaves would finish. After that, whether they won or lost, she'd promised to return Gerard to the mortal realm. And then...

Then, Lorelei would have to watch him willingly walk back into the heart of the Serafin

Empire, away from her and along a path that led only to ruin and death.

She knew exactly how Emperor Otto II would react to his Imperial authority being questioned by a dangerously popular member of his private council. He'd already shown his hand to the world with his first Imperial high priest's arrest.

For better or worse, Gerard de Moireul had always followed the god of both war *and* justice and respected the gravity of the law. His emperor felt no such personal restraints.

So, no, tonight couldn't be the start of anything real and true—but it was still Lorelei's last chance. So it wasn't so much that she threw herself at him as that she finally stopped *holding herself back*.

When she landed on his lap and his arms closed around her, the relief felt overwhelming. His strong legs were a sturdier throne than any she had ever ruled from; her palms molded around his big shoulders as if they'd belonged there from the beginning. Perhaps they always had, after all. Goddess knew, she'd been drawn towards him like a lodestone from the very first night they'd met—and that need was clearly mutual. The delicious proof was pressing up against her core, driving her wild, while his lips sought hers with unhidden hunger.

Thank Sylvana she'd chosen this dress with its skirts made of daringly mobile strips! The petticoat underneath was scandalously short; it slipped easily up her thighs, allowing her to wrap her legs around his waist like a vine binding itself around an oak tree, making him utterly hers . . . for this one night. Gerard's heartbeat hammered against her chest, all of his usual impenetrable calm vanished, as their lips met and breath mingled.

She didn't only want to ravish this man—she needed to *meld* herself into him until she'd embedded her scent into his skin and he would remember her with every breath he took, no matter how far apart their destinies took them. Sylvana knew, *she* would never be able to forget this moment; it was only fair that he share that poisoned blessing.

She didn't even notice the cool wetness sliding down her own cheeks until she tasted sudden salt in their kiss. "*Lorelei.*" Gerard drew back, breathing hard, and brought his hands up to cradle her face for a too-keen inspection. His thumbs swept out, calluses rubbing with delicious friction against her skin, and brushed away her tears with a care that threatened to shatter her completely.

"Oh, don't worry about those," she said lightly. "They're nothing! Completely meaningless. Just ignore them, for my sake."

She tried to lean forward, to reclaim his lips and *make* him forget, but he held her in place, his grip gentle but implacable. "Lorelei." His voice was pained, but his lips quirked into a small, rueful smile. "We truly do not have to do this. I swear to you, none of my commitments will change if you don't want—"

"Oh, yes, we *do*!" she said fiercely, and grabbed hold of his uniform jacket before he could escape. "I've been waiting seven *years* for this moment. If you're going to be cruel and tease me now, after everything we've been through—!"

"You are weeping," he reminded her. "*Something* is clearly wrong."

"What absolute rubbish." Lorelei lifted her chin and sneered up at him. "Darling, I *always* weep at times like this. That's simply the way I am."

"And *that*, my darling, is a flat-out lie." His voice was a deep rumble that vibrated through her, with a tenderness that made her frantic. "You never willingly let *anyone* catch any glimpse of vulnerability."

She narrowed her eyes dangerously. "I believe you're thinking of yourself now, General."

"No, I'm thinking of *both* of us." He shook his head slowly, never breaking her gaze. "Haven't you noticed yet? We're two of a kind."

Her lower lip wobbled horrifyingly at the truth of his words; she sucked in a bracing breath and shook her head right back at him. "Careful!" she said and attempted a scornful laugh. "If anyone ever heard the famously noble Golden Beacon compare himself to the most notoriously immoral queen on the continent, whatever would they think?"

"Regardless of what *anyone* may think, you're not immoral," he said calmly, "and I am finished with self-delusion and fencing around the truth. I'm in love with you, Lorelei."

Oh, goddess, no, I can't bear this. "Don't—!" Lorelei began.

But he was already continuing like the inexorable force he always had been on every battlefield in his life. "I have loved you for years, I think, though I was too cowardly to admit it to myself until now."

Was he, of all people, calling himself a coward? *Lorelei* was ready to wrench herself free and flee into the night . . . if only the warmth of his palms around her face didn't feel so meltingly addictive, as if she'd finally found a home where she entirely belonged.

Her pulse thumped frantically at her throat, like a bird battering at its cage, and her attempt at laughter sounded half-strangled. "Goodness, such high drama, and I haven't even removed any of my clothing yet! Are you always so sentimental with your lovers before they've satisfied you?"

"I wouldn't know," he said simply. "I haven't had any lovers until you."

Oh, Sylvana. Is this meant to be torture? Of course Lorelei had known he was rumored to be chaste. But to have it confirmed—to have this gorgeous miracle of a man offered up to be all *hers*, if only . . . !

She was so wrapped up in the shock of his revelation that he slipped his next words like a dagger through all of her guards. "Are *you* always so unwilling to accept real love when it's offered to you?"

"Argh!" Lorelei let out a muffled scream, squeezing her eyes shut against him and every impossible temptation that he offered. "This *isn't* real love. You know it can't be. You, of all people—"

"*I* know I haven't been able to get you out of my mind or my heart for seven years," he said as easily as if he were relating a perfectly ordinary, everyday fact and not tossing an incendiary device into her life and future. "I know that no one in my life has *ever* gotten under my skin the way you do."

"Like a stinging insect?" She opened her eyes to roll them pointedly at him.

"Like a *soulmate*."

The sincerity in his amber gaze made her bones feel as if they were melting, braced muscles and pride only barely holding her upright and her voice rising in panic. "What would you know of soulmates? You've never even had a single lover before me!"

"And you've had plenty," he said calmly. "But tell me, Lorelei, did you care for any of them as strongly as you do for me now? When you look back on all of them, did *any* of them feel like such a perfect match?"

Lorelei lifted her chin into her haughtiest expression and did not respond.

His smile was slow and glorious, and she couldn't wrench her eyes away as it lit up his face. "Lorelei, we *fit*. You feel that, too, don't you?"

She pressed her lips tightly together, but he nodded anyway. "That's what has you so afraid now."

"Damn you," Lorelei gritted out, "I told you before—I am not afraid of *anything*." Green shoots pierced the silken floor around them, thrusting upwards with aggressively sprouting leafy vines to wrap themselves tightly around Gerard and Lorelei's entangled figures, locking them in place together. Supported and cradled by her own creation, Lorelei glared mutinously at her nemesis, who looked infuriatingly unaffected by their new cage of vegetation. "You see? There is literally *nothing* you can do to hurt me!"

"One day," he murmured, "you'll allow yourself to believe I never would—because I love you, too."

Wait—"too"? Panic flipped Lorelei's center of gravity, leaving her breathless. "I did not—! I *never* said—!"

"It's all right," Gerard said patiently. "You don't need to say the words. I know you love me, Lorelei. That's why you kidnapped me in the first place."

"*Ugh!*" He was impossible. He was the most stubborn and enraging man she'd ever met. Without a doubt, he would be her undoing. But when she tugged upwards against his grip with a desperate, wordless moan, he let her move, his strong hands sliding down to her waist to pull her even closer.

Giving up on debating her way to victory, she sealed her lips to his and rubbed herself against him, instead, to claim it by different means. *No more talking.* No more perilous, life-disrupting words could be allowed to escape into the too-seductive warmth and privacy of this tent.

From now on, she simply wouldn't let him speak.

But it was impossible to miss the message he was sending her with every movement that he made. She might be keeping his lips safely occupied, but the slow, warm stroking of his thumbs around her waist was a terrifying statement of care in itself. Wriggling within the constricting cradle of vines that surrounded them, she reached between their tangled bodies to yank his troublesome hands up and place them firmly on her breasts, determined to get this intimate encounter back on track, just like any other act she'd shared with other lovers across the years . . .

But—*oh, goddess, save me!*—that was a terrible mistake. When Gerard's big, capable hands closed around her sensitive breasts through all the layers of her bodice, they *fit* as no one else's hands ever had, as if they had been made to her own personal specifications—made for *Lorelei* from the very beginning. Her back arched against her will, and hot sparks shot through her skin in a moment of near-divine revelation. Had she been looking and waiting for *this* singular man all along, without realizing?

The twin groans they let out at that shattering moment of contact felt perilously like a shared prayer of gratitude.

Damn it, she was *not* in love with Gerard de Moireul, no matter what that unyielding force of a man might think. No matter how right his body felt against hers—no matter how perfectly they fit together as partners both on and off the tournament field—no matter what a subversive *delight* it was to spark off him in arguments or conversation!—he had not been made for her, nor she for him.

But it was impossible to make herself focus on that stern reminder when his fingers were exploring her shape with a slow, relentless thoroughness that threatened to destroy her completely. Closing her eyes, Lorelei tipped her head back with a helpless moan of pleasure and despair.

He'd always been much too adept at spotting weaknesses in her armor. Now, his hungry lips closed around her throat without hesitation, the bristling golden stubble on his cheeks and the delicate scrape of his blunt teeth against her skin making her shiver uncontrollably. Silk shifted against her chest as he tugged at her bodice; she let out another, embarrassingly raw moan as his warm, calloused palms closed around her newly revealed, bare breasts.

Goddess help her, he was taking her apart! If she didn't retake control of this encounter soon, she'd end up in a puddle of melted willpower, helplessly agreeing to anything he wanted. It was unthinkable. No, *intolerable*.

"*Enough!*" Her voice was a pitifully breathy rasp, but her power swept out without fail, tipping their cradle of vines onto a newly made bed of soft, green grass. Those vines vanished an instant later, leaving Gerard flat on his back on the fresh greenery before her, covered in golden glitter she didn't even remember shedding. The sight was intoxicating enough to make her light-headed, but Lorelei pushed herself up anyway to straddle his waist, while chains of lushly scented, de-thorned roses wound themselves around his outstretched arms and legs to pin him down.

"*My* turn," she announced smugly.

His amber gaze fastened on her exposed bosom, which spilled over her loosened bodice as she sat triumphantly over him—and his lips curved with an unexpected wickedness that made her breath catch in her throat.

"I yield," Gerard said gravely, "and can only hope that the conditions in which you keep your prisoners of war are not too burdensome."

"Oh, they're just *terrible*," Lorelei assured him. She tried to keep her expression appropriately stern, but as she met his wicked grin—Gerard de Moireul, of all people, grinning up at her like a rake and playing delicious games in bed!—she found herself smiling helplessly in return, a years-old knot inside her chest melting in a sudden wave of warmth.

Still, she hardened her voice as she laid down the only law that could allow her to survive the rest of this reckless encounter with her heart unscathed. "From now on, you have to lie back and let me do *everything* to you."

His head tilted; rapid calculation shifted across his face. Before her eyes, despite his prone position and the unbreakable bindings that held him firmly in place, she saw her wickedly amorous captive transform once more into the dangerously brilliant and ruthlessly determined strategist who'd countered her every daring move for seven long years. "We'll see about that," he murmured.

Gerard had spent years fantasizing against his will about exactly this situation. In reality, though, even the sight of her gloriously lush breasts hanging over him—the most mouthwatering of offerings, maddeningly just out of reach—couldn't blind him to the glaring truth: Lorelei was still running scared.

She wanted to make it clear that this was just another meaningless encounter, no different to her than any others she'd indulged in. She was gambling that, if only she stayed firmly enough in control, she wouldn't be affected by any of it.

Gerard was more than willing to be sensually tormented by this particular woman . . . but he would be *damned* if he let her keep her own emotions out of it.

"Do you know how often I've dreamed of you in exactly this position?" He couldn't move his arms or legs, but as she sat scandalously astride him, deep instinct drove him to roll his hips, pressing firmly up against her center. Her lips parted into a silent O, and molten heat flooded through all of his bound limbs, gathering at that single point as he rocked up against her again and again with focused intent. "Do you . . . have any notion . . . of just how you've tormented me across the years?"

She bit down on her generous lower lip, eyes fluttering closed and fingers flexing into fists in the air beside her as if she were grasping for something just out of reach. "I . . . think you're the one tormenting me at the moment." A stifled gasp ripped out of her throat as he shifted to a different angle, and her eyes flew open. "Aren't you supposed to be a *virgin?*"

"I am inexperienced," he agreed, "but I know how to pay attention." He'd been obsessively studying this woman for years. It was a nearly vicious pleasure to learn new nuances of her expressions now as he deliberately tested her reactions to every possible approach.

"Well, maybe I can teach you a few new things." She fluttered her lashes flirtatiously, and vibrant specks of rainbow glitter showered through the air around him. They were the fierce, bright colors she used for showing off to the world, not the pure gold she shed by nature whenever passion overcame her—and that observation put him on guard even before she reached down to unbutton the placket of his trousers.

Jovar, keep me strong. He swallowed hard, bracing every muscle as she released him from his confines.

As her soft hands closed around him, shock lanced his body, shooting white fire through his limbs . . . but he forced his eyes to stay open and fixed on her face.

"Lorelei . . ." His voice was hoarse, his head a pleasure-blurred jumble, but he still refused to surrender. This was the most vital battle of his life, so he fought for words through the flaming chaos. "This is you. Me. *Us*, together."

Her small fingers stilled for one telltale moment before they began to move again, this time working with a firm confidence that left him gasping. "Well, I am glad you haven't lost your memory, darling, and forgotten who we are. But if you can still think clearly enough to speak, I may be doing something wrong."

"Don't need...to think...to know the truth." As his back arched against his will, every muscle straining against his floral bonds, Gerard forced his eyes open wider and levered his head up from the impossible grass that made his bed—one more reminder of the jaw-dropping powers of this woman, as if her touch weren't magical enough—until he was staring directly at his tormenter, meeting her veiled gaze with all of his own shields lowered, emotions open and defenseless. "I *love* you...Lorelei. You...love *me*. It's like this now...because it's *us*. Together."

She looked momentarily stricken as she wavered in her upright position, swaying closer...

And then she rallied, because this brilliant, headstrong hurricane of a woman would never offer him an easy victory. "Well, if there's really only one way to make you finally stop talking...!" Dropping him a lascivious wink, she rose over him, shifted aside her skirts and petticoat...and then sank down to take his full length *inside her.*

Flames shot through him, and his vision whited out.

When he could finally see again, he found Lorelei's head tipped back in an arc of wordless pleasure, her own eyes closed and their bodies still impossibly, incredibly connected. Every muscle urged Gerard to move, to power them both towards fulfilment—but he kept himself torturously locked in place, waiting.

Her eyes finally reopened, pupils so dilated that she looked utterly drunk on the sensation of him inside her. As if *he* were her most powerful intoxicant.

As Gerard met her gaze, he felt their connection in every tingling inch of his skin. "*Us*," he gritted out through clenched teeth and shifted his hips in deliberate tandem with his statement.

"Oh, goddess... *yes*, Sylvana help me, us!" The words came out in a broken moan as Lorelei's eyes crossed at his move. "But only this once. Do you understand?"

Her inner muscles squeezed tightly around him as she spoke, and he lost his own voice to a new, blazing madness . . . but he made a silent vow as they battled together towards a fiery completion that laid waste to every careful, logical plan he had ever made for his future.

Not just once, he swore.

Forever.

23

Lorelei had the unnerving feeling that she might have made a fatal mistake.

As she lay, limp and warm and *far* too comfortably plastered over Gerard's big body, with gorgeous waves of pleasure still rippling beneath her skin, she could almost hear Ailana's skeptical voice and see those elegant dark eyebrows rise in older-sisterly disapproval.

"Is that really how you plan to protect your heart?"

The icy Queen of Nornne had warned her countless times before that Lorelei opened herself to pain with every new lover she recklessly allowed into her bed—but ever since the last betrayal, none had even come close to piercing her diamond-hard emotional shields.

In the past hour, Gerard de Moireul had shattered them completely.

He shifted under her now, nuzzling her disordered hair with an open affection that made her traitorous body melt even more into him. "Do you think it might be safe to release me now?" His voice was rueful, his breath warm against her skin.

"Ha!" Lorelei snorted. "I haven't lost *all* of my common sense yet, so, no. You are *never* harmless." Even so, she let the vines slip away from his magnificently splayed arms and legs, making sure to let the blossoms slide like kisses against his skin ... and she couldn't bring herself to move even when he closed his arms around her in a dangerously tender embrace.

"Liar," he whispered against her hair. "I'm the only man you do trust. Remember? You already admitted that to me."

She blinked ... and then remembered: oh, yes, he *had* asked her, the night before, why she hadn't partnered in the tournament with anyone before him. Somehow, she'd been fool enough to let it slip that, of all the men she'd ever met, she'd trusted only him to fight by her side.

Clearly, that had been yet another mistake on her part ... but wait! Lorelei pushed herself up, bracing her hands on his strong shoulders, to look down at him triumphantly. "There *is* another man I trust not to knife me in the back nowadays—Saskia's consort, Felix."

Gerard's eyebrows rose with interest, but his arms remained relaxed and warm around her. "The Estarian Archduke?"

"Oh, I've forgiven him for that part." She waved away Felix's title with easy dismissal. "He'll be the official Kitvarian Prince Consort soon enough. At any rate, I don't doubt his loyalty to Saskia and the Queens of Villainy anymore."

"'Anymore' ... ah, yes." Gerard's eyes narrowed. "You did mention, back at our armies' meeting on the Kitvarian border, that you had something to make up to him. What did you do that was so dreadful even *you* regretted it?"

"I..." Lorelei winced, her gaze sliding away from his as she plucked uncomfortably at the glitter-covered blue wool of his jacket. "Well, I *may* just possibly have kidnapped him. Briefly. Almost by accident. Really, it was all just a terrible misunderstanding."

"I see." Gerard regarded her for a long, silent moment before shaking his head with grave disappointment. "So, I'm not your first, after all."

"Wha—? It wasn't like that, and you know it!" Letting out a huff of startled laughter, Lorelei crossed her arms on his broad chest and rested her chin on her clasped hands. She was *not* gazing adoringly at him, absolutely not. Still, it was a revelation to see the crinkle of amusement around his eyes and the tiny curve of his stern lips. "You really do have a sense of humor, don't you?"

"I find it's best to develop one after being brutally kidnapped," he told her in a philosophical tone. "It helps to bear the trauma."

"Ha." Narrowing her eyes, she freed one hand and ran a fingertip experimentally down his side, slipping it beneath the untucked shirt at his waist to venture even farther. "Has it been too, too *utterly* traumatic, darling?"

His throat flexed convulsively above his stiff uniform collar and cravat as he swallowed. "Utterly. Entirely. Please do feel free to continue everything you're doing, though. I have been trained to withstand torture."

"You beast! Just for that, I *will* stop." But she was laughing as she raised her hand once more, and her palm somehow ended up cupped around one big shoulder, rubbing affectionate circles with her thumb there instead.

She would get up in a moment. *Obviously.* Staying here for too long, undeniably *cuddling*, would give him entirely the wrong idea. But it was hard to summon up any motivation to leave when she felt so very relaxed and at ease . . . and, clearly, so did he.

Who could have imagined Gerard de Moireul having a secret well of playfulness hidden behind that famously stoic demeanor? Was this what he might have been like all along if he'd only had a different kind of upbringing? If he'd acted like this when they'd first met... oh, it would have been impossible to resist him for so long! She would have been forced to kidnap him *years* ago.

But the idea of any other woman discovering what this man was really like in bed...

"Is there a reason why you suddenly look ready to commit murder?" he inquired with unruffled interest.

"I'm just... considering the future." From now on, she would have to order her ladies-in-waiting never, *ever* to pass on any newspaper articles or gossip about the Empire's Golden Beacon. Lorelei had never approved of jealousy... but she had to confess, in the privacy of her own twisted heart, that she wouldn't trust herself *not* to set a thornbush growing directly from the heart of the next woman lucky and clever enough to maneuver herself into Gerard's arms.

Unlike him, she truly was a villain.

It took her a moment to realize that she'd stopped rubbing circles against Gerard's shoulder and was digging her nails into it instead. She jerked her hand back—and found Gerard watching her with far too much comprehension.

"Panicking again, my darling?"

How dare he take *her* meaningless endearment and turn it into something entirely different? When he called her *his* darling in that deep, rumbling voice...

No. Suddenly reinvigorated, Lorelei pushed herself upwards, and he—of course—immediately let her go. She did *not* regret the loss of that warm hold one bit as she jumped to her feet and adjusted her gown back into a semblance of discretion. She didn't *want* to be persuaded into staying, deceptively safe and dangerously happy, in the comfort of his arms. It was *excellent* that he wasn't wasting his breath trying to change her mind about that.

So she gifted him with her most dazzling smile as she tossed back her hair over one shoulder. "Well! That was certainly a very pleasant diversion"—Sylvana knew, if it had been any *more* pleasant, she wouldn't be able to walk now—"but we do have a final day of trials left tomorrow, so we had better both get some sleep."

"Very sensible." He didn't move from his comfortably prone position, but there was a subtle tinge of amusement in his tone that made her instincts tingle in warning.

Lowering her eyelashes, she regarded him suspiciously. "Then I'll see you again in the morning."

"As you say." Rising with the fluid ease of a man who did calisthenics every single morning by choice, he removed his uniform jacket.

Lorelei truly didn't mean to lick her lips at the sight. It was just... *remarkably* pleasurable to watch those objectively impressive muscles flex through his white cotton shirt. When he pulled that shirt over his head to reveal his bare, hair-dusted shoulders and strong arms—and oh, the dangerous temptation of his broad, golden-furred chest, calling out for her hands to carefully shape every ridge and tangle her fingers in that short, curling hair!—she had to bite down hard on her lower lip to hold back a whimper of pure hunger.

Damn it. She was supposed to be done with him now!

Digging her nails into her palms to stop herself from reaching out for what she *could not* keep, Lorelei spun around and stalked onto her official bed without allowing herself to look back.

Behind her, as she descended with perfectly queenly grace onto her own, individual resting place, she heard the unmistakable sounds of his thick woolen trousers and belt slipping to the ground.

Lorelei dropped the last half a foot onto her bed of leaves with an embarrassingly awkward *thump*, but did not whimper.

Willpower. Self-control, she reminded herself and signaled the will-o'-the-wisps above them to fade out of sight and let darkness fall before she could lose both qualities entirely.

The new darkness should have provided a respite, but even as she lay in that lovely, leafy hollow that had felt so comfortable last night, her senses remained attuned with agonizing acuteness to the soft whispers of sound nearby that signaled Gerard settling into the neighboring bed of grass that she had created for them earlier.

He wasn't even trying to join her. *Of course not.* Safely hidden by the darkness, her features drew into a mutinous scowl. Even after they'd made lo—no, *shared a diversion*—he was still too much of a gentleman to enter her bed without an explicit invitation.

... Which was *excellent.* Exactly what she wanted and what made most sense for both of them, regardless of all that sentimental nonsense he'd spouted earlier under the influence of his first *diversion.*

Goddess, but his arms had felt so warm and right around her.

Had she made a horrible mistake tonight?

Sleep didn't arrive for hours.

She knew immediately that she was trapped in no ordinary dream.

Lorelei had lived with the breath of a goddess brushing the nape of her neck since the day she'd been born. She knew all too well the disorienting, overwhelming sensations that came with the glow of a divine being's attention.

This time, though, it wasn't her own, familiar goddess who had summoned her in her sleep. Any visit with Sylvana came with the vibrant scents of green, growing things all around her, warm wind caressing Lorelei's face and new life coursing through her veins like liquid sunshine.

Now, she stood dwarfed by monumental grey statues in a vast stone hall with a hard, bright light shining down on her to pin her in place. Each flagstone was at least ten times the length of her bare feet; each giant statue portrayed a grim-faced warrior holding a shield and sword, bayonet or musket, in a seemingly endless line that marched far past the limits of her vision. Their styles of armor shifted along the way, along with the types of weapons that they bore, from the sleek modern weaponry of those closest to her to bows and arrows, lances, and then rough knives and clubs in the far distance, combined with wild, waist-length beards caught in stone.

But every face, no matter its surroundings, showed the same expression of noble determination as each warrior faced a terrible end without flinching, making themselves into walls between the innocent and injustice without any complaint—and when she turned slowly in place to look behind her, at the statues marching on into the future, the first one she saw lanced her with instant recognition.

"No!" Lorelei leapt forward.

Gerard did not—would *never!*—belong here, trapped in stone.

Yes, he projected an image of impenetrability to the world. That shield was all that most people would ever be allowed to see: the carefully built illusion that *was* the Golden Beacon. But she had seen the man beneath smiling and teasing her—and scorching her with his passion. He was no frozen object. He *felt*, deeply and undeniably.

There was so much more to him than the terrible, blank-faced statue that rose before her now, pinned forever on a platform of cold stone.

But oh, the uniform he wore on that statue was only too painfully familiar. She recognized the carefully recreated smudge that was a grass stain, not from tonight, but from a battle earlier that day. He clasped his own sword against his stone chest, along with the familiar shield he'd won in a tournament trial.

And his eyes . . .

Oh, goddess! Lorelei bit back a cry.

The rest of his expression might be blank, but his eyes held the bone-deep resignation of a man who knew his certain doom and had surrendered to it without complaint.

Lorelei had *not*—and she was *done* listening to common sense over the screaming of her instincts! Homicidal fury billowed up within her as she spun around in that vast, echoing stone chamber. Thorn-tipped green vines erupted at her command from the slim cracks between the flagstones, ready to take on even the most powerful of opponents.

She knew exactly which god had brought her here to warn her off His chosen champion. But Lorelei had been chosen by a different divine being, and she would *not* be intimidated.

"I don't care if You think You own him," she gritted through her teeth to the acknowledged head of the Imperial pantheon and the stern Divine Father of Justice and War. "I worship Sylvana, not You, and I *will never* let him go."

She *had* made a nearly fatal mistake, after all—but it wasn't in letting herself take such soul-shattering pleasure from the gorgeous, aggravating man who slept in her tent now. No, her mistake had lain in allowing either of them to believe that she would *ever* stand back and let Gerard walk away from her to certain death, no matter how glorious or noble it might be.

They'd struck a binding bargain when they'd first arrived in Efaelen: She *would* have to return him to the mortal realm in exchange for his participation in the tournament . . .

But she'd never said *where* in the mortal realm she'd take him. Gerard had only assumed that return would mean his freedom. Even Lorelei had spent long enough in the mortal realm, by now, that by the end of their second day of trials, she had decided to provide that freedom rather than lose her partner's trust.

Not anymore.

Divine Jovar might well crave another stone martyr for His gallery of heroes, but Lorelei was a Queen of Villainy with urgent, personal needs of her own. No matter what her high-minded lover might imagine—or any gods *or* goddesses demand of her from this moment forward—she had no intention of releasing her captive ever again.

24

Gerard knew from the moment he woke that something had shifted in the air.

Lorelei was scheming.

Unlike the previous morning, she had woken well before him—if, that was, she had slept at all. There was a nearly imperceptible humming tone, like the echo of far distant chimes, vibrating through the tent as she paced back and forth along the silken floor, past the lush green rectangle of grass where he lay. Watching her through his lowered lashes, Gerard saw her long, tousled curls lift away from her shoulders as if by static, reacting to internal lightning he couldn't view.

But then, who had ever managed to predict this irrepressible woman's thoughts for long? She was a force of nature in more than one way... and satisfaction rolled, long and leisurely, through Gerard's body as he stretched along his bed of grass and felt pleasurable reminders of the night before in every muscle.

Before Lorelei, endless chastity had never seemed an intolerable burden. Now, he was already impatient for the end of today's trials and his next opportunity for intimate exploration.

Apparently signaled by his movement, Lorelei whirled around... but unlike the night before, she didn't avert her eyes from his nearly undressed body. This time, her gaze stroked over him with the heat of a physical caress, and her face flushed with some unknowable combination of strong emotions. Arousal? Defiance? Determination?

He couldn't wait to find out.

"Good morning, my darling." Giving her a small smile, he flexed his stomach muscles, rising to a seated position without the use of his hands. She blinked rapidly at the move, half a dozen golden sparkles shifting free to scatter across her cheeks, and his smile grew against his will.

It was enormously satisfying to find a whole new range of weapons suddenly at his disposal in the challenge that had always lain between them... and he hadn't forgotten the way she'd watched his calisthenics the day before. Thinking of that now, he shifted position to begin his usual morning round of one-handed push-ups—and savored the telltale hiss of her breath behind him.

As he'd learned years ago, though, the Queen of Balravia could never be kept off guard for long. Soft footsteps sounded behind him. An instant later, it was his turn to suck in a harsh breath of arousal as her small fingertips trailed a light but fiery arc across his flexing rear end through the thin cotton of his drawers. Fire licked through his body; he nearly doubled over at the force of his own response to her touch, after everything that had passed between them the night before.

"Mm, this *is* a lovely way to start my day," Lorelei purred above him. "Really, it is a pity to have to leave so soon for the day's entertainment."

It . . . was? Gerard wasn't fool enough to show his surprise, so he forced himself to continue his push-ups with easy, regular moves as he considered that marked shift in her attitude.

At the point when he'd fallen asleep last night, she'd still been hiding in a separate bed, insisting that their lovemaking had been a singular event that could never be repeated. What had changed for her since then?

It might be pleasing to imagine that she'd spent the night reconciling herself to the truth of their emotional connection and was ready to confess her love . . . but that idea was laughably implausible. He had never once known Lorelei to make such a linear progression between any points A and B. No, her dazzling mind always shot off in wholly unexpected directions first . . . and as he prepared to find out which angle to defend against next, his lips stretched into an all-out grin of anticipation.

Was there any wonder he'd fallen in love with this woman? He'd never had so much fun in all his life before she'd kidnapped him.

Regardless of whatever clever scheming lay behind it, that stroke across his drawers just now had been a challenge in itself. He would *not* back down from answering it. Finishing his last push-up, he rose to his feet without bothering to reach for any of the pieces of his uniform that lay scattered around him. "How long do we have before the trials begin?"

Lorelei regarded him with her eyelashes lowered but a teasing grin playing across her lips. "Not long enough for me to teach you any new tricks yet, General."

"You think not?" Raising his eyebrows, Gerard prowled closer, the tent seeming to draw tighter around them with every predatory step. "I've always been a fast learner."

"Oh, I'm quite sure you are." Her magnificent bosom rose distractingly with the deep breath she drew. "But we don't have time for a full meal."

"Then how about an appetizer?" Keeping his gaze locked on her face, Gerard dropped to his bare knees on the silk floor before her.

Her eyes widened; her tongue darted out to swipe across her upper lip as her breathing quickened. "I suppose . . . I could hardly let you fight your final battles without *any* nourishment beforehand."

His *final* battles? Gerard's eyes narrowed, but he set that clue aside to deal with later. For now, he had only a few minutes to work with—and an intoxicating new challenge to master.

Moistening his lips in enthusiastic preparation, he drew aside the daring strips of skirt that surrounded her and set out to conquer new territory.

Delightful golden waves of pleasure were still rippling through Lorelei's skin as she stepped out of the tent into the cool morning air just over ten minutes later, one hand laid delicately atop Gerard's closest arm.

He was, of course, covered once more in the stiff—albeit grass-stained—uniform he'd worn the day before, just as Lorelei wore yesterday's gown. She hadn't dared leave him alone in the tent long enough to visit the mortal realm for new supplies—not after Oberon's threats last night—and there hadn't been enough time left for such a visit by the time Gerard woke up.

But oh, had he made impressive use of the time they had shared afterwards!

Golden sparkles shamelessly covered the bodice of Lorelei's gown, Gerard's dark blue uniform jacket, and, though no one else could see them, her legs, too. To absolutely no one's surprise—had this man ever met a challenge he hadn't been determined to win?—he had indeed proven to be a quick study. Just the memory of those big, blunt fingers and that demanding tongue were enough to make another gorgeous internal earthquake shiver through her now.

Her own fingers tightened ever so slightly on the unyielding support of his arm, but she kept her expression sunny and unembarrassed. Here in Efaelen, there was none of the judgmental prudishness of the mortal realm, which twinned women's so-called virtue to a prim aversion to physicality. No one *here* would be scandalized by the idea of Lorelei taking a lover! And as no one here knew Gerard's identity, no one could be horrified on his behalf—or likely to send any dangerous reports to Otto in the mortal realm.

Today was their last day of freedom and happiness, so she planned to savor every moment to the utmost. By this time tomorrow, Gerard would hate her for twisting their bargain and keeping him a prisoner. He would have every right to do so, but until then...

Winning the Tournament of Leaves would be the perfect proof to her competitive lover of just how well they worked together, to help him eventually forgive her and even want to be partners again.

One day.

Possibly.

Ugh! No, she couldn't let herself think about any horrible consequences now. The idea of Gerard's steady amber gaze icing against her in betrayal—turning against her just as her first two lovers had, this time due to her own choices—made every lingering golden ripple disappear, replaced by a sick churning deep in Lorelei's stomach.

Enough. Being a queen meant making unbearable choices for the sake of her people's safety, even when "people" meant a stubbornly noble general. For now, she needed all of her focus for the next set of challenges. As she and Gerard neared the field, the noisy, enthusiastic crowd parted easily around them, revealing their final three pairs of competitors waiting ahead. Oberon, magnificent in swathes of deep copper and umber silk, stood by the throne in low-voiced conversation with some of his usual hangers-on.

Hmm. That particular grouping looked significantly smaller than the day before. Could it be a sign that the court was turning against its temporary host? One could always hope, after the public tantrums he'd thrown the day before.

Smiling serenely, Lorelei gave him a courteous nod as he turned to face her and her partner. Oberon's upper lip twitched with distaste as he glanced up and down their rumpled, grass-stained and sparkle-covered outfits . . . and then his gaze moved past them, over Lorelei's left shoulder, and his lips compressed into a tight but disturbingly smug smile.

What was he plotting now? As Lorelei took her smiling place by the other contestants, she aimed a discreet glance in the direction he had turned. One of Oberon's missing sycophants was hurrying towards them from the woods beyond, beaming with the confidence of a pet who knew he'd earned a great reward.

Gerard leaned close, his whisper brushing warmth against her skin. "'Ware the lackey."

Of course he'd taken note as well. Lorelei nodded infinitesimally, shifting even closer to his side and drawing strength from the reminder.

Whatever Oberon threw at them, they would face together—and there was no one here who could defeat them as a unit. Of that, she was entirely certain, even as a cold breeze flew across the tournament field and made her shiver with the first bite of oncoming winter.

At Oberon's signal, the usual herald stepped forward with her golden hunting horn. As she raised it to her ivy-green lips, the air itself seemed to withdraw in a deep, pulsing, expectant breath—and then she blew a long, ringing peal that echoed across the field, through the crisp autumnal air, bringing the big, rustling crowd to attentive silence. The magic of so many fae's gathered energy and attention formed a palpable pressure in the air, and Lorelei felt her heart beat faster with the thrill of it.

For so many years, she had sat in those outskirts, looking on as a mere guest. Now, she was finally an active participant, proving to everyone at her mother's court that she *did* still belong here, among them, no matter where else her mission had carried her.

"*Welcome,*" Oberon proclaimed, his voice magnified to echo across their audience, "to the final day of our sacred tourney, the day in which we choose a final pair of competitors to share this shining victory." He raised his hands in a slow clap. When he drew them apart, a single golden arrow lay across each of his palms. "Any bearer of this sign will be ever welcome at our highest tables, the pride of Efaelen forevermore."

Lorelei didn't need any golden arrows to earn her usual place at her mother's table as a diplomatic guest of state. Still, every muscle in her being tightened with fierce yearning at the sight of future triumph made tangible. When she finally wrenched her gaze away to glance up and to her side, she found Gerard's keen gaze fixed on those golden symbols, marking them as his target. *Of course.* Neither of them would ever fight for anything less than first place.

Perhaps they really were two of a kind.

"Only three more challenges lie before you," Oberon announced, his gaze passing over all four pairs of competitors. His smile was gracious and his voice honeyed ... but when his gaze landed on Lorelei, he closed one eyelid in the briefest possible wink. The hairs on the back of her neck lifted in warning. "Each pair will be given a different clue before being dropped into position to solve your joint riddle. The first to find the prize, of course, will win. And now, if everyone will bear with me a moment as I hand out those clues ..."

Lorelei's eyebrows drew together as she watched him stroll towards the closest pair of competitors, a tall dryad and a shorter swamp hag, and lean over to whisper into the dryad's ear. Where had all this nonsense about secret whispers come from? In every trial thus far, each pair's hints had been visible to the audience at large, so that the onlookers could vicariously enjoy that deeper challenge. There was no reason not to let the audience see or hear these clues, too ...

Unless Oberon was planning to cheat.

As he moved with unhurried grace to the second pair, the first pair huddled together for an urgent private conference. Did they look *too* excited by what he'd told them?

Damn it, she couldn't *stand* not knowing her enemies' plans! Where were Ailana's spies when she needed them? Lorelei set her teeth together, trying not to let her anxiety become visible in foot tapping or any other telltale movements. She was nearly shivering with the effort of staying still—until Gerard's free hand closed over hers, warm and steadying.

Silently, she let out a long breath, letting herself absorb strength from his big figure beside her. Whatever trickery Oberon might attempt, they would handle it together. Whatever . . .

"Now." Oberon's smile was a fierce peeling-apart of lips around his teeth as he stepped into place just before them. "Which hint *was* I meant to give you two, to help you succeed in this challenge?" he murmured. "Let me think . . . oh, yes. I *do* remember now." Vicious triumph lit his face as he leaned even closer and whispered with the full force of his magic: "*Gerard Emmanuel de Moireul, I command you by your true name to kill Lorelei, your partner.*"

"And now!" he said brightly to the field as a whole. "Let the trial begin!"

The world shifted beneath their feet. Colors whirled sickeningly around them as they were swept away into the setting of their next trial.

Lorelei landed with a painful thud on rocky ground—and Gerard wrenched his arm violently away from her as he reached to draw his sword.

25

"*Get away from me!*" Gerard bellowed the words with all his might—but they emerged only as a hoarse and desperate whisper from the moving cage of his body, which was no longer under his control. As if caught in a nightmare, he felt his own hand reach against his will to grasp the hilt of his sword while Lorelei stumbled backwards, mouth wide open in shock, nearly tripping on the rocky mountainside where the two of them had been dropped.

Other competitors were racing around that same mountainside, intent on the tournament's official quest, but he took no notice. He couldn't have turned his head to look at any of them even if he'd cared anymore.

"Gerard." Lorelei's voice trembled with emotion as she ignored his frantic orders and stayed exactly where she was, in excruciatingly imminent peril. "*My* darling. This is not your fault. It is not!"

Jovar's hells, why wasn't she running from him? She'd heard Oberon's enspelled command just as clearly as he had; she *knew* what was about to happen.

Gerard had spent decades building his willpower into an unstoppable force, but now he couldn't even stop his own damned arm from drawing his blade from its scabbard.

"*Bind. Me!*" He forced the words out in harsh fragments of sound as his sword hissed free.

Thick green vines leapt out of the ground to twine around him in answer—but they only slowed him for an instant. His blade flashed forward, arm muscles working with well-practiced ease, to slash himself free. Damn it, even the vines' leaves were soft. What was she thinking?

"*Thorns,*" he rasped. "*Poison. In me!*" She couldn't afford to be so gentle with him now! He'd been trained to kill from the time he was a child. She *had* to fight him like the ruthless opponent she always had been.

He'd spent years dreading the day when he would be forced to meet her in battle, but he had never imagined this.

"I . . ." Shaking her head, Lorelei finally began to back away, but she wasn't moving nearly quickly enough. "I *can't*," she whispered, her voice breaking. "I can't hurt you."

Gerard had sworn to her only the night before that, unlike her earliest lovers, he would never hurt her, either. Now, stinging tears leaked out of his eyes for the first time in decades. Inside his head, he screamed in absolute refusal of Oberon's magical order. Following it would break him forever—yet he couldn't stop his own right arm from swinging back in preparation for a killing blow.

With all of his strength, he forced one final command from his lips: "*Kill me. Now!*"

It was the only outcome he could bear.

"*As queens, we do what we must, not what we would prefer.*" Her mother's words, spoken so long ago, echoed in Lorelei's head as she backed away from the impossible choice playing out before her.

Even she couldn't break the hold of a true-name command while she and Gerard remained in the fae realm—and there was no way to *leave* the fae realm now without violating its most essential code. If Lorelei publicly broke her sworn word by abandoning the tournament midway through, she would be exiled from Efaelen forever after, never allowed to visit her mother or her first home again.

Was it only a few minutes ago that she had gazed covetously at those golden arrows and seen a promise of full acceptance here at last?

Oh, how smug Oberon must be feeling. He'd finally found his perfect revenge . . .

And she knew exactly what Queen Morgana would tell her to do, no matter how painful it might feel.

No one in the assembled crowd of fae onlookers would blame her for sacrificing her mortal partner, even if they knew why he had turned upon her. Everyone would understand that it was the only option Lorelei had had to save herself and her home.

Even *he* was begging her to do it.

Until this week, the Empire's Golden Beacon had never allowed her to see any of his deeply buried true emotions. Now, tears shone in Gerard's anguished amber eyes as his right arm drew back, raising that lethal sword in preparation . . . and a final knot of tangled emotions melted away in Lorelei's chest, leaving her path laid out before her with perfect simplicity. For once, her instincts and cool logic were in full agreement.

She spun one forefinger through the air as his blade arced towards her. Its steel tip landed—and stuck—in a shimmering, rapidly growing fae portal that hung in the air between them. Caught off-balance, Gerard stumbled.

Lorelei drew a deep, final breath, absorbing that gorgeously rich and familiar land-magic that drenched the air in Efaelen and caressed her skin with loving delight ... and then she leapt forward, flinging herself on Gerard's big body, to knock him fully into the portal. As they fell together through it, she didn't cast a single look back.

She had been a fool ever to imagine that she could harm this man, whether for the sake of her people, her goddess, or any other higher cause.

He *was* her true home, and some part of her had known that from their first meeting. She would never let him go.

They landed in a tangled heap in night-darkness, with a hard *thump* against wooden flooring that knocked the breath out of Lorelei's chest. It would certainly leave bruises later, but even as she gasped for air, deep relief suffused her.

No magic tingled in this room except the lingering traces in each corner where her familiar, lush pink roses bloomed, long out of season but thriving in her care. She knew every inch of this polished wooden floor. If she'd had more time to properly focus her portal, she would have aimed it three feet over, to set them both on the big four-poster bed, but she didn't care about her own bruises now.

"Gerard!" Scrambling off him, she gently touched his closest shoulder, which was hunched against her and unmoving. Had he been badly injured in the fall? Knocked unconscious? No, his muscles were locked tight; he must be awake. Was he afraid to move in case the spell took hold again? "My love," she murmured, "you're safe now. We're in Balravia, in my bedroom, in my own secure hunting lodge. Oberon can't touch you here or ever again. I swear it."

She couldn't imagine the violation he must feel. For such a tightly controlled man to be worked like a puppet against his will ...

Rage lit deep within her belly, only waiting to spread and become a wildfire.

For the sake of her mother's partner and diplomatic relations between Efaelen and Balravia, Lorelei had allowed Oberon to survive his attempted assault by love potion upon her. As she watched a tight shudder shake Gerard's big figure now, she swore she would not show such mercy again.

She fought for control, but her voice shook with fury even as she gave his bunched shoulder a long, soothing stroke. "I am so, *so* sorry that that was done to you, but darling, I promise it will *never* happen again. Oberon has made his last mistake. I swear to you, he *will* pay for it. I won't let you be hurt or used like that ever—"

"*Lorelei.*" Gerard abruptly rolled over to face her. She couldn't make out his expression in the unlit room, with blackness pressing against the glass windows to their side, but his voice was ragged. "How can you bring yourself to touch me? I could have killed you. I *would* have killed you with my own sword!"

"No," she said firmly, "you would not." Leaning forward, she cupped her palms against his cheeks, cradling him with the utmost care. "*Oberon* would have killed me through you, but he couldn't, because both of us fought against it—and *you*, you impossible man, actually told me to kill you to protect myself. Did you truly believe I would ever do that?"

"I prayed that you would," he said quietly. "I couldn't have survived your loss regardless. Lorelei . . ." He took a deep breath. "You are the first—the only—true joy I've ever known."

In the darkness, emotions billowed up through her until they filled her throat, nearly choking her. She couldn't speak.

But she felt his sudden jolt of realization against her palms. "*Wait.* You brought me here to save us both, but the tournament hadn't ended. What about your sworn word? You told me . . ." He jerked himself abruptly upright into a sitting position, and her hands slipped away from his face. "Lorelei, they'll never let you back again! How could you have forgotten? I would *never* expect you to give up—"

"Oh, you foolish, foolish man." Lorelei had never taken such a frightening step in her life, but she forced the words through her tight throat, risking everything. "Aren't you the one who told me first? I've been in love with you for *years*. How could I ever make any other choice?"

There was a long moment of stunned silence. Then he lunged for her in the darkness, and she met him with a thankful cry.

As his big hands plunged into her tangled curls, she met his lips with a kiss full of relief, passion, and desperate tenderness—and he met and matched her with a new desperation of his own.

There *was* a bed only three feet away—but that thought slipped from Lorelei's mind like a will-o'-the-wisp winking out of view as they tumbled together to the polished wooden floor, scrambling and pulling at each other's battered clothes. She wasn't in charge this time, but neither was he. There was no space left between them for control. Everything was pure *sensation:*

The rough cloth of his jacket against her palms as she grabbed at him.

The incineration of his kiss and the furnace of his skin through his clothes as their bodies pressed against each other with urgent need.

His big fingers cradling her head—then sweeping downwards, shaping every inch of her form as if to reassure himself that she was truly here, no mere illusion, still alive and unharmed and openly loving him at last.

They were really here, together.

"Us," Lorelei panted as his lips left hers and drew a hot trail down her throat.

"*Us,*" he growled back and sucked her skin between his teeth until she let out a moan of helpless pleasure. "Only us, Lorelei, from now on. Swear it."

At any other time, she might have teased him—or challenged him to make it *worth her while*. Now, she was too shaken to give him anything but honesty.

"Forever," she murmured, and it was the truth. How could she ever settle for a lesser man once she'd known this joy with him?

She tipped her head back against the floor, arching against him, and the glorious scent of summer filled the room. Soft rose petals showered over them in the darkness, scattering across Gerard's broad back and kissing against her own cheeks and hair in celebration. Her lover paused in his explorations for a startled instant to capture and inspect a handful of falling blossoms—and then he let out a laugh of pure wonder.

"Of course." He shook his head ruefully down at her. "What else could I have expected?"

"Oh, my darling..." Lorelei's lips curved with delighted anticipation. "You've seen *nothing* yet."

Those blossoms had arisen from sheer emotion, unguided by thought. At a wave of her hand, a whole green bower sprang into place around them, rustling with life and vivid beauty. Tall, cherry-red tulips and purple irises nodded down at them from the exuberant living bouquet that surrounded them. Every stem, leaf, and blossom was lit by the warm golden sunshine that shone down from above, while a thick, berry-studded circular hedge shut away the rest of the world. Humming sounds signaled smaller creatures busily at work among the plants, while the steady, soothing ripple of moving water signaled a stream nearby.

Propping himself on one elbow, Gerard turned to take in every sumptuous detail, his eyebrows rising. "Illusion or real?"

"A bit of both, but *mostly* illusion this time." Lorelei shrugged with entirely false modesty, savoring every instant of his focused attention on her work. "What do you think of it?"

"*I* think," he said slowly, "that whoever wins the Tournament of Leaves this year should thank you every day for surrendering that chance. You are remarkably gifted, and you know it. But that's not all."

"Oh, no?" Stretching like a cat under the stroke of his praise, she purred the question. "What else?"

As he turned back to her, Gerard's lips curled into a shockingly mischievous smirk. "I think I *still* haven't seen you fully unclothed!"

With a lightning-fast move, he yanked down her bodice like a scoundrel.

"Why, General. How *very* forward of you!" Laughing with giddy delight, Lorelei shimmied in place to help him work her puffed sleeves down, too, and then kicked herself free of all the rest until she lay, bare skinned and glowing with happiness, before him.

She hadn't laid herself so open to any lover in years—which had nothing to do with nudity and *everything* to do with the way she lay back now and let her busy mind pause, for once, to luxuriate in his slow, worshipful exploration. Heat and light spread with every brush of his warm, calloused hands against her skin, shaping every inch of her into something new and bright beneath him. No—with endless patience, he was tracing the shape of *herself*, the Lorelei she'd truly been all along, beneath every illusion and shield, finally exposed in full for him . . .

And oh, the look on his face as he did it! She met his gaze—amber eyes gleaming with an irresistible mix of hunger and amazement—just as he slipped a second big finger inside her, inexorably testing the pressure he'd already wound within her to breaking point . . .

And Lorelei detonated against him. Gold sparkles filled the air as she ripped at his uniform, pulling off that last obstacle between them and letting his buttons fly. She couldn't *stand* any distance for even a second longer. She needed him—not the Empire's famous Golden Beacon but *Gerard*, her beautiful, ethical, stubborn lover—*now*, his skin bare and hot against hers, burning her up as she pulled him to her.

She tipped her head back to meet his gaze as she yanked him that final distance—and as he surged inside her, she wrapped her legs tightly around him to seal him in place.

Birdsong sounded, high and joyful, like the pealing of bells. Somewhere in the distance, Lorelei could have sworn that she felt the whole house shudder, as if even its longstanding magical shields had felt the impact of their union...

But she could only focus now on Gerard's wild eyes, his pupils dilating more and more as she tightened around him, until all she could see was a thin rim of amber circling that desperate black. Lorelei couldn't look away—could barely even breathe—as he shifted his hips to move inside her with a steady, powerful rhythm that carried the resonance of holy ritual.

His hands reached for hers—and she reached up to wrap her fingers around his without breaking his gaze for an instant.

Sylvana, I beg You to forgive me. I'm no longer only Yours.

Her fingers tightened around Gerard's as she cast up the prayer... and then all words were lost.

A long time later, she came back to herself, her body filled with golden light. Still shuddering with pleasure, she clung to him with her arms and legs, holding him close. His softly furred chest worked like a bellows against her cheek as he panted for air, his warm weight pressing her down to deliciously prolong the moment.

No worries or distant dangers could intrude in their illusory green bower...

Until the sudden rap of a fist against wood sounded much too close nearby. Lorelei startled, Gerard stiffened into a defensive crouch above her—and although Lorelei couldn't see her bedroom door, Katrin's voice sounded clearly through it, sharp and urgent.

"Lorelei! Your shields are down, and we have visitors approaching."

26

"*Darlings!*" Lorelei caroled less than five minutes later.

It had taken a frantic scramble behind the scenes, but she was ready for her public performance just in time, sitting with her skirts spread about her on a plush, rose-velvet love seat by the fire in her favorite parlor while Ilse sewed placidly on a sofa across the room and thick, plum-colored curtains held out the winter cold. Standing just behind Lorelei with one strong hand resting atop the love seat's gilded frame, Gerard had buttoned his uniform jacket over his irreparably ripped shirt and looked as calm and composed as if nothing extraordinary had happened to him at all.

As Katrin opened the parlor door for the intruders who'd smashed through her magical walls, Lorelei clapped with a perfect approximation of delight . . . and prayed that the illusion that kept her hair seemingly in place—and the grass stains off her gown—wouldn't drop before she could rid herself of her two closest and most valued political allies. "How wonderfully unexpected to see you both!" she exclaimed. "Why, I'm so happy, I can't even recall inviting you."

"Ha!" The Witch Queen of Kitvaria stalked into the room, her long black hair pulled free from its usual plait to hang thick and wild about her shoulders, tangled with sticks and leaves from her own magical journey. Saskia's crimson gown swished with every impatient step as she glowered at Lorelei in the low light. "We invited ourselves."

". . . Because you left us no choice," finished the third Queen of Villainy. Raising a single, elegant eyebrow, the Ice Queen of Nornne looked from Lorelei to Gerard and back. "*Really*, Lorelei." Sighing, Ailana slowly shook her head. "Do you have *no* impulse control whatsoever?"

Just like a disapproving older sister! Biting back a groan, Lorelei batted her eyelashes and sent rainbow sparkles floating through the air. "Oh dear. Was the journey here *terribly* difficult without any of my lovely portals to carry you? Don't worry, I completely forgive you both for being so grumpy. Perhaps once we've all enjoyed some cake—"

"Lorelei!" Magic crackled like a building storm in the air as Saskia threw out her arms. "Do you have *any idea* how much trouble you've caused everyone with your nonsense?"

Ugh. Behind her, Lorelei sensed Gerard stiffen. No doubt he was already lashing himself with worry over whatever was happening in the Empire without him now—and feeling damnable guilt over having actually dared to enjoy himself, for once in his life, with her.

Couldn't they have had a few more minutes of happiness before the world came crashing in to taint everything?

Leaping to her feet, she stood before him like a shield. "Perhaps the three of us should retire to speak separately and . . ."

Gerard spoke at the same time, his voice a low rumble. "*Ahem.* Your Majesties, you may be interested to learn that Queen Lorelei has been working to *all* of your benefits over the past few days."

Wait. Eyebrows shooting upwards, Lorelei twisted around. Was *that* what had made him stiffen up? Irritation that they were chastising *her*?

Gerard kept his watchful gaze on the queens across the room, but he reached across the love seat to extend one hand—and as Lorelei took it in hers, Ilse stopped sewing to let out a muffled squeal. "*I knew it!*" she stage-whispered to Katrin across the room.

Standing sentinel in a corner by the door, Katrin didn't respond in spoken words . . . but her lips stretched into a knowing smirk.

Neither of the other two queens responded with the same cheering enthusiasm.

"Oh, gods." Saskia groaned and clapped one palm to her forehead. "Lorelei, has it even occurred to you that the high general of our greatest enemy is *not* a sensible toy for you to play with and discard?"

"Gerard is no toy." Lorelei's eyes narrowed to dangerous slits as her fingers tightened protectively around his. "And—"

"Of course no one could ever seriously imagine him as anything so frivolous." As Ailana turned to Gerard, her usual diplomatic mask slipped back into place along with a rueful, sympathetic smile. "General de Moireul, I believe I speak for all of us when I say that you have our deepest respect *and* regret for any inconvenience or indignities that may have been inflicted upon you this week. Your sense of honor is so well-known and admired, I know you would never dream of pursuing any *personal* revenge through your exalted position. Still, regardless of what may have passed between you and our friend and ally . . ."

"I'm not *discarding* him," Lorelei snapped. "I'm keeping him."

Ailana blinked rapidly, several times in a row. "I beg your pardon?"

Ha. Apparently even the queen of ice and spies didn't know everything after all! Lifting her chin to meet the other woman's gaze full-on, Lorelei said, "You may be the first to congratulate us, if you like. Gerard is going to be my consort."

"But . . . but you *can't!* *He* can't." Ailana spun around to stare at all the other silent observers in the room. "Are you all hearing this madness?"

"I heard it." Frowning, Saskia crossed her arms . . . but unlike Ailana, the witch queen looked more thoughtful than disturbed. "I *thought* something odd was happening between you two at the battlefield last week. I suppose this explains it after all."

"Doesn't it?" Lorelei beamed at her with perfect satisfaction. Saskia, of all people, knew how it felt to fall hopelessly in love with an official enemy; *she* wouldn't be foolish enough to hold Gerard's past allegiance against him in the coming years. "I knew he couldn't hold out against me forever. I *am* irresistible, you know."

Gerard let out a quiet, ironic huff of breath . . . but squeezed her fingers in wry agreement.

When he spoke, his words were aimed at Ailana, and his tone was perfectly calm. "Your Majesty, may I ask which particular aspect of the situation most concerns you? As you can see, I have no intention or desire for revenge. Lorelei's intervention was not only of personal benefit but professionally timely. Her warning about the Emperor's ambition to adopt Purification as a directive was a gift I won't ignore—and I will promise you, as I've promised her already, that I will *never* lead any troops under that banner. We haven't yet had time to discuss all the details of our future plans . . ."

He slid Lorelei a glance, and she shivered at the delicious reminder of what they *had* spent their time doing since their return. Gods, if only the others had let them have another hour! The things she wanted to *do* to this man . . . !

"But my own current plan," he continued calmly, "is to enact a slow and carefully managed retirement from my role. I have a clear responsibility to remain Imperial high general long enough to persuade the

Emperor and his private cabinet against the conscienceless course of action which he is currently considering. Afterwards, though, I should be able to tender my formal resignation and, soon afterwards, shift to Balravia for good."

"Wait, I haven't agreed to that plan." Lorelei's brows drew down into a scowl. "It would mean spending *months* apart. If not years!"

"Really?" He raised his eyebrows, a tiny, private smile tugging at the firm line of his lips. "For most people, it might. But I have heard rumors that one particularly scandalous queen is capable of creating extraordinarily powerful fae portals—and can use them to enter my own quarters at will, even in the very heart of the Empire. Surely, such a remarkable woman could find a way for us to spend a *good deal* of time together, regardless of my official residence or any outward appearances."

Even so . . .

"I truly appreciate that thoughtful approach, General. However . . ." Ailana sighed. "What you two may *not* yet know is that we've run out of time for any quiet, peaceful strategies. If you don't return to the Empire within the next hour, we may all be doomed."

"He will *not*—!" Lorelei began hotly, turning back to her.

Gerard said, "What do you mean? What has happened?"

"You've been found out, Lorelei," said Saskia. "The Emperor knows his Golden Beacon is missing, and fae magic was sensed at the scene."

"What?" Lorelei's stomach sank. "*How?* It's only been two days in mortal time! Gerard wasn't even due to arrive in the capital yet. I made certain, with the note I left . . ."

"Unfortunately," said Ailana, "the Emperor doesn't share your lover's patience. Apparently, Otto wasn't willing to wait long enough for General de Moireul to travel back across the continent with the troops in a slow procession, as planned. Instead, he sent a messenger by rail to *demand* General de Moireul's immediate presence and report—and while the general's soldiers did their best to shield his privacy, once a Gilded Wizard was drawn into the mix and sensed fae magic, all was lost."

Oh, Sylvana. The world fell away from Lorelei like a chasm opening up before her feet, simmering joy transforming into abject horror. *I have failed You after all.*

She didn't need anyone to tell her what the consequences would be.

Emperor Otto II had been desperate for months to find a suitable public excuse to adopt Purification. He would *leap* at this opportunity to blame the fae—and, by association, all other non-human creatures—for the abduction and loss of the public's beloved Golden Beacon.

It was every Purifier's dream come true: a foolproof way to pull the human continent together in united enmity. And if—when—that fae abductress was revealed to be Lorelei herself, Otto would whip up his populace behind the patriotic need to invade and annex Balravia in righteous vengeance.

"The messenger returned to Fiora just tonight," Ailana said quietly. "The Emperor has summoned his private council into session now."

"So there is still time." Gerard's grip on Lorelei's hand was as warm and steady as his voice. "We can avert this. Lorelei will send me through a portal directly to the Imperial winter palace, so I may explain to the Emperor and the rest of the council that only a misunderstanding occurred. I am neither injured nor in need of any vengeance."

"If only I hadn't . . ." The words fell out from Lorelei's numb lips like pebbles sinking into a deep, dark well.

If only she hadn't trusted so confidently in her own instincts. If only—

"No." Gerard released her hand, but only so that he could stride swiftly around the love seat that filled the space between them. He closed on her an instant later, his amber gaze intent and his broad shoulders blocking her view of the room and the disapproving friends around them as he caught up both of her hands in his. "Don't even think it! If you hadn't come for me when you did, Otto would have found another excuse soon enough—and when that one came, we both know I wouldn't have had the strength of will to refuse him."

His tone was bitterly self-deprecating, and it made her frown. "Don't talk about yourself that way! You have a conscience. You would have argued against him, even then. I know you would have."

"And I agree—but once he gave up listening and issued me an official order?" Gerard squeezed her hands tightly, but his tone was unrelenting. "I would have loathed it with every ounce of my being, but I would have followed his commands. I would have thought I had no choice."

"And now?" Lorelei whispered.

"Now I know how it *truly* feels not to have any choice in following a ruler's orders." As the memory of their last moments in Efaelen passed between them, Lorelei shifted even closer, her throat clenching at the shadows of pain in his face. "Even under a fae truename command," Gerard continued evenly, "I could never have forgiven myself for what I did if you hadn't saved me from it. To go against my conscience once again, this time in the mortal realm, *without* any actual constraint but my own fears?" He shook his head slowly, keeping his haunted gaze fixed on hers. "That wouldn't be patriotism or duty. It would only be weakness, after all."

"You are the strongest man I know," she murmured.

"And you have the most remarkable mind for strategy," he told her firmly. "*Yes*, this move had unexpected consequences—but that's the way of war. You can never predict every outcome. You only have to be ready to shift with the results . . . and although this particular outcome does carry some urgency, you *are* still on the winning side overall."

"She is?" Saskia's skeptical voice came from behind his back.

Gerard didn't turn away from Lorelei as he nodded. "After this small hiccup is resolved, the Queens of Villainy will still have the high general of the Serafin Empire firmly on their side. Isn't that worth a bit of anxiety along the way?"

Despite everything, Lorelei let out a gurgle of laughter. "Darling, just because *you* never show any anxiety doesn't mean it's unimportant!"

"... Says the woman who's delighted in tormenting me for seven years," he murmured under his breath, too quietly for the others to hear.

Beaming, she leapt up on her toes, and he met her halfway in a kiss full of sweetness, passion, shared laughter, and a promise that rang like fae bells through her whole body.

Ilse's sentimental sigh sounded as they finally drew apart, drawing another giggle from Lorelei ... and giving her the strength to step around Gerard's big figure to face her friends and allies, still holding one of his hands in hers.

Katrin was smirking silently in the corner where she now leaned, no longer stiffly alert against the wall. Even Saskia had sprawled down across a luxuriously cushioned seat with an indulgent smile that reminded Lorelei that the Queen of Kitvaria was enjoying a wild romance of her own and understood the need for such displays.

Only Ailana remained standing in the middle of the room, her slim figure tense with concern and her cool brown eyes shifting worriedly between Lorelei and Gerard ...

So Lorelei aimed her next words at the Queen of Nornne. "Fine. Gerard and I will portal to Fiora now." Every instinct rebelled against the idea of letting him step into danger, but he *was* her true partner, as the Tournament of Leaves had just proven to all of Efaelen. They always worked best in tandem, and this cause was too urgent to avoid the risk. "I'll cast an illusion over myself for invisibility, and—"

"No!" Both Gerard and Ailana spoke at once. As their voices clashed, Gerard hesitated for an instant—and Ailana seized the opportunity to continue, her voice urgent. "Lorelei, there *cannot* be any implication of coercion if General de Moireul is to succeed. If you're discovered hidden by his side, everyone will immediately assume he's being forced into his stance."

"Then I simply won't *let* myself be discovered," Lorelei snapped. "If you had any true understanding of the strength of my illusions—"

"I *do* understand and respect them," Gerard said, "and I am certain that no one in that palace could break them against your will—but, my darling, there are magical guards, fail-safes, and alarms laid throughout the council meeting area specifically to protect against eavesdroppers or observers. Those alarms might not be able to break any illusion that you cast—but they would absolutely alert the Emperor and his Gilded Wizards that fae magic was present and hiding from them. They would draw their own conclusions."

"General de Moireul is correct," Ailana said quietly. "No magic-worker of any sort can get through to that private council chamber without setting off its warnings. Believe me."

If even the continent's most powerful and discreet spymistress couldn't manage that . . . then, curse it, it probably was impossible after all. *Argh!* Lorelei wanted to turn and pace the room for inspiration, but she didn't dare release Gerard's hand in case he took that chance to stride merrily away to martyr himself.

"He *cannot* go alone," she said to her fellow queens as calmly and reasonably as she could. "Saskia, would you let *Felix* walk into any of the Emperor's palaces on his own, without you or any magical guard to protect him?"

At that mention of her own consort, the Queen of Kitvaria's dark brows drew together in sudden shared concern, but Gerard only tugged Lorelei closer to shake his head down at her. "You do realize that I've spent a good deal of my life in that palace for the last several years and have never been harmed in any way?"

"That was when you were Otto's loyal man," she pointed out tartly, "and even loyalty didn't save the last high priest!"

Sighing, he lifted his free hand to stroke his fingertips lightly down her face in a caress that made her suppress a shiver, his lips curving into a rueful, tender smile. "You are the only person in the world who has ever thought I needed protection."

"Pah." She would *not* be soothed into allowing this, no matter how his touch made her body want to melt against him. "A whole continent adores you."

"No," he said, "they adore the *Golden Beacon*. That's an entirely different thing."

"And yet... he *is* adored," Ailana said softly. When Lorelei glanced at her ally, she found Ailana's eyes narrowed in deep thought. "General, you've worked hard to build a reputation that stretches far beyond the Empire itself... and you've been careful never to misuse it yet."

Gerard frowned. "... Yes?"

"So, I *think*," Ailana said slowly, "that you should be ready to use that as your guard tonight. Ensure that everyone in that council chamber is aware of exactly what will happen if you speak out against them to the newspapers that love you so much—and remind them that *no one* will believe the kind of claims made about the last high priest if Otto tries that course again with you."

"Well, then, they'll want him *dead* to keep him quiet!" Lorelei snapped. "How is that an improvement?"

"My darling," Gerard said with maddening overconfidence, "even Otto won't order me assassinated in the council chamber. He may have traveled further down that path than I'd cared to admit until now, but the Empire *hasn't* yet. The other council members won't stand for any bloodshed directly in front of them."

Lorelei rolled her eyes. Could no one else see the truth? "The high priestess is Otto's *sister*."

"And yet..." Gerard's brows compressed. "I've never heard any ill of her."

"Have you heard any *good*?" Lorelei demanded. "What does she actually say in those private meetings?"

"Nothing," he admitted. "She maintained an unceasing silence in the only meeting we shared before my departure for Kitvaria. But before her recent elevation, I only ever heard of her in combination with charitable activities and good causes."

"She used to care about justice and what was right." Ailana's voice was low and strained. "But that was a long time ago."

Eyebrows arching, Lorelei exchanged a quick, baffled look with Saskia . . . who shook her head with equal confusion.

At any other time, Lorelei would have pounced on the opportunity to delve into their tight-lipped friend's most intriguing secrets, but there was no time to discuss years-old gossip. She had a consort to save from his own noble intentions and very little time left to do it.

So she crossed her arms, raised all of her power in readiness, and smiled with ferocious sweetness at all the friends ranked around her. "Gerard is *not* walking into that trap without protection. I won't let him."

It was the moment of truth for all of them, now—the moment she'd been dreading.

Perhaps he would never forgive her for this high-handed decision. If he closed his heart against her now, the pain would be indescribable . . . but she would far rather risk his hatred than his life. There was no doubt left in her.

Across the room, Saskia's eyes narrowed, but she sat back in her seat, clearly withdrawing herself from the debate; she, at least, knew what it was to have a partner to protect. Ailana's brown eyes iced over with dangerous silver, though, and a perilous cold chilled the room as the ice queen's powers mantled in return, the first thin layer of transparent ice forming on the floor around her feet. "Lorelei, this is no time for one of your sudden whims. The fate of the entire continent is at stake! You *cannot* risk everyone and everything we care about for a personal distraction, no matter how compelling he may be."

"Can I not?" Setting her teeth together, Lorelei called on the grace given to her by Sylvana. Summer heat swept through the air, melting the ice into puddles.

She raised her arm in preparation for battle . . .

But Gerard closed one hand around it and gently turned her. "Lorelei," he murmured, "love of my life, look at me."

Mulishly, she set her jaw, refusing to raise her eyes. She couldn't afford to weaken now, no matter how hurt or furious he was. But . . .

With his free hand, he gently tilted her head—and the unhidden gratitude, love, and wonder in his gaze trapped her in place like a butterfly caught in amber. She had been fighting for so many years to break through his stone-hard shell. And now—!

"No one in my entire life has ever tried to shield me as you do," he murmured huskily. "I cannot even express to you how much it means to me."

"You. Are. Mine." Her words were a bare whisper, but she knew he could hear every word. "I am a queen. I know the stakes. But I *will not* let you sacrifice yourself and become a martyr."

Once again, that terrible vision of Jovar's hall of heroes rose to chill the blood in her veins more effectively than Ailana could ever manage. Gerard had worn this same grass-stained uniform coat in that vision, hadn't he? If Sylvana had mercy, Lorelei *might* have already averted that prophesied fate by rescuing him from Oberon's ruse in Efaelen today . . .

But she wouldn't take that chance. She couldn't.

"My mother gave me up for the sake of a greater cause," Lorelei said softly, "and it nearly broke me. I will *never* do the same to you."

"You won't have to." Ailana spoke, breaking their spell of intimacy, but this time, there was no ice in her tone, only regret. "Forgive me, Lorelei. I didn't realize how deeply you truly felt."

Gerard released her chin, and Lorelei turned slowly to face her longest-standing political ally. Ailana's eyes were shadowed but no longer silvered, and her expression was grave.

They had been friends for years. And yet . . . "I told you he was my consort," Lorelei said. "How did you *think* I felt about him?"

"I heard you. And yet . . ." Sighing, Ailana made a graceful, flowing gesture that spoke without words of all the years Lorelei had spent painting a picture of herself to the world as a heartless rake.

She'd always assumed that her two closest allies must know her better than to *believe* in that self-presentation... but as she met Ailana's gaze now, she realized that they had all been keeping far too many secrets from one another, despite their binding vows of alliance.

If the Queens of Villainy were to take on the Serafin Empire—and survive—they couldn't afford to keep any self-protective shields raised within their private meetings any longer.

With a sigh, Lorelei released the illusion that had held her hair neatly in place to their vision until now. Dirt and grass stains reappeared on her skin and clothes. Wholly imperfect, smudged, and real, she looked from one ally to another and spoke the plain, unvarnished truth. "He has my whole heart in his keeping."

"I see." Ailana drew a deep breath and then released it as Saskia nodded in silent acceptance. "In that case, we will all have to make certain that you do not lose him."

27

Gerard stepped through Lorelei's portal alone, but he felt her worried gaze cling to his back until the portal sealed shut, leaving him alone in a dimly lit but familiar gallery of Imperial family portraits. A grand altar to Jovar at the far end cast a warm glow from the holy flames that burned in the marble bowl at its center, but their height indicated that they'd already had their hourly visitation from an Imperial priestess, leaving Gerard free to move past unobserved.

As high general of the Serafin Empire, he should probably have felt more concerned by the discovery that the Queen of Nornne somehow knew the palace layout and routine well enough to direct Lorelei's portal to the safest spot for an arrival at this time. Tonight, though, he felt nothing but relief that no courtiers were there to be astonished and distracted by his magical arrival and informal appearance... which, he grimly accepted, was far from ideal for the meeting ahead. Unfortunately, by the time all the arguments in Balravia had finally ended, it had been too late to change out of his grubby uniform or even shave the unaccustomed stubble from his face.

Gossip would be unavoidable once the story of his return spread through the court—but at least it couldn't slow his mission now.

At a purposeful stride, it was a mere eight minutes' walk to the wing where Otto's private councils were held. It could have been shorter, but Gerard took the back ways to avoid all company, and the only maid he nearly met along the way made enough noise to allow him to step swiftly out of sight before she could see him and spread the news. Only when he neared the guard post outside Otto's private council chamber did he finally step into a central corridor and walk confidently to greet the two Imperial guards stationed there.

"High General!" They both stood to attention and saluted, but the covert glance they shared was too full of speculation for Gerard's comfort.

Apparently, Otto had not been discreet with his opinions about Gerard's recent decisions at the Kitvarian border. That did not bode well for the battle to come.

Still, he'd taken on worse odds before. With a firm nod, Gerard released them from their salutes and handed over his sword, as usual, for them to guard during the meeting. "I believe I'm expected."

The younger guard opened his mouth, looking eager to expound on that topic—but was glared into silence by the older one, who merely said, "Yes, sir."

Hmm. As members of the Imperial guard, meant only to protect Otto and his close family members from attack, neither of these men officially reported to Gerard, who headed the armies that fought for the Empire as a whole. However, in practice, few important secrets had ever been kept by the guard from the high general . . . until, of course, the last two weeks, when the late high priest's downfall had seemingly come out of nowhere.

Uneasiness prickled against the nape of Gerard's neck now, although he kept his expression unperturbed.

That older guard's hesitation to share any excess information *might* be perfectly harmless. Still, he found himself suddenly glad, after all, of the precautionary measures Queen Ailana had enacted upon Lorelei's insistence. The last high priest had been taken by surprise when the guard descended upon his undefended home and arrested him from his bed in the middle of the night, bundling him off to prison before his allies could even awaken to protest. The queens' clever plan meant that Gerard's own villa, two streets away, would be a *far* safer refuge.

Keeping his head high and his posture relaxed, Gerard stepped forward, and the others made way for him.

Of course they did.

Blowing out a silent breath once he was safely out of sight, Gerard strode down the final turn of the corridor to the massive, magic-deflecting iron door that protected Otto's most private meeting room, and confidently turned the handle.

"Ugh!" Lorelei stalked back and forth behind Ailana in a small, round office perched dizzyingly high above the snowy Nornne landscape in a tower that looked, inescapably, like an icicle. Really, there was such a thing as going *too far* with decorating on theme! "What is the *point* of devoting your life to spywork if you can't tell what's happening when it most matters?"

"We saw General de Moireul walk past my ice to the meeting room." Ailana spoke without lifting her gaze from the ice-covered desk, where an empty corridor was still on display. "The shard of ice my spy has placed in this outer corridor will melt long before their meeting is over, but I'll keep watching until it does, just in case—and I have eyes on the streets outside to warn us if he's attacked on his way home. Once he's safely locked inside his villa, the mirror-box my spies have placed inside his house will give him the chance to contact us for help."

"And if someone tries to murder him *inside* that council chamber, where he's without his sword?" Lorelei demanded.

Letting out a heavy sigh, Ailana finally turned away from the ice to cock a skeptical eyebrow at her. "I may not have personally witnessed the entrance of every council member tonight, but I have never *once* seen a single armed guard or Gilded Wizard step into any of Otto's private council meetings. The only people likely to be in that chamber right now are Otto and his highest advisors. Meanwhile, *your* paramour is the high general of the Serafin Empire and built like a steam train made of muscle. Do you really think he couldn't fight all of them off by himself if necessary?"

Lorelei slumped against the closest rounded white wall, all the righteous indignation flooding out of her as she slid down to the blue-and-white tiled floor, summoning warmth to protect her skin from the chill. "You're right," she admitted. "I *am* being absurd. I just . . ."

"You're just in love. Of course you are." Shaking her head, Ailana turned back to her viewing post. "I did warn you this would happen, didn't I? You can't expect to keep your heart protected when you invite every man you like into your bed. You might *intend* to keep emotion out of the equation, but—"

"For your information, I fell in love with Gerard *years* before I let him into my bed." Lorelei let out a sigh of her own as she contemplated her grubby skirts. "It wasn't something I did by choice—although . . ." Her jaw tightened as irritation rose to overcome her other emotions. "Even if I had, what of it? I don't recall hearing you lecture Saskia like this when she fell in love with Felix! If you could respect *her* choice, then why not mine?"

"Felix," said Ailana with maddening patience, "is the Archduke of Estarion. Their pairing directly averted a war and granted us a major diplomatic advantage."

"And mine won't?" Lorelei snorted. "Gerard is the Imperial high general. If you, of all people, can't see the advantage in that—!"

"You want to know what I see? What I *truly* see before me now, Lorelei?" Ailana spun around in her seat, an uncharacteristic flush high on her light brown cheeks. "I see my oldest friend and ally suddenly ready to shatter into pieces if anything should happen to the man she loves. After *years* of admiring your power and independence, I see your heart captured and sent out to wander the world, unprotected, in the body of a man who strides onto lethal battlefields *by choice*. In other words, I see every possibility of tragedy looming ahead of all of us because *you* couldn't keep your own emotions locked under control, *exactly* like what happened before and ruined ev—!" She broke off with a snap, her eyes flaring.

"'Ruined everything'?" Lorelei straightened against the wall where she sat, her gaze narrowing in on her ally's face. "What happened to frighten you so badly, Ailana?" she asked quietly. "Back when Saskia first announced her troth with Felix, you told me you believed in true love because you'd seen it . . . and *that* was why you took such care to protect yourself against it. Did you mean that you'd experienced it yourself, before we met? Or—?"

"No." Ailana's voice was coated in ice. "True love will *never* be allowed to infect me."

"Hmm." Lorelei regarded her skeptically. "Is this related to what you mentioned about knowing the Imperial high priestess in the past? Was *she* the one—?"

"Enough!" Ailana snapped. She turned back to the ice on her desk, her spine rigid and her words tightly controlled. "I met the high priestess only once, when we were both *far* too young for that sort of emotional connection. She has nothing to do with this, I promise you. It was another couple who served as my example and taught me a lasting lesson."

"So . . ."

"No more, Lorelei." Ailana's hands gripped the edges of her desk, new trails of ice spreading out from her clamped fingers to run along the wooden corners and legs. "I'll watch out for your consort, as promised. Just . . . don't ask any more of me right now."

"Very well." Frowning, Lorelei rose to her feet. As she stood, she took in, for the first time since her arrival, the sheer emptiness of the room about them . . . and the utter silence, apart from the whisper of falling snow as it brushed against the high, plain windows.

Even in the earliest years of Lorelei's reign, when she'd been surrounded by danger and betrayals in her own court, she'd had Katrin and then Ilse by her side to keep her loyal, loving company. Saskia, too, had been surrounded by a motley family of trolls and ogres and goblins ever since the years she'd spent in hiding as a child.

In all the years that she and Ailana had worked together, though, had Lorelei *ever* witnessed any signs of other caring relationships in the ice queen's life? Right now, she couldn't think of a single one. Ailana did have an excellent and efficient marshal of her realm, much like Lorelei's own reliable Balravian Chancelloress. But when it came to family, friends, or any other personal relationships . . .

Were she and Saskia all that Ailana truly had?

The last of Lorelei's irritation fell away as she regarded that tensely watchful figure who had worked so tirelessly across the years to protect and advance not only her own nation's interests but those of her allies, too. If the price of that fierce loyalty was an aggravating sisterly lecture about Lorelei's choices every now and then . . .

Well. As Lorelei had lost her own mother's protection long ago, perhaps she should finally stop complaining and consider the addition of a caring older sister to her life as the gift from the gods that it truly always had been.

Slipping across the tiled floor now, she darted in to embrace Ailana from behind, ignoring the other woman's twitch of surprise, and dropped a swift, soft kiss on her friend's cool cheek. She also added an affectionate scattering of rainbow sparkles simply to muss up Ailana's elegant perfection. "Thank you," Lorelei murmured, "for looking out for Gerard as well as for me. I hope you know we'll both do the same for you, forever."

"Ah." Ailana swallowed visibly, eyes wide with startlement. How long *had* it been since anyone had dared to hug the ice queen? "Well. That is excellent. Of course. Our alliance will remain strong."

"Always," Lorelei promised. "Our friendship, too. But now I'll leave you to concentrate and stop fretting at you."

Ailana twisted around in her seat to give Lorelei a warning look. "And you'll be listening out for messages, this time, instead of ignoring them?"

Lorelei rolled her eyes and tapped the pink silk reticule that hung from a silver belt around her waist now, holding an enchanted mirror-box for communication. "As if I'd ever risk your wrath that way again!"

Laughing, she drew a portal in the air and stepped into it.

Her riding gryphon, Bluebell, wouldn't mind her fretting in his company as long as it was accompanied by a good grooming. It had been far too many days since Lorelei had visited her luxuriant stables. She couldn't think of a better distraction from her worries now than to comb out Bluebell's gorgeous neck feathers and then take an exhilarating ride through the winter air on the gryphon's furry back...

But as she stepped into the portal, its path abruptly shifted before her, twisting and writhing out of her control.

It shouldn't have been possible. Surely *no one* carried enough power in a magical signature so close to Lorelei's own that they could seize and overwrite her private portals! And yet...

She landed in a sinuously shifting, silver space that felt immediately *wrong*—not part of the fae realm, but not within the mortal realm, either. The aetheric tunnels in between were meant to be passed through in a heartbeat whenever fae used them to travel by portal; now, the silver walls of aether trapped her in place, rippling, upending themselves, and circling around her with nauseating effect.

Swallowing down acid bile, Lorelei forced herself to turn in a circle of her own, to take full stock of the eerie limbo where she'd somehow landed. All she saw was silver upon shifting silver fog until...

Ohhh. I should have known.

Several feet behind her stood the only living creature who could have achieved this feat of magic; the only one with a signature so close to her own but even more powerful... and one who had every right to be furious with Lorelei now.

The eye-wateringly ancient and impossibly beautiful Morgana of Efaelen regarded her errant daughter with lips pursed and power fully gathered to vibrate through the air in warning. Ominous disapproval marked every line of the *true* fae queen's features.

This would not be a happy reunion.

28

The moment Gerard stepped into the private council chamber, he knew that everything he'd been told by the Queens of Villainy was true, and every nonhuman on the continent was in more danger than he could have imagined only a few days ago.

Otto, of course, was sprawled in the large, cushioned, and gilded chair that faced the iron doorway, while everyone else gathered around him in a circle of smaller, uncushioned chairs as supplicants in the windowless room. The council members who'd already assembled were a disheartening assortment of spineless young flatterers and sycophants more versed in fashion than in government. Clearly, none of them had possessed either the principles or the political power to protest the addition of one of the Empire's most despicable figures to their circle.

The Imperial high priestess, who sat at her brother's left hand, resplendent in her usual flowing robes and golden headdress, looked as serene as ever . . . but as every voice silenced in the shock of Gerard's sudden arrival, she caught his gaze and gave a miniscule tilt of her head, subtly directing his attention to that horrifyingly familiar new member of the council who sat directly to Otto's right in a place of honor:

The lean and hollow-eyed fanatic who had become the official leader of the Purification movement, Feodor Rapenthe.

Despite appearances, the man had been born into the highest ranks of the aristocracy forty-some years ago, and Gerard was confident that he still possessed an impressive family fortune. However, tonight, as had become his well-known custom, Rapenthe wore a ragged, floor-length, black tunic ornamented only by a plain length of rope that served as a belt around his gaunt frame, claiming the appearance of a poverty-stricken saint. His flowing black hair was matted and uncombed, his beard reached nearly to his waist, and Gerard marked a glint of cold cunning in the man's gaze before Rapenthe lowered his chin and gaze in a courtesy nod for the arrival of the Emperor's high general.

The Emperor himself wasn't nearly so restrained. "Good gods, man! What did they *do* to you?" As Otto leaned forward in his throne-like seat, self-gifted military medals of honor glinted from the chest and shoulders of his padded, gold silk jacket. Copper eyebrows rising high, he openly gaped as he looked Gerard up and down from stubble to stained uniform and muddy boots. "Thank Jovar you've escaped! Apparently, my Golden Beacon really *is* unbeatable, eh?"

Otto turned his head to gather the other council members' reactions. Most of them murmured in assent before he continued, "We'd all assumed you must be dead by now! Whatever godsawful tortures those creatures inflicted on you, never fear, they *will* be punished for it. That's what we've all come together to act on tonight!"

"Your Majesty." Gerard lowered his upper body in a deep bow of respect and used that instant to regather his scattered composure after the shock of Rapenthe's unexpected appearance. Matters were *far* more advanced than he'd expected, even after the queens' warnings—which meant that he had no time to lose. "I beg your pardon," he said calmly as he straightened, "but I believe that there has been a profound misunderstanding."

"A . . . what, now?" Frowning, Otto sat back in his seat and tapped out an irritable beat against one golden chair arm with his heavily beringed fingers.

"A misunderstanding," Gerard repeated. "As I made clear in the note I left for my men, I was called away on an urgent personal mission. No abduction was involved. I can assure you, there has been no torture."

. . . Or at least, none that he hadn't thoroughly enjoyed. Certainly, when Lorelei had used her powers to hold him down while she'd ravished him last night, he *had* experienced a few agonizing moments from not being allowed to touch her in return.

Still, he didn't allow his lips to curve at the memory. A heavy silence had fallen in response to his words, and he could feel lethal peril hanging like an axe above his head.

Even Otto's tapping fingers had stilled. Every member of the council but the high priestess froze, waiting with their gazes fixed on Otto's rigid expression.

Finally, the Emperor spoke, his voice strained. "No . . . abduction, you're claiming now?"

"No, Your Majesty. I did explain as much in my note."

"And . . . you weren't even tortured a *bit?*"

Gerard allowed a single eyebrow to rise. "Fortunately not."

"But—Jovar *damn* all of this for a pile of bullshit!" Otto's fist crashed down on the arm of his chair, making every other member of the council except his own sister flinch. "Fae magic was *clearly identified* in your tent and on that letter!"

"As you say, Your Majesty." Hands clasped behind his back,

Gerard held himself perfectly still in a relaxed but respectful pose, not permitting a single muscle in his shoulders to clench. He drew on every decade of practice he'd had in keeping his true emotions from his face as he regarded his emperor. "The mission was brought to my attention by a fae citizen who had been helpful to my work in the past and called upon me for urgent assistance in return."

At that news, Rapenthe visibly twitched, upper lip lifting in a sneer above discolored teeth. The other council members glanced back and forth, wide-eyed, but didn't speak. The high priestess continued to smile complacently, apparently unaware of the tension mounting in the air.

Otto's face mottled with color as he squeezed his hands around the arms of his chair. "You . . . abandoned your post . . . to help *a fucking fae?*"

"A fae citizen of your empire, yes," Gerard said. "It is my duty, as Imperial high general, to stand for all of your citizens in need, is it not?"

"It was your *duty*," Otto snarled, "to get your arse back to Fiora to report to me about the *total fiasco* at the Kitvarian border, where you threw aside everything I'd planned and tried to turn me into a laughingstock!"

"Your Majesty?" Gerard tilted his head, careful to keep his tone mildly curious. "I believe the newspapers have universally applauded us for our work in arresting the traitorous Chief Minister of Estarion, who dared to feed you such criminally false information about his archduke's wishes. Our army *heroically* freed Estarion from that corrupt, dangerous influence—and Archduke Felix himself informed me that our military support would not be needed after all, due to the newly peaceful relations between Estarion and Kitvaria. There should be no more danger at that border, which is now thankfully secure in your keeping."

"I didn't want it *secure*," Otto gritted, "I wanted it *erased*—and you damned well *knew* that was the real goal, no matter what balderdash we had to feed the newspapers."

"I beg your pardon?" Gerard's fingers tightened in their clasp behind his back, but he kept his gaze steady and unaffected, the very image of an honest and straightforward soldier without nuance. "I'm afraid I could only operate on the field under the orders that I had been given—and as you'd instructed me to lead our troops in *support* of the Estarian Archduke, I could hardly refuse to follow his command to withdraw our forces."

"Yes, well, Estarion's Archduke has clearly been bewitched out of his mind by that harridan in Kitvaria!"

Estarion's Archduke was undeniably head-over-heels in *love* with that so-called harridan . . . but Gerard only said, "I assure you, Your Majesty, that no such magical crime has been committed. The captain of the elite corps of Gilded Wizards that traveled with my own soldiers confirmed that Archduke Felix is under no spell."

The wizard had also revealed something far more startling about that same archduke's abilities—but Gerard would not volunteer such a closely guarded secret of his own accord, and he'd commanded the wizard's silence on the matter from then on.

Before Otto could argue any further, Gerard turned his gaze to survey the rest of the council chamber. "I would happily answer any further questions from Your Majesty or my fellow council members, but . . ." His gaze landed, pointedly, on Feodor Rapenthe. "I see a most untrustworthy visitor has intruded upon this meeting. As your loyal high general, I must strongly advise that we avoid uttering any more classified information in his presence."

Shocked breaths hissed in response from council members around and behind him, but Gerard turned his expectant gaze to the Emperor without backing down. This was a battle that could only be won by immediate and unqualified resistance—and while the rest of the council might prioritize their positions over their principles, Gerard had sworn an oath to defend the Empire and *all* its citizens. He would not betray it now.

In the corner of his vision, he saw Rapenthe close his eyes and begin to sway in a slow, sinuous, back and forth motion that had surely been designed to capture the attention of an audience, but Gerard held his emperor's gaze and refused to allow the charlatan's theatrics to distract either of them.

Otto's eyes narrowed dangerously. "General de Moireul, you are apparently under a misapprehension. *I* invited Messer Rapenthe tonight myself, specifically to address the dangers presented to our empire in the light of your recent abduction."

"In which case, he may rest easy in the knowledge that he is no longer required," said Gerard evenly, "as I've clarified that there was no abduction after all ... and therefore his ignorant, hysterical, and bigoted views *won't* require any distasteful hearings in the Empire's highest chamber."

Urgent whispering broke out from the councilors behind him, but it was swiftly overwhelmed by a low, throbbing drone that emerged from deep within Rapenthe's throat, beginning quietly but rising to an ominous, wordless vocalization so loud and so hoarse that it clamored and echoed through the small room like polyphonic hammers against every pair of ears. Chairs scraped against the ground as council members retreated from the cacophony. Even the Emperor cringed.

Gerard stiffened his muscles, refusing to flinch or to shift back as the man rose to his feet. Ragged, black cloth sleeves fell to Rapenthe's bony elbows as his arms curved in a melodramatic arc of challenge and ended, in a sudden, pulsating silence, with two long, knobbly forefingers pointed in accusation at Gerard himself.

"Your Majesty!" Rapenthe's voice was a harsh rasp of warning as his heavy lids finally slid open to reveal eyes fully rolled back in their sockets with sickening effect. Only the whites of his eyes showed as he intoned, "The gods have spoken to me and revealed all. This man who stands before us all has been tainted by fae magic! He is no longer the loyal servant you knew but only *their* false puppet, sent here tonight to deceive and defeat you."

Gasps sounded. Otto's eyebrows shot upwards. The high priestess's peaceful smile did not falter, but her copper eyelashes lowered to veil her hazel gaze.

Gerard didn't even try to hold back his snort of contempt. "That is easily disprovable rubbish. Call in any Gilded Wizard, and they will confirm to the council that I am under no magical influence whatsoever, regardless of this performer's claims."

"The gods have *spoken!*" growled Rapenthe.

"This is a *waste of our time*." Gerard spoke even louder, allowing impatience to lash through his voice like a whip. "If the gods wished to convey a true message to the Emperor, we all know They would choose Their own holy high priestess, sitting just beside him, to deliver it."

Heads swiveled around the room, looking to the Imperial high priestess for a response to that challenge. She offered no answer to any of them but an unaltered smile, her downturned gaze calmly fixed on the hands that she had crossed in her lap.

"The gods move in mysterious ways," Otto muttered, with a quick, surreptitious glance of his own at his younger sister. "Clearly, we all have much to discuss and consider. For now, though . . ." His gaze flicked warily between the two standing figures of Gerard and Rapenthe. "I'll call tonight's meeting to a close. We'll all convene again tomorrow, no doubt."

"Your Majesty." Gerard bowed in assent, but he couldn't ignore the itch of warning in the back of his head as he witnessed a long, wordless look pass between Otto and the Purifier . . . and then a silent exchange of nods.

What would *Lorelei*, who so hated the Emperor, expect to happen next if she were here?

It was Gerard's fervent hope that Otto did not actually share Rapenthe's malevolent beliefs, much less trust the man's ludicrously self-serving claims of an overarching holy mission unknown to any actual priests of the gods. *If* Otto saw Rapenthe as no more than a useful tool, then with time and patience, he could eventually be convinced to drop the whole hateful political strategy, as Gerard had originally planned.

But if Otto nourished private intentions of continuing tonight's meeting with Rapenthe *without* any powerful dissenting voices there to observe and object ... then, it suddenly occurred to Gerard, there might not actually *be* as much time left as he'd imagined.

Those royal guards outside had been uncharacteristically evasive in their answers to his questions. His own soldiers were still at least a full day's march away from the capital.

He had handed over his sword.

Perhaps it made him a traitor after all to imagine that his ruler would ever partake in any of the dark, unethical scenarios whirling now in the back of Gerard's mind—but only a fool would carelessly disregard any suggestions from the cool-headed Queen of Nornne. So, as he straightened from his bow, he raised his voice to halt all the other councilors who were rising from their seats. "If I may have a moment ..."

Otto's brows lowered, but he waved his assent, and the room went obediently still.

If Lorelei was right—and he'd learned at last to respect her instincts—this might be Gerard's final chance to make a stand. So he chose his words with care, even as he began to mentally plot the safest and swiftest path back to his villa after this meeting. "My loyalty to our empire is steadfast." Regardless of what his parents had done, he had fought to prove himself for years, and he saw grudging acknowledgement of that truth in every face turned towards him now. "My record speaks for itself, as do the honors Your Majesty has granted me. When you first appointed me to this role, I swore to Jovar Himself, before all the world, that I would follow my vow as your high general to serve and stand in all your citizens' defense."

Otto's face tightened into a suspicious frown. "And what exactly is all that supposed to preface, *General* de Moireul?"

"It means," Gerard said gravely, "that I will not allow a simple misunderstanding around my own personal movements to be used as an excuse for any acts of violence or whipping up of hatred against innocents now. Nor will I ever, under *any* circumstances, agree to lead troops against our own citizens, humans or nonhumans alike. Furthermore..."

He turned his gaze to look with chill disdain upon Rapenthe's ominous glower. "I will *never* allow any of my soldiers to engage in hateful acts of so-called 'Purification,' even outside our own borders. I certainly hope that everyone here can agree"—he turned his head in a slow, watchful sweep of the room and saw gazes drop guiltily away from him on all sides—"that such hypothetical events would be despicable and unjustifiable under any circumstances. However..."

Finally turning back to Otto, he met his emperor's rage-filled gaze and invested his own expression with all the grim, unyielding determination that he felt... the same determination that, as they all knew, had won seemingly impossible battles again and again over the years. "If Your Majesty truly believes that this statement of intent disqualifies me from my position in your service, then I will regretfully but obediently tender my resignation tonight. Then, to avoid any possible confusion, I will make it clear to every newspaper in the Empire *exactly* why I did so."

His final words fell like stones into a deep, dark well from which there would be no returning. No diplomatic rephrasings from now on could ever return him to the Emperor's favor... and Otto had always had a dangerous thirst for revenge.

Thank Jovar Lorelei had insisted upon that mirror-box device for magical communication being planted in Gerard's Fioran villa. With luck, he wouldn't need to call for an urgent portal to safety... but from the moment he reached his own home tonight, he would make certain to have it in hands' reach at all times, just in case.

...If he made it that far. For a single heartbeat, Gerard wondered whether Otto might actually lose control and physically lunge at him in front of everyone.

But then, even more unnervingly, the fury abruptly vanished from the Emperor's face, replaced by a broad, indulgent smile.

"Ah, General. You have had a difficult week of it, haven't you? There's no need to rant at any of us about absurdities like *resignation* after all your famous honors and achievements. Everyone here knows how hard you've worked for so long, and how weary you must be by now! In fact . . ."

Rising to his feet, Otto reached up to clap Gerard companionably on one shoulder, his eyes glinting with a nearly manic cheer. "Instead of dragging yourself all the way back to your own humble villa tonight, why don't you bunk down in some real luxury, for once? Let's put you up in one of the suites reserved for royal guests! You've certainly earned that treatment by now, haven't you?"

"Ah . . ." *Jovar's hells!* Gerard's mind raced as he fought to keep his tone uninflected. "I thank you for your generosity, Your Majesty, but there is no need for such an honor. I find the short walk to my home quite invigorating, so . . ."

Otto's fingers curved around Gerard's arm and squeezed tightly to cut him off. "Oh, no, I *insist*." Bared teeth showed in the Emperor's ferocious smile. "I won't hear any more protestations. After all, a man with *your* famous record of achievements deserves all the honors and protection the Empire can devise. In fact, I believe I'll even station a few of my own men outside your room tonight to guard your sleep and make certain that no more 'misunderstandings' can occur!"

Forgive me, Lorelei. I should have believed you sooner.

Gerard looked into the face of the man he had loyally served for years and saw the promise of his own demise.

How had he ever convinced himself that he could talk this petty, vengeful man into pardoning the former high priest? There certainly wouldn't be any such mercy for himself.

For the first time in years, his grandmother's words rang once more in his ears—the words she'd spoken to him in judgement as they'd witnessed his own parents' execution: *"This is the price of weakness and treason."*

She wouldn't be surprised by this moment, would she?

Numbness slipped between Gerard's ribs like a knife, spreading a heavy, distancing chill through his chest. As if from very far away, he took in the facts of the situation and ran them through his strategic brain.

Queen Ailana's watchful shard of ice in the corridor outside must have melted by this point. She would not see what happened next or know to alert Lorelei and mount a magical rescue. Any attempt to flee on his own would be useless. Every Imperial palace was full of guards. Resistance would only give Otto the perfect excuse to order him cut down before Gerard could even attempt to spread the news of the truth behind his arrest and whatever "crimes" they might claim he had committed.

Cool logic mingled with the leaden inevitability of fate.

Every honor he'd won, every challenge he'd mastered since he was only eight years old—they'd all been fought to stave off this outcome. *His parents' ending.* Had he ever truly believed he could escape it in his turn?

Despair felt as heavy and inescapable as the weight of memory. Still, he followed the lessons he had been taught, and he kept his face as impenetrable as stone.

"Your Majesty." He bowed obediently under the weight of every watching eye. Then he turned to walk with calm, unhurried steps out of the room and down the corridor towards his latest prison chamber.

This time, there would be no escape.

29

For years, Lorelei had both anticipated and dreaded each new, rare, and inevitably public encounter with her immortal mother. This, though, had to be the worst possible timing to be trapped in their first private conversation in over two decades.

"Mother." She nodded politely but did not curtsey—because in this liminal realm outside either of their worlds, they were neither of them ruler, and she knew better than to relinquish her authority. Still, around her mother, it was always a struggle to keep her voice light and unaffected. "It is, of course, a pleasure to see you, but I'm afraid that at the moment, I do have a rather urgent—"

"What could possibly be more urgent than explaining your *abandonment?*" Morgana demanded.

Lorelei's mouth fell open for a long, stunned moment—brought about not only by the accusation itself but by the shockingly emotional tone of her own mother's voice, after decades of courteous but distant communications.

When she finally regathered her composure, she asked with unhidden incredulity, "*My* abandonment?"

"*I* just returned from an entirely fruitless and disheartening set of meetings with the encroaching court of Faennor," Morgana snapped, "only to discover my own court in turmoil, because, apparently, *my daughter* had arrived without any prior warning, insisted upon inserting both herself and an unknown human partner into the Tournament of Leaves, disrupted the proceedings with her personal lovers' quarrels, and then publicly chose to *break her own vow* and dishonor one of our most ancient rituals, expelling herself from my realm before the trials were over—without ever stopping to share a *single word* of explanation with her own mother!"

There was so much wrong in that summation that Lorelei couldn't even begin to summon a sensible or diplomatic response. Instead, the words that somehow escaped her lips were, "Why would I expect you to *care?*"

Oh, goddess, what a mistake! Humiliation burned beneath Lorelei's skin. She gritted her teeth and forced back into place the lid of the mental box where she'd *thought* she had safely buried all of her most embarrassingly childish emotions about her mother years ago.

Queens do not have the freedom to allow their own feelings free rein. That had been one of her earliest and most important lessons. Perhaps it was the turmoil of her current fears for Gerard—in combination with his cracking of all the old defenses around her heart—that had loosened her grip on those older, more inappropriate emotions, too. Regardless, she drew a deep, calming breath through her nose and began once more in a placating tone. "That is . . ."

"You didn't expect me to *care?*" Morgana sounded every bit as incredulous as Lorelei had a moment before. It was the first time that Lorelei could ever remember seeing her mother look genuinely baffled. "You are my only child."

Apparently, this was the day for *all* of Lorelei's most dangerous and tumultuous emotions to be uncovered, dragged out in public, and riffled through like playing cards for other people's entertainment. Setting her teeth together, she said coolly, "We both know you haven't thought of me in that way for decades, but that is of no matter now. In the meantime . . ."

"What nonsense are you speaking?" Morgana stared at her, green power curling and twisting around her in unhidden consternation. "Has someone been poisoning you against me? Feeding lies into your ears? Your father, before he died—no, wait. Is it that *human* lover you've taken up with?" Her upper lip curled in scorn.

Lorelei rolled her eyes. "I never trusted a word my father spoke to me, and Gerard has nothing to do with this." Nothing except the revelation that *some* exceptional people could, after all, be trusted with the keys to her heart . . .

But that list did not include the beautiful, powerful fae woman who stood before her now, holding her trapped in the shifting silver aether. No urgent messages could reach Lorelei here, no matter how desperately Gerard might need her help . . . and it was *that* reminder that helped her refocus on what mattered now: escape. "You're the one who's been fed lies," she said briskly. "I *did* send you a letter before I arrived, regardless of what Lord Oberon may have intimated. Ask enough of your courtiers, and you'll find someone who saw him publicly wave it in my face before the tournament began."

Morgana's deep-green eyes narrowed, and the lighter green vines that held her long plaits of hair in place lengthened to creep around her like decorative armor. "You truly believe that he would intercept my letters?"

"I *saw* it," Lorelei said firmly. "Just as I saw *and* heard Oberon whisper a true-name command into my partner's ear the moment before our final trial began, ordering Gerard to murder me."

In an instant, Morgana's eyes shifted from forest green to venomous black. "He did *what?*" Thunder echoed in her voice.

"That was why I had to leave," Lorelei said. "It was the only way to save us both."

"The *only* . . . ?" Morgana shook her head violently, and leaves scattered from her autumn-brown hair with the force of her agitation. "Are you trying to convince me that you were at risk of true death from a *human?* When you stood in Efaelen, with all of your powers and the land itself at your call?"

Lorelei drew a deep, steadying breath as she looked into her mother's eyes and forced herself to speak without emotion. "I couldn't harm him," she said. "I never will, and I won't allow anyone else to touch him, either. He is my chosen consort."

"*Ah*—!" With a choked-off sound of frustration, Morgana turned a quick circle in place, her gold-and-orange gown swirling about her legs. If they had stood on solid ground, Lorelei had no doubt that thorns would be bursting out of the grass in response, loyally seeking to defend her mother from whatever enemy was causing her such distress.

It had been a long time since Lorelei had felt that she was *pleasing* her mother . . . but the force of that open disappointment now burned against her with unexpected force.

Finally, Morgana stopped her pacing. "Did it never occur to you to call upon me for help?" she asked tightly.

"I beg your pardon?" A startled laugh fell from Lorelei's throat. "You'd left the court in *Oberon's keeping.* Despite everything he'd done—"

"I left it in my consort's keeping," Morgana snapped. "Unfortunately, Reynard was taken unexpectedly ill after I'd already departed on my diplomatic mission. It was decided by the advisors I'd left behind that his son would be the most natural replacement. As I hadn't the time or energy to return and sort matters out myself . . ."

"You trusted *him* to take your place? Really?" Lorelei couldn't help the raw hurt that crept into her voice.

Morgana frowned. "He paid the price for his only true offense against me with his time of exile. When he returned, Reynard assured me that his remorse was sincere. I know he offended you, too, some time back, with an ill-judged attempt at romance, but you sorted that out yourself, didn't you? Whatever you did made him the butt of every jest at court for ages afterwards. Are you truly so petty as to still hold a grudge? By now, you must be accustomed to dealing with courtiers whose company you don't happen to enjoy. As queen..."

"As *queen*," Lorelei gritted through her teeth, "I would never allow a man who attempted to overpower my daughter's will with a *love potion* to set foot in my court ever again—much less allow him to wear my own crown in my absence."

There was a long, pulsating silence. The silver walls and floor shifted sickeningly around them.

"A love potion?" Morgana said at last, her voice without expression.

"Slipped into my glass of wine," said Lorelei with icy calm. "He had it all planned out. You see, I had already refused all of his more politely expressed offers."

"And you felt no need to tell me what he'd done?"

Lorelei looked at the woman who'd been no more than a distant idol to her for decades . . . and the long sigh she let out combined sorrow and relief. Perhaps this conversation was necessary after all. It was certainly long overdue. "You haven't let me close enough to speak of such matters since I was a child. You surrounded us with witnesses every time to keep me at a distance."

I couldn't bear to risk losing even that remaining place in your court. She didn't speak the words, but that obvious truth resonated between them.

Morgana's cheeks hollowed as her eyes widened. "You believed I would choose him over you?"

"I begged you to choose me once before," Lorelei said quietly. "But even when I was finally allowed to come back and visit..."

It had been as if the warm and loving mother she remembered had disappeared, replaced by a cool and elegant moving statue who looked as if from a vast, impassive distance at the child she'd once rocked in her arms.

Morgana swallowed visibly, her long throat flexing. More leaves fell from her hair like tears, twirling slowly through the air. "Giving you up as I did... sending you to fulfil Sylvana's promise..."

"I know." Lorelei stiffened her shoulders and forced her voice not to crack. "You didn't see it as a choice. You followed your duty as a queen for the sake of your people, under the direction of a goddess."

"... And it nearly destroyed me. Did you not understand that?" Her mother's voice carried echoes of falling rain. "I didn't eat for months after you left. My handmaidens feared I might simply fade into the trees. I couldn't bear to taste any food. Any pleasure. Any..."

She stopped, looking suddenly achingly fragile and nothing like the indomitable figure Lorelei had known all her life. "It took me years to fully come back to myself. And when I did..." She moistened her lips. "When I did, the scar ran so deep, I didn't dare reopen it. The land had mourned with me in my grief and fallen into endless cold rain, misery, and hardship. The court erupted into chaos and turned bloody knives upon itself in answer. It took all I had, once I finally recovered, to wrest Efaelen into order and bring it back to health. That was why I couldn't risk allowing you too close again on any of those rare, precious visits when I was able to see you. Human lives are so unbearably short." Tears glittered in Morgana's ancient eyes. "The first time I lost you, I almost shattered everything I had sworn to protect. I couldn't allow myself to risk that again."

Lorelei's stomach lurched. It was unbearable—unjust!—to navigate this terrible conversation here, of all places, with no solid ground to stand on and no allies or lover nearby to support her.

Conflicting emotions rocked through her like warring armies, and she fought to keep her balance in the morass of shifting silver.

Her mother *had* loved her and truly grieved her loss. Her mother still loved her, apparently. And yet . . .

Lorelei forced a wry smile instead of a sob. "So you chose the needs of your court over the needs of your daughter not once but *twice*, after all. I see."

Morgana's mouth dropped open. "I was in *pain*! If you understood how much I'd suffered—how much any mother would suffer—"

"Do you think I didn't?" Lorelei's laugh was shrill. "I was a *child* when you sent me into a court where I was universally loathed—and then, when I finally saw you again, you didn't even offer me comfort or reassurance. Instead, you made it perfectly clear to me and everyone else that I'd lost not only my first home but also the only parent who had ever loved me."

Her mother rocked back as if she'd been physically struck. "You still don't understand," she whispered. "I had to—as queens, *we both* have to make impossible decisions all the time. You must have learned that for yourself by now! Do you imagine I *wanted* to lose the only child I've ever been lucky enough to birth? Sylvana *showed* me: If I were selfish enough to keep you with me, every fae in the mortal realm would have paid the price in blood! Even here in Efaelen, we would have suffered and faded, in the end, from the loss of that vital connection with the mortal realm. Would *you* have chosen any differently, as an adult?"

Lorelei breathed deeply, taking the time to think through her words before she spoke. She wasn't a child anymore to take instructions—or to vent her tumultuous emotions without care. "As queens, we do have to make painful, impossible choices," she finally agreed. "*That* is why I made the choice I did today and broke my vow. Believe me, it wasn't what I wanted, either."

"No?" Morgana's voice trembled like a leaf in cold wind.

"No." Lorelei swallowed hard. "If I'd seen any other way to save us both... but I didn't. So I would make that same choice again without regret."

Her mother's eyebrows arched in reproach. "You know I can't set foot in the mortal realm."

"Nor can I step into the fae realm from now on." Lorelei didn't lower her gaze. She refused to pretend to any shame over her actions. "That's why you chose this space for our meeting."

Morgana waved off her words impatiently. "This once, yes. But—"

"It won't disappear, will it?" There was a part—a large part—of Lorelei that wanted to step back from this tentative brink and shield herself in self-defensive distance before she could be hurt again.

But that was exactly what her mother had done to her all those years ago... and Lorelei had no desire to repeat the example.

She wasn't ready to lower all of her shields. Not yet; perhaps not ever. The lessons she'd learned across her life were real. But she had recently realized that not all of her shields were necessary... and she had loved her mother enough as a child to risk a single step forward now—if Morgana did the same.

"We can meet again like this," Lorelei said. "We can even try to do it on a regular basis, to come to know each other once again... but only if you finally let down your guard. If you want me in your life, then *treat* me as someone you care about. Respect me and my choices—*and* ensure that Oberon's attempt to murder me and my consort receives the punishment it truly deserves."

Lifting her chin, she looked at Morgana with all the haughtiness of the powerful queen her mother—for better or for worse—had made her, not the child who had simply yearned for her parents' love. "I have my own eyes in your court, as you do in mine. I *will* find out if you decide once again to choose the comfort of others over my and my consort's safety."

Ire flared in Morgana's eyes. The immortal Queen of Efaelen was not often spoken to in such a manner... but she held her tongue for a long moment. Finally, she let out a carefully controlled breath, like a gently unfurling bud. "Oberon has been a challenge to my patience since I first met him. I've granted him as much leniency as I could for Reynard's sake ... but until now, I never understood how far he was willing to go. He will *not* overcome this offense. I swear it."

Lorelei lifted a single brow, mantling her own power around her. "And if Reynard protests again? Weeps and swears to Oberon's true remorse?"

The small, wry smile that twisted Morgana's lips told a bitter story in itself. "Unlike you, apparently, I chose a consort who would never claim too much territory in my heart. It seemed the safest choice."

... *After your father*, the sentence finished silently between them.

Lorelei lowered her head in a slow nod of understanding.

They had both reacted in their own ways to her father's betrayal, hadn't they? She might never forgive all of her mother's choices, but for the first time in decades, she could glimpse the possibility of a true relationship between them as adults, based not in either of their own queendoms but in this permeable, shifting middle space.

"Very well," she said. "You know how to reach me with a message."

Morgana inclined her own head gravely. "I won't capture you without warning again."

Twenty years ago, Lorelei would have flown into her mother's arms for a final tight embrace before they parted. Today, she only said, "Until next time," as she felt the silver walls of aether turn pliant to her will at last.

As she landed in her own warm stables, Bluebell looked up at her with a pleased, welcoming chirp, his golden fur shadowed in the darkness and his massive beak still bloody from his latest meal. Stepping towards the gryphon, she felt a lightness in her chest that she hadn't known in years.

Perhaps she hadn't lost quite all of her first home or family.

Even as she had that thought, though, she realized that the mirror-box in its silk reticule, still hanging from her belt, was vibrating—and with such intense agitation, she could only imagine it must have been trying to alert her the whole time she'd been trapped and unreachable in the aether.

With a muffled groan, she snatched it out of the reticule and flipped the box open, pressing her side against Bluebell's big, leonine form for strength. Even his familiar warmth and the affectionate nuzzle of his feathered head against her shoulder couldn't comfort her as she took in Ailana's grim expression in the mirror.

"Lorelei! *Finally*," Ailana breathed. "Come quickly. We may already be too late to save him."

30

There was, of course, no lock inside the door of the luxurious bedroom to which Gerard had been led. From the richly gilded mirror on its nightstand to the elaborate designs etched on the low-burning gas lamp and the silk hangings on its large four-poster bed, it had clearly been designed for royal guests—and *if* Gerard had somehow lost all of his wits, he might have believed Otto's words and imagined this stay to be an actual honor.

However, he didn't miss the lack of any windows—or the click of a heavy iron bolt being fastened into place on the *other* side of the door.

"This is the price of weakness and treason..."

Memories flashed across his vision, still brutally vivid after all these years. The executioner lifting his axe high, again and again, while the voracious roar of the crowd filled Gerard's ears to bursting... and his own body sat paralyzed with fear and horror beside his ferociously smiling grandmother.

Her fingers had gripped his closest arm like bejeweled claws.

"*This is the price...*"

He'd been running from those memories for years, with his meticulously polished reputation and his obdurate refusal ever to look beyond the blinders of his duty.

The iron bolt closing him in now was a mere formality... which, frankly, seemed unnecessary, with two armed guards already stationed outside to prevent escape and his sword in their keeping.

Perhaps he should have been searching the room now, constructing radical new weapons by hand and strategizing brilliant plans for escape despite all the odds. That was surely what the rest of the world would expect from the famous Golden Beacon.

But Gerard had constructed and maintained that reputation as a shield against exactly this moment... and now that it had come to pass anyway, he felt as numb and frozen as if he were still trapped in that seat beside his grandmother, a silent witness to brutality that could never be altered, only endured.

Truthfully, if he had ever been set against his two Imperial guards on any battlefield, he was confident that he would win the fight. However, the idea of bursting through his door now to murder a pair of young men for doing their duty made acid twist and spiral deep inside his gut.

He could have so easily been in the place of either of those boys, ordered to guard an enemy of the state and believing that he was doing the right thing. In fact, he *would* have been trapped in that situation, still fighting with all his heart and mind for an emperor devoid of conscience, if Lorelei hadn't been clever and reckless enough to steal Gerard from his bed and rip the comforting illusions from his eyes. The amount of damage that would have been on his conscience, then...!

No. He would defend himself if attacked—and he wouldn't trust any food or drink sent in to tempt him—but he *would not* voluntarily cut down innocents in an escape attempt doomed to failure. There were too many guards in this palace for him to take them all on. More than that, he'd known the risks he was taking when he stood up to Otto tonight. He wouldn't be callous enough to make others pay the price for his own choices.

"*This is the price* . . ."

Taking a deep breath, Gerard strode forward to study the room before him. With luck, he would have several days left before a show trial and execution could be organized. He would stay alert and ready. If any true opportunity for escape showed itself, he would seize it. But if this proved to be his last night—if Otto chose *not* to risk handing him the kind of public platform a trial would provide—then he would make damned certain he used the time he had left wisely.

There were letters to write and strategies to formulate. If he could find any means to spread the news of Otto's plans to at least a few of the right ears, he would not consider his final hours wasted.

If nothing else, he could hide letters around the room in hopes that one of Queen Ailana's spies might uncover them.

. . . In which case, he could write a final letter to Lorelei, too.

Lorelei. Pain burned through Gerard's chest, overwhelming the numbness that had filled him until now. For an agonizingly long moment, he couldn't even breathe. The thought of never again hearing her mischievous, bubbling laugh . . . never seeing that triumphant glint light her eyes whenever she bested him in a challenge—or that shocking, world-upending tenderness she'd shown him earlier today . . .

What would she think when she learned what had happened here tonight? Would she remember him only as the latest man to ignore all of his promises and abandon her without a thought?

Or . . .

Wait. Cold certainty sliced through his pain as he realized the true outcome that would result if he was executed tonight.

Lorelei, heartbroken and furious, would *absolutely* fling herself into wreaking bloody and brutal vengeance upon Otto for Gerard's sake, regardless of the danger—and with a whole empire ranged against her...

Oh, gods, no.

Sudden clarity splashed across him, dissipating the last of the numbness that had gripped him ever since Otto's decision.

He might be physically trapped in this room now, but he didn't have to remain emotionally trapped in that seat beside his grandmother anymore. He was an adult ready to forge his own fate now, not a child ruled by fear—and after fighting back-to-back over the past few days, there was no doubt in his mind that Lorelei would come for him the moment she worked out where he was.

Nothing mattered more to him than making certain that whatever happened here tonight, Lorelei would survive its fallout. She was the price that he would never pay, no matter how many enemies were ranked against him.

All those diplomatic letters and political strategies would have to wait. First, Gerard needed to fortify the bedroom door to hold off his final battle as long as possible...

And make it as safe as he could for his reckless partner to save him.

In all her life, Lorelei had never had to fight so hard not to give in to her feelings. Even in the midst of killing rage and terror, though, her instincts *all* agreed that she couldn't conquer the entire Imperial winter palace, filled with armed guards and Gilded Wizards, by herself in time to save her consort's life. For Gerard's sake, she needed a real strategy, preparation, and reinforcements.

So she arrived in Ailana's castle a tooth-grindingly long ten minutes after their first conversation, riding through her portal on Bluebell's back with her hair carefully pinned up out of the way, an enchanted dagger hanging lightly by her side, and her gryphon protected in shining battle armor.

She almost wept when she saw Saskia already there, too.

Lorelei had spent the last several days hiding from her allies for fear of their judgements, and yet here they both stood now in the great hall of Ailana's icy castle, ready to fight for her regardless. Ailana's riding gryphon, Bluebell's hatch-mate Frost, stood alert beside his armored queen, beak held high and one set of big claws already scraping at the flagstones in anticipation. Saskia had no companion of her own and carried no visible weapons, but on the belt around her velvet gown were hung at least a dozen sacks and bottles that glowed with power to Lorelei's deeper senses. They would be full of magical compounds, the witch queen's own most lethal preparations for any battle.

Lorelei had spent decades learning that real trust was too dangerous an emotion to allow. Now, she had to blink away tears of overflowing relief and gratitude before she could give her loyal, trustworthy allies an appropriately dazzling smile. "Darlings! Are we ready to give Otto's nose a good tweaking?"

"We can try," Saskia said grimly. "We *will* try. But we've run into a problem."

Lorelei's forced smile vanished like the autumn she had left behind in Efaelen. "What *problem?*"

"General de Moireul isn't being held in any of the Emperor's standard cells," Ailana said with crisp certainty. "It's not surprising that he wasn't taken to an ordinary prison, but when I heard he hadn't left the winter palace with the others, I'd expected that he'd be kept in one of the rooms used for political prisoners in the outer west wing, where I have multiple informants. Unfortunately, I've now received confirmation that he isn't there—but they don't know where else in the palace he could be. There's only one maid in my pay who works in the wing where tonight's meeting was held, and I haven't been able to reach her at all."

Lorelei's stomach sank. "So, he could be almost anywhere." Otto's winter palace, rebuilt from the first Serafin Empire's ruins, was a massive, labyrinthine complex that stretched across the Fioran hills. Even with all three queens working together, it would take hours to search.

"I tried to find him using the same spell that worked to find you," Saskia said, "but there's no sense of him anywhere in Fiora. Of course, they *might* have locked him in somewhere with iron to prevent us finding him with magic, but it's also possible that—"

"No!" Lorelei hissed. "He has *not* been killed yet."

Ailana arched a single eyebrow. "Do you know that for a fact? Or do you only hope it to be true?"

Setting her teeth together, Lorelei met the ice queen's gaze full-on. "I *know*," she gritted.

She would *never* give up on her partner.

Ailana's eyes narrowed in open skepticism . . .

. . . and Lorelei realized that her whole body was shaking in long, shivering waves of tension. *Gods damn it.* She was usually so good at putting on convincing shows of confidence! She'd spent decades practicing and perfecting those skills . . .

But the last week had ripped away too many of her shields. Desperately, she closed her eyes and forced herself to slow her racing heartbeat. *Sylvana, help me, I pray to You with all my heart. Help me save him, I beg You!*

It was useless. She knew that much even as she sent up her plea to the goddess she'd worshipped all her life. As Sylvana's chosen avatar, her purpose in the world was to prioritize the divine mission she'd been set, not to risk everything to save her own lover.

She felt no hint of any divine response to her prayer. Still, when she reopened her eyes to face her two allies again a minute later, at least her body and mind were safely back under her control.

Her shields hadn't been miraculously rebuilt, but she'd found a more important core of certainty at her center.

"Darling friends," she said softly, "I won't lie to you. I *believe* that he's alive, but I cannot swear to it. Still, if he is, and if I don't even try to save him . . ." She shook her head with slow inevitability. "I *have* to try everything I can, but I'm not so reckless that I don't see the risks. I won't force you two to walk into danger with me. I'll release you from our vows of alliance if you'd prefer."

"Well, of course we're not going to just leave him there." Saskia's brows lowered together into a scowl. "Do you think I'd abandon Felix in that situation?"

Lorelei let out a hiccupping laugh of startlement. "Darling, I'm surprised you even managed to leave him safe at home tonight. Was he truly happy to let you walk into danger without him?"

"Ah . . ." The witch queen looked abruptly shifty, her dark eyes lowering and pale skin flushing. "I . . . may not have mentioned quite how much danger we'd be in, or where we were going tonight."

"Saskia!" Ailana let out a heartfelt groan as she reached to massage her forehead with elegant brown fingers. "Who do you think he'll blame if you do get hurt?"

"Felix would never blame either of you," Saskia said defensively. "He *knows* me." She lifted her chin mulishly. "Anyway, I have a whole argument prepared to explain why his coming would only have put me in more danger. He'd have been a potential hostage for the Emperor to take against us."

"Good luck convincing him of that," Lorelei said dryly. She'd never seen a man more sweetly besotted with his partner—nor more shockingly capable of convincing stubborn Saskia to see reason. "I foresee a *long* night ahead of you once he finds out what you've done."

Saskia shrugged, clearly confident in her adoring partner. "He likes General de Moireul. He'll understand."

"Hmm," Lorelei said and turned to their other ally.

Ailana was still frowning. "I meant what I said to you before," she told Lorelei, "but the situation has undeniably changed since then. If we don't know exactly where we're going, we can't hope to slip in and out without being identified. We have to be prepared for this act, tonight, to be taken as an open declaration of war upon the Serafin Empire from all three of our nations."

Lorelei's sigh was heavy, but it held no regret. "We've known for years that war was coming. It's why we formed our alliance in the first place—and we couldn't have a better general on our side once we do rescue Gerard."

Saskia nodded in grim assent.

The political direction of the continent as a whole had been aiming towards this moment ever since Otto II took the Imperial throne. It had only ever been a question of *when*, not *whether*, it would finally happen.

Ailana said tightly, "I do take your point. But we can't just leap into the center of that enormous palace and expect to find him without a plan. We need to—ah, wait a moment." One of the long, divided skirts of Ailana's cool blue riding habit had suddenly begun to vibrate, no doubt carrying a message from one of her countless spies.

Eyebrows rising, the Queen of Nornne reached into a hidden pocket and pulled out a miniature mirror-box. "I beg your pardons." She turned away from the other two queens to open the lid . . . and then, for the first time since Lorelei had met her, she let out an audible gasp of astonishment.

Ailana's whole body went as still as an ice sculpture as she stared into the mirror.

Lorelei traded a swift, astonished glance with Saskia . . . and then both queens abandoned all semblance of courtesy to hurry after their ally and peer together over Ailana's slim shoulders.

Gazing confidently into that mirror was a smiling face that Lorelei recognized both from younger portraits and from recent newspaper stories. Light freckles covered the woman's strong nose and generous cheekbones, while a tall, gold headdress atop her deep-red hair announced the divine authority of the new, famously silent high priestess of the Serafin Empire...

...Previously known to the world as the Imperial Princess Clothilde.

A sudden breath of fresh spring air brushed past Lorelei's cheek in an unseasonal caress, and she tipped back her head with a prayer of gratitude, eyes stinging and warmth filling her chest. Neither of her allies had abandoned her—and neither had her own goddess, after all.

"Oh, good, Ailana, you *are* there," the high priestess said through the mirror, sounding as comfortable and relaxed as if she made this sort of illicit magical call every day. "Forgive the intrusion, but sending a message through more regular channels would have taken too long, and I thought you'd want to know as soon as possible: General de Moireul has been sentenced by my brother to a private execution, tonight. I can tell you exactly where he's being held, but you and your friends will have to hurry if you hope to save him... and even if you don't succeed, you will owe me an *impressive* favor afterwards."

31

The bedframe presented a challenge.

Gerard had already managed to shove the heavy chest of drawers in front of the bedroom door, along with the wooden nightstand. However, the massive four-poster bed was well beyond his strength. Standing back, he eyed the closest of the posts that held up the heavy canopy in the low light of the gas lamp.

There. Using the post's weakest point as his lever, he snapped off a three-foot-long section with a *crack!* that mingled with the pained *creak* of the canopy as it sagged over the bed.

"General de Moireul?" one of the guards called through the door. "Is everything all right in there?"

"Perfectly, thank you," Gerard called back as he weighed the new weapon in his hand. He would have preferred his sword—not to mention the fae shield that he'd won in the Tournament of Leaves. But the wooden bar that he now held—sturdy in the middle and raggedly sharp at each end—was a good start.

Was it too much to hope that he could break the mirror into shards of glass large enough to be usable, too?

Low, unhappy muttering sounded outside the door. Even without being able to make out any words, Gerard had a strong suspicion that his time was running out.

Swiftly, he scooped up the closest two pillows and ripped off their cases, wrapping the soft, gathered cloth in thick swathes around his left hand.

Footsteps sounded in the corridor outside.

Many footsteps, far too many for the two guards he'd already met.

The familiar thrill of upcoming battle coursed through Gerard's skin, erasing his fatigue and setting every sense alight.

Jovar, guide and hold me true.

Gerard scooped up the hot brass hook of the still-lit gas lamp with his cloth-wrapped hand, gripped the wooden bar in his other, and prepared to fight not only for his life but for his and Lorelei's joint future.

Between the high priestess's detailed instructions and Ailana's smuggled map of the winter palace, Lorelei was certain—*nearly* certain—that she was aiming her portal in the right direction. As she drew it, she sensed a warning numbness nearby that signaled lurking iron—the bar that had latched and hidden the room's door when Saskia had made that earlier search—but she aimed directly inside the bedroom itself . . .

And saw only pitch darkness through the portal. She hesitated, straining her vision. Was she about to step into a locked wardrobe? The map hadn't included any helpful notes on furnishings . . .

A sudden *crash* sounded through the portal as she wavered, and a streak of light flashed past. Men's voices yelled. Then the sharp report of a rifle sounded—and Lorelei urged Bluebell into the waiting darkness without a second thought.

They landed in the deeply shadowed back corner of an impressively large bedchamber that looked as if it had been hit by an earthquake. The bed was a crumpled mess in the center of the room. Beyond it, a stack of broken furniture lay scattered by the door. That crash must have been the door being broken down, while the flash of light had come from—who else?—her own lover, the Golden Beacon himself, who stood facing the incoming throng of royal guards alone, lit by the swinging light of a gas lamp that hung from one big hand.

He was one man against who knew how many, all of the others armed with rifles or swords, but he faced them with his head held high and his massive shoulders squared, emanating as much confidence as if the wooden bar in his right hand—or was that a stick?—was an impenetrable shield.

Of course. This man would never accept defeat in any challenge—and with her and her allies at his side, he would never have to.

Laughing with breathless delight, Lorelei nudged Bluebell into action. The gryphon galloped forward, letting out a terrifying battle screech.

Every rifle swung their way. Lorelei only flicked her fingers. Chains of ivy surged from the floor, climbing over the broken furniture as the guards yelled with alarm. Her magic couldn't touch the iron weapons, but her green chains swarmed around all of the closest guards, pulling their arms to their sides and slamming them down to the floor.

More guards surged forward to take their place—but Gerard hadn't so much as twitched at the sound of Bluebell's battle cry. The rest of the continent might think of Lorelei as flighty and fickle, but he had clearly never doubted that she'd come.

"Watch out," he said calmly to her over his shoulder . . .

And then he swung his left arm back, light streaking once more across the room, and sent the burning gas lamp flying through the broken doorway, directly into the swarming group of guards.

"Huh!" Saskia let out a grunt of surprised approval as she stepped through the portal behind Lorelei. The only light left in the once-elegant bedroom was reflected from the flames that now lit the outer corridor, catching hold of furnishings and lush carpeting and spreading rapidly.

"Well done," Ailana said briskly from her position on her own gryphon's back, waiting in the opening of the portal. "General de Moireul, are you ready to make your departure now, before they can summon any Gilded Wizards as reinforcements—*or* that fire can spread inside the room?"

"Oh, nothing's getting in here. Trust *me* for that." Saskia flung a handful of white powder at the opening to the corridor, and a shimmering wall of air and magic appeared to fill it, blocking the way every bit as completely as her magical border had blocked Kitvaria from armed intruders for over a year.

That wall couldn't stand against *too* many Gilded Wizards all attacking it at once, but it was more than enough for the moment.

They were all more than enough whenever they stood together . . . and Lorelei intended to make the most of the extra time Saskia had granted her.

Whatever either of her allies might think, flirting with her lover was always a *top* priority.

"Well, General?" Taking full advantage of the height that Bluebell gave her, Lorelei dropped a mischievous wink at Gerard from across the room.

Seven years ago, she had met that mountain in a uniform, and he'd set her a seemingly impossible challenge.

Tonight, she knew with giddy delight that she had won it . . . just as he had won her heart along the way.

"*Shall* we take our leave now?" she drawled in her haughtiest tone as flames leapt outside the bedroom. "This party is becoming terribly dull, you know. It might lead to the most embarrassing gossip if we chose to stay longer."

"And we *all* know how much you fear scandal." Warm amusement sounded in Gerard's voice as he strode around the broken bed to meet her.

The Imperial palace continued to burn beyond him. Screams and yells of both alarm and command sounded in the distance.

Otto's unmistakable shout of rage rose above all the rest . . .

But all that Lorelei cared about was the tender smile that cracked the familiar, chiseled face that had been set like stone against her for so many years.

The warmth of Gerard's strong hands closed around her waist, and she slipped from Bluebell's back into his waiting arms.

"It's time to go home," she told him. "Together."

32

Of course, it wasn't quite that simple. Before he and Lorelei could go anywhere, the other Queens of Villainy had to be returned to their own homes—but with Lorelei in his arms and his would-be assassins left behind, Gerard found himself more than happy, for once in his life, to linger and take time along the way.

They landed first in a long, narrow hall with stained-glass windows shaped like snowflakes and cool blue draperies hanging from the walls. It took no great leaps of intuition to guess which queen claimed this as her home, even before Ailana slipped gracefully off her gryphon.

"At least *that's* finished," she said, "but we'd better meet again once we've all had some rest. We'll need to set our new plans in motion as swiftly as possible."

One arm still curved around Lorelei's soft waist, Gerard bent forward in a respectful bow. "I hope you'll allow me to assist in any plans devised by your alliance, Your Majesty. I won't forget the aid you all gave me tonight."

"I appreciate that, General. In that case..." Her brown eyes narrowed in speculation. "How would you feel about beginning your repayment tomorrow morning, as early as possible?"

"Tomorrow?" Gerard blinked. "If you hope for me to lead any armies, I'll need—"

"I was thinking of a more tangential approach." The Queen of Nornne tapped one finger against her side. "Why don't we start by following through on your earlier threat to Otto?"

"Speaking to journalists, you mean?" Relief cascaded through him at the idea of *any* strategy that might delay the inevitable moment when he would have to lead troops against his own former men in battle. Still, he couldn't bring himself to be dishonest with any of the women who had saved him. "Depending on Otto's reaction tonight, the newspapers may not be willing—or able—to print the truths I share with them. They may not even believe me if Otto tells the world I'm a traitor... especially once they learn that I am now partnered with Lorelei."

There were more than a few journalists, he knew, who would leap on that particular development with malicious glee—*bad blood showing itself at last, as always; a traitor after all, just like his parents!* Even now, that prospect sent a trickle of acid into his gut—but with Lorelei at his side and his own principles untainted, he was finally ready to stand tall against oncoming scandal.

"They may not take your word on the matter," Queen Ailana agreed, "but if nothing else, it will plant the seeds of contrary ideas into their heads... and I know others who will be far more inclined to listen and believe you immediately."

"Of course!" Letting out a gurgle of delighted laughter, Lorelei nestled even closer against him with an open possessiveness that soothed his tension. "Every soldier in the Empire respects the Golden Beacon *far* more than they do poor Otto. Unlike him, you actually *earned* every medal you've been given, and they know it! All you have to do now is find a way to address your old troops directly . . . and luckily for you, my darling, your fabulous new consort is *more* than willing to help you travel anywhere you want to go from now on. We can portal directly to your last encampment tomorrow morning, if you'd like, and explain exactly what's happened before Otto has the chance to spread any of his libels beyond the capital."

"Even in Fiora, not everyone can be fool enough to believe him," put in the Queen of Kitvaria with her customary brusqueness. "They may be keeping quiet about it for now, but Otto only *just* got rid of the old high priest by telling all sorts of awful stories about *him*. When he starts spreading claims about his high general, too, there's bound to be more suspicion."

"A good deal of suspicion," Queen Ailana agreed, "and as the newspapers have spent the last decade and a half working tirelessly to make General de Moireul a shining hero in the eyes of the public, it will be even harder for Otto to quell the rumors this time round."

"Ahem." As Lorelei glowered at the ice queen, her grip tightened protectively around Gerard's waist. "*My consort* worked to make himself a hero. The newspapers only reported on that fact."

Queen Saskia raised one hand to cover her mouth but didn't manage to disguise her snort-laugh as a cough. When Lorelei turned her warning gaze to the witch queen, Saskia only shrugged, smirking. "It's just . . . fascinating to see how quickly things can change."

"Hmm." Lorelei's ominous scowl deepened.

"Weren't you the one who said, only last week—?"

Lorelei's glower shifted into a far more dangerous smile, and Gerard braced himself for trouble. "Oh, but darling Saskia, we've kept you for *far* too long tonight already," she purred. "I know how much you must be missing your own lovely consort by now. He does still consider himself to be your librarian, does he not?"

"Ah . . ." Queen Saskia's brows lowered in suspicion. "Why would you—?"

Before she could even finish the question, Lorelei drew a swift circle in the air. The new portal opened to reveal a cozy, circular library, lit by a crackling log fire as well as the warm glow of a gas lamp. The room was filled with towering piles of books and papers, high wooden bookshelves that stretched up for multiple stories . . . and the Archduke of Estarion himself, studying an ancient-looking manuscript at the closest table while a crow napped by his elbow.

"Yoo-hoo!" Lorelei caroled through the portal, waking the crow up with a jerk. "Felix, darling, we've brought your lovely consort back to you perfectly safe and sound. Don't worry—she wasn't injured in the slightest when she marched into the Emperor's own winter palace in Fiora tonight and took on a whole squadron of his guards!"

"Why, you—!" Queen Saskia's mouth dropped open in outrage.

Giggling, Lorelei leapt forward to push her taller friend through the portal. She snapped it shut while Saskia was still sputtering in the library beyond.

Queen Ailana sighed and shook her head as she turned to Gerard. "You've always seemed such a reasonable man, General. Are you aware of what a menace your new consort truly is?"

Gerard smiled as he tucked Lorelei once more against his side, where his mischievous partner belonged. "Your Majesty," he said gravely, "I will look forward to working with all of you, beginning tomorrow."

"Tomorrow," she agreed with a regal nod.

Lorelei was already drawing a new portal in the air with dancing, multicolored sparkles that were nearly as eye-catching and irrepressible as she was herself. Gerard stepped through them without a second thought and felt the closest sparkles cling to his hair and coat like a welcome brand.

The room they landed in was familiar—Lorelei's bedroom in the private lodge where she had first brought him—but Lorelei's sudden gasp startled him into full attention. He followed her shocked gaze to the bed, where a single golden arrow had been laid across one pink silk pillowcase.

Gerard's eyebrows rose as he turned back to her. "Was there some clause I missed in the rules for the Tournament of Leaves?"

"Oh, no. We certainly didn't win. We couldn't have. But . . ." Lorelei's smile wobbled as tears glistened in her eyes. "I believe that must be a message from my mother."

"Ah." There was a good deal to unpack in that statement—something important had clearly passed between the two of them while he was gone—but even as Lorelei dashed the tears from her eyes, relief was paramount in every weary line of her body. So Gerard set aside that conversation for later and made his chest a wall that she could lean against tonight.

Tomorrow, they would talk over everything that lay ahead, both for them and for the continent as a whole. Hard consequences would inevitably follow tonight's victory, along with challenging new battles to fight. War was coming, and for the first time in years, Gerard couldn't be certain that he would stand on the winning side of that battlefield, with all of the Empire's forces mounted against him rather than under his command.

Tonight, though, after so many years, he and Lorelei were finally together—not only as partners for a single tournament, but for the rest of their lives. Whatever came next, they would face it all together . . .

And that night, when he dreamed, she was at his side again.

Lorelei recognized that vast stone hall immediately. She grabbed Gerard's hand in hers before he could take a single step forward to be claimed by Jovar.

"You can't have him for your hall of heroes yet!" she announced into that endless, echoing hush. "He's mine for the rest of our lives. You'll have to wait!"

Standing beside her, Gerard cleared his throat. "Lorelei... who are you talking to?"

"Can't you tell?" She snorted, waving her free hand at the stone statues in frozen procession around them. "We've been summoned here because I dared to flout a direction from your god."

"Summoned into a summer garden?" He frowned down at her.

She blinked up at him. "I beg your pardon?"

As they stared at each other in mutual incomprehension, the scene shifted around her... and, from Gerard's start of surprise, around him as well.

Suddenly, the stone hall didn't look nearly so austere.

Green vines climbed lovingly around the statues. Scented flowers bloomed and hung from the high ceiling. And, spotlighted at the far end of the hall, an immense, stern, and bearded divine presence cracked a miraculous smile, while the shining goddess who rested in His arms laughed out loud, the sound of Her open delight filling the hall with joy.

Lorelei's mouth dropped open. "You two have been planning this together all along?"

Gerard, always more sensible, was already on his knees and tugging her hand to join him.

Still staring, she lowered herself to the ground. Soft green moss covered the hard stone floor, cushioning her knees, and Sylvana's breath brushed over them both in answer.

"PARTNERS."

It was the sound of a gentle, cooling breeze after a long, hard day's work. It carried the scent of roses blooming after a bloody battle...

And it felt like a gift from the goddess who'd claimed Lorelei before her birth... or a reward from the god Gerard had followed with such devotion.

Either. Both?

Oh, yes. Definitely both, working in tandem, unexpected but utterly perfect in combination . . .

Just like them.

As Lorelei woke in her own bed in Balravia, the first hints of dawn shone through the gaps in her velvet curtains, and she laughed out loud through her lingering tears of wonder.

Lying on his back beside her, Gerard shook his head in awed disbelief. "Were we really . . . was that actually . . . ?"

"Oh, yes," Lorelei said with relish. "And do you know what else? They woke us up a full *hour* before we have to get out of bed and go anywhere!"

His eyes widened. Then they narrowed with a sudden, dangerous glint—and her serious, stoic lover abruptly rolled over to pin her beneath him, trapping her between his braced forearms. "In that case . . ."

"Why, General." Lorelei fluttered her eyelashes up at him, scattering sparkles with abandon. "Are you by any chance attempting to take *me* prisoner?"

"It seems only fair." His lips twitched, but his amber eyes burned with intensity. "Considering how often *you've* played that game . . ."

She pouted theatrically, blood thrumming with excitement as his big, nearly naked body hovered tantalizingly close above hers. The gods knew, this man was a veritable furnace of energy and tightly controlled passion even in ordinary times; now, the heat from his bare skin flared through every inch between them and sent flames licking across her own, making her shift restlessly against the trap of his strong arms. "Unfair, darling! I've only kidnapped two men so far."

"Two men *ever*," Gerard intoned. The muscles in his upper arms flexed deliciously, making her throat go dry, as he lowered himself to breathe his words into her ear. "No more kidnapping other men, Lorelei. Never again!"

"Aww." She couldn't reach him with her arms still pinned, but she turned her voice into a teasing caress of its own. "Do you really want to spoil all of my fun?"

"Never." His low growl sent warm breath ghosting across the sensitive skin of her neck, making her shiver. "I want to *share* all of your fun from now on. Feel free to kidnap me as many times as you like."

"Oh, I definitely will." Tipping her head back on her pillow, Lorelei beamed up at him. "But you'll have to promise to try to escape every time. That's part of the game."

And just to prove it . . .

Their bed suddenly lurched into the air. Caught off guard, Gerard fell back for only an instant before he reached for her again—but Lorelei had already seized her chance to slip away. The vines she had commanded to sneak up from the floor released the bedframe as she leapt off it, and it fell back into place with a juddering thud to slow his chase even more. Giggling, she sprinted for the door, showering taunting sparkles in her wake.

Strong, bare arms closed around her waist and scooped her up off the ground before her fingers could touch the door handle. "You should have drawn a portal if you wanted to escape," Gerard whispered into her hair.

She wriggled happily in his unyielding embrace as his warm breath ruffled her skin. "Would you have given up on catching me if I had?"

"Never." A hot, open-mouthed kiss sucked at her throat, making her whole body shiver with delight. "I will *never* give up on you, my nemesis. My love."

"That's good, because you're all *mine*." Lorelei wrapped her arms around his, binding him in place, as she tipped her head back to give him a stern glare. "And you'd better understand, I will *never* let you step into danger without me ever again. Last night was unbearable!"

His lips curved in response. "Why would I want to go anywhere without my partner? We fight best together, always. Didn't the gods themselves just confirm that?"

"They certainly did." She smiled dazzlingly, content in their mutual victory... but she made her voice prim and proper, because she wasn't finished with their game. She would *never* be tired of playing with this man! "Personally, *I* think we ought to give thanks for that. Don't you?"

His amber eyes narrowed. "What exactly did you have in mind?"

She stood on tiptoes to whisper the shocking answer in his ear... and he let out a shout of laughter that no one else in the world would have expected from the sober and stoic Golden Beacon.

Then they lunged for the bed together.

Laughing—and then shivering and moaning—with delight, Lorelei spent the rest of that early morning with Gerard fully celebrating the gift their gods had given them.

EPILOGUE

Queen Ailana of Nornne was meeting with her chamberlain to go through her accounts early that same morning, firmly holding back every yawn that wanted to escape, when a letter suddenly fluttered into place on the small side table beside her.

It wasn't unusual for mail to be delivered in that fashion. Any number of her spies had magical access to her. She only spared it a quick glance as she continued to calmly deliver her instructions...

...until she spotted the letter's crimson wax seal, where the icons for every god in the Imperial pantheon had been stamped in a full circle of power.

Clothilde.

She didn't even realize she'd stopped speaking until her chamberlain politely cleared his throat. "Your Majesty?" His head had cocked in question, his quill pen held ready in his hands.

"Ah . . ." There was no reason not to continue their meeting now and wait to read Clothilde's—no, the *Imperial high priestess's*—letter later. No matter which favor might be demanded in exchange for the unexpected help given last night, it could surely wait for at least half an hour. After all, it might be after nine o'clock, but the winter sun hadn't even risen here in Nornne yet.

So it made no sense whatsoever that Ailana found herself breaking the seal open anyway with hands that felt suddenly out of her control.

"Just one moment, if you please." At least her voice remained steady; her chamberlain nodded and sat back without any sign of concern.

Ailana pulled on the ice that could always be counted on to chill her veins and took great care, as she unfolded the letter before him, not to allow her expression to reveal anything but the coolest of interest.

This was only one more diplomatic missive of many; yet another in the series of quiet favors and repayments that had helped her spy network spread across the continent and earned Nornne a position of power once more after her parents' reign had come so close to shattering everything.

She didn't allow her eyes to widen as she read. She forced herself to breathe slowly and deeply as she absorbed every word of the proposal laid out before her.

Then she set down the letter in her lap and counted in silence for several seconds until she felt able to speak out loud again. When she did, her voice sounded strangely distant to her own ears, but it was, at least, perfectly controlled, as she always would be.

"Oh, and one more note," she told her chamberlain. "We'll need to prepare for a public celebration very soon. It appears that I am to be married."

Acknowledgments

Thank you so much to my dauntless beta readers, Jenn Reese, Deva Fagan, Y.S. Lee, and Patrick Samphire, who cheered me through my first draft of this book.

Thank you to Deva Fagan for supplying the perfect wording for three of the riddles that Lorelei and Gerard had to solve.

Thank you to Molly Ker Hawn for being the best possible publishing partner and champion for this book and everything else I've written in the last 10+ years we've worked together—I feel *so* lucky to have you as my agent! And thank you to Emma Lagarde for doing such a phenomenal job at selling the Queens of Villainy around the world.

Thank you to my parents for supplying me with dozens of books of fairy tales as a kid and multiple visits to our local library every week. Without having imprinted so hard on those stories as a child, I would never have had the ideas for any of the fae trials my characters faced here!

Thank you to Erika Tsang for thoughtful edits that made all of my queens and their partners shine brighter, and to Gillian Green for doing such an amazing job of bringing the queens home to the UK!

Thank you to Conni Covington for careful copyediting, Jennifer McClelland-Smith for marketing, Alexis Saarela for publicity, and Luisa Rozo Castañeda for all her assistance.

Thank you so much to every single member of my Patreon (patreon.com/stephanieburgis) for our monthly book clubs, patron Q&As, Discord hangouts, and more! Your support makes a real, tangible difference to my writing life, and I deeply appreciate it.

And to every reader who enjoyed this book and/or *Wooing the Witch Queen*: Thank you so much for joining in with my wicked queens, sharing my fun, and tagging me in your amazing photos of my book out in the world!

Sign up to my newsletter to get advance sneak peeks at Book 3 and more: www.stephanieburgis.com/newsletter.

Turn the page for a sneak peek at the next book
in the Queens of Villainy series

MELTING THE ICE QUEEN

Ailana of Nornne was famous—some might say infamous—across the continent for the ice that she manipulated with her magic and the equally cool control that she maintained over her emotions in every situation.

Unfortunately, her two closest and most trusted allies seemed determined to test that self-control in this meeting.

"What do you mean, you're *getting married?*" Queen Lorelei of Balravia gaped at Ailana with deeply aggravating shock from her perch atop one of Ailana's favorite elegant, high-backed chairs. Ivy leaves glistened within the curls of the fae queen's hair as her deceptively guileless blue eyes narrowed upon her hostess. "Darling, is this your idea of a bad joke?"

"I don't think Ailana *does* tell jokes," said Queen Saskia of Kitvaria. The witch queen's brows lowered as her suspicious gaze swung back to Ailana, her eyes dark against the pale skin of her face. "Is this part of some political ruse? Will you only be *pretending* to be wed, to cover up some complicated spywork? That would make much more sense for you."

Oh, *really*. Ailana set her teeth together with a nearly inaudible *click*.

It had, she reminded herself, been wise to form an alliance with the only other queens on this continent who led kingdoms of their own, independent from any overbearing husbands *and* from the ever-hungry Serafin Empire that had already annexed so many other nations on this continent. The fact that both of the other Queens of Villainy possessed magic strong enough to rival Ailana's own—and thus felt no intimidation when it came to her powers—should, theoretically, be a bonus.

Politically and practically speaking, she was *glad* they didn't fear her.

Every so often, though, they did make it difficult for her to remember that.

Ailana gently lowered her teacup to the table beside her and spoke with unruffled calm. "It is neither a joke nor a ruse. The ceremony will be private and unannounced until after its completion, but as my closest allies, I wanted to pay you the respect of alerting you ahead of time . . . especially as it may have implications for all of our plans."

"Well, you certainly can't get married without *us*." The fae queen's pink slippers lay carelessly discarded on the carpet beside her as she perched cross-legged on her seat, blonde hair flowing in wild curls and feet scandalously bare, but she raised her eyebrows at Ailana with all the outraged haughtiness of a society grande dame witnessing a sordid scandal. "Did you really think we wouldn't clear our schedules to attend?"

"There is no need for anyone to attend," Ailana said crisply. "It isn't that sort of arrangement, as I was about to explain."

"So, it *is* a ruse." Saskia nodded in satisfaction and picked up the first of the cardamom biscuits from her plate. "I knew it."

Ailana drew a deep, sustaining breath. These two women weren't only her closest allies. They were also the closest she had to real friends. The closest she had ever had . . .

Apart from one brief moment nearly two decades ago, at that ill-fated political summit that had changed her life forever. For years, all she'd remembered from that summit was the devastation in its wake, but lately...

Lately, other memories had been sneaking through without permission. Disconcertingly vivid memories of clear hazel eyes and a confident smile that shone with the irresistible, beaming warmth of a hearth fire in winter. *"There you are, at last! I've been waiting for you."*

Ailana shook off that pointless, distracting flash of recollection. There had been far too many of those ever since an Imperial announcement had shaken the continent two weeks earlier.

"The Imperial high priest has been arrested on charges of vile corruption and treason to the state. While prosecutors have requested a sentence of execution for the former high priest's crimes, Emperor Otto II has appointed a new Imperial high priestess..."

The girl Ailana had met all those years ago would never have colluded to accuse a peace-loving, honorable old man of treachery only to clear the way for Imperial expansion. *That* girl had been honest and forthright to a terrifying degree. Now, though, not one of Ailana's hardworking spies had uncovered any evidence of the new high priestess expressing even the faintest disapproval of any of Otto's brutal plans.

The princess Ailana had once known was clearly long gone, regardless of the unexpected messages—and aid—that Clothilde had sent Ailana four days earlier.

"This will be a true and binding marriage... of political convenience. Unlike either of you, I haven't fallen prey to romance or any sentimental feelings." She smiled coolly as she poured a steaming arc of tea from an elegantly decorated white-and-blue pot into her empty cup, careful to hold her powers in check. Nothing ever really warmed her nowadays, but that first sip of hot tea always offered some relief. "However, if you *would* care to offer me a wedding gift, I would gladly accept your aid in transporting my bride here in the first place, to aid with speed and secrecy."

"Of course," Lorelei said impatiently. "But why would it need to be a secret if it's a matter of political conven—? Oh, *no!*" The fae queen abruptly stiffened, trading a look of deep alarm with Saskia. "Ailana, we all know you're a mistress of calculating risks, but this . . . darling, this might be too much for even *you* to handle."

"I beg your pardon?" Ailana raised her eyebrows in an unmistakably quelling message.

Naturally, her fellow queens ignored it.

"Wait, are we talking about the Imperial high priestess?" Saskia demanded.

"Of course we are!" Lorelei groaned. "Didn't you see the way Ailana looked when Clothilde appeared in the mirror-box the other night? 'No romance or sentimental feelings' my arse!" Eyes narrowed, she swung back to her hostess. "You two knew each other when you were younger, didn't you?"

"*Briefly.*" Ailana bit off the word. "If you'd take a moment to listen, though, and stop jumping to conclusions—"

"Oh, no. She's the Emperor's sister." Saskia—*Saskia*, of all people, who barely paid any attention to anything outside her own laboratory except her smitten consort!—shook her head at Ailana as pityingly as if she were conveying brand-new, startling information, as if Ailana's own massive, carefully built and meticulously tended spy network weren't the source of all the crucial information that the three queens relied upon to manage the lethally shifting ice floes of politics around them. "His *sister*, Ailana!"

"I am aware of that." Drawing ice through her veins, Ailana held fast to control. "But if you'll recall—"

"Oh, we all know she helped us last week," Lorelei said impatiently, "and I'll be grateful for that forever, but darling, you *must* understand: That doesn't mean we can trust her. For all we know, Clothilde could have done all of that as a ploy to win your confidence!"

For one instant of self-indulgence, Ailana allowed her weary eyelids to fall shut. How long had it been since she'd had a true night's sleep? "Lorelei . . ."

But the fae queen barreled onwards, irrepressible as ever. "Everyone knows that you control the most dangerous spy network on the continent. *Of course* Otto must know that, too—so he'll know exactly how much trouble that could cause him when he sends his armies out to invade the rest of us! What could possibly be better for him now than sending his own sister into your home to ferret out all of your secrets—weakening you *and* all the rest of us!—just in time to aid in his long-awaited expansion?"

"I could think of a few easier methods," Ailana muttered as she forced her eyes open to face her allies once more.

"Could you?" Lorelei tilted her head in challenge. "Could you really? We *know* you, darling. You would never allow any ordinary spies close enough to you to learn anything, no matter what clever role they were playing. A wife is the only one who could ever manage it."

"So, that *is* a possibility." Saskia scowled, crossing her arms. The still-untouched cup in front of the witch queen lifted into the air and began to circle dangerously around her empty plate, conveying the force of her mounting ire . . . and spilling tea with every move. "When Clothilde helped us the other night, she said you would owe her a favor, didn't she? So, was this it? Did she tell you that you *had* to marry her?"

Lorelei's answering gasp of outrage accompanied chains of thorns stabbing upwards through the floor of Ailana's parlor, ripping holes in the cool blue carpet and piling in furious tangles around the fae queen's seat. "If she thinks she can force *any* of the Queens of Villainy—!"

"*Enough.*" Metaphorical ice crackled through Ailana's tone, but it was physical ice that shot across the floor as she rose to her feet, freezing every drink in its delicate cup, wilting Lorelei's vines, and turning the three queens' breaths into visible clouds as the air chilled around them with an audible *snap*. "No one is forcing me into anything, now or ever again. She has not called in the favor yet; she's only offered me a proposal, one that *I* chose to accept with a full understanding of all the potential nuances involved.

"Clothilde may well be lying when she claims to secretly oppose her brother's aims, but I, of all people"—dangerous memories crashed in the distance, but her ice held them safely at bay—"know better than to ever allow myself to be deceived by any member of that family again. We will be wed in name only; I can assure you that no feelings will be involved, now or ever. *If* she's telling the truth, we will have gained a strong advantage in the war to come. But if she isn't?"

Ice silvered Ailana's vision as she looked at the only two allies she completely trusted. It was the same ice she had used to such terrible effect the last time her family's trust in an alliance had been unforgivably betrayed . . . the ice that had run in her veins ever since. "I know very well how to deal with my nation's enemies."

Saskia didn't answer; she only frowned more ominously than ever, without even hunching her shoulders against the cold.

With a flick of her small, fair-skinned fingers, Lorelei created a bubble of summer warmth around herself. "Very well." She met Ailana's gaze steadily, but with unmistakable warning. "We won't argue anymore if you've really made up your mind, but we will *both* come with you when you retrieve your new bride. She needs to know exactly what she's in for."

About the Author

Stephanie Burgis grew up in East Lansing, Michigan, but now lives in Wales with her husband and two children, surrounded by mountains, castles and coffee shops. She writes wildly romantic adult historical fantasies (including *The Harwood Spellbook*, with more than 20,000 self-published copies sold) and has had more than forty short stories for adults and teens published in magazines and anthologies.